WHAT EVERY MOTHER NEEDS

WHAT EVERY MOTHER NEEDS

EMILY SHINER

bookouture

Published by Bookouture in 2025

An imprint of Storyfire Ltd.
Carmelite House
50 Victoria Embankment
London EC4Y 0DZ

www.bookouture.com

The authorised representative in the EEA is Hachette Ireland
8 Castlecourt Centre
Dublin 15 D15 XTP3
Ireland
(email: info@hbgi.ie)

ISBN: 978-1-83618-672-4
eBook ISBN: 978-1-83618-670-0

*For everyone impacted by Hurricane Helene.
Come hell or high water, we are Appalachia strong.*

PROLOGUE

My hands shake a little as I take the baby. She's perfect, with a little upturned nose and pink cheeks. Her onesie is soft, an off-white with little rosebuds all over it. Even though it's chilly outside, the heat is on in here, so her arms and legs are warm, but I still take a striped blanket and wrap her up in it before pulling her closer to my chest.

The last thing we want is for something to happen to her, so I'll do whatever it takes to protect her.

I babysat all through high school and have held a lot of my friends' babies. I know how to protect their head. I know how to snuggle them just right. It's all in the support. Babies this age are wobbly little things and can get hurt so easily.

But she's safe in my arms. It's funny, the hormones that fire off when you hold a baby, how you already know immediately that you'll never let anything happen to them.

Dipping my face towards her, I take a deep breath and inhale that amazing baby scent.

It's their trick, you see. To smell amazing. To be soft and loving. To look at you with big eyes so full of love and trust that you don't have a choice but to love and protect them.

To never let them go.

"What do you think?" The woman speaking interrupts my focus on the baby, and I fight to keep from glaring at her.

"She's perfect," I say. "Absolutely perfect."

"She really is. The first time I held her, I couldn't believe it."

A pause, like she's nervous to continue, so I speak up.

"Why don't you go rest? Or do you want to go for a walk by yourself? Just take some time to be alone. I'll take care of her."

The smile on her face is so genuine, I almost feel bad for what I'm doing. Almost. My mom always told me that I have the kind of face that anyone would like. That they would trust. That I had the unique ability to walk into a situation, read it correctly, and do whatever it took to make people feel more comfortable.

And that's exactly what I did here.

She trusts me.

I smile at her, then turn my attention back to the baby in my arms. From the corner of my eye, I watch as she finally leaves the room.

She shouldn't.

ONE

Help Needed

Looking for a kind, reliable, detail-focused housekeeper and cook, 10+ hours a week.

We are a family of two located in Redville, North Carolina. My daughter is six weeks old, and I will be going back to work.

This position requires up to five hours on Fridays spent deep cleaning the house. This includes laundry, scrubbing the floors, putting away dishes, and cleaning out the refrigerator. Trash must be taken to the dump.

An equal amount of time will be spent on Monday. I will make a menu and need the person hired to do all of the shopping and prepare meals for the week. Overtime may sometimes be needed, and advance warning will be given if possible. This is not an overnight or live-in position. It is also not a childcare position. The nursery is off-limits, and at no time will the housekeeper be left alone with the baby.

The ideal candidate has the following:

- Previous experience cleaning homes
- Previous experience batch cooking for a week
- A clean driving record
- High school diploma
- First aid certification

In this position the candidate will be expected to do the following:

- Grocery shop on a given budget
- Handle all cooking
- Pick up the kitchen
- Keep the house clean, ensuring that all weekly and monthly cleaning tasks are completed.

TWO

TUESDAY

Charlotte

Lawrence has been dead a month.

Well, thirty-five days, to be exact.

The funeral has come and gone. The casseroles neighbors brought by remain stuffed in the freezer, but most of them are untouched. I need to throw them away, but the thought of loading them into a trash bag and taking the garbage can down to the street is too much for me right now.

This is so much harder than I thought it would be. Not that I thought Lawrence dying would be all sunshine and flowers, but I sure didn't expect to miss him as much as I do.

Right now? I'm in survival mode. I'm exhausted. And eventually I'm going to have to go back to work, and I have no idea how I'm going to balance everything.

It doesn't help that Jordan won't settle.

I hear her crying in her room, and I push myself off the sofa, standing still for a moment to steady myself. Stress makes me not eat as much as I should, and when I don't eat a lot, I tend to get dizzy.

She's still wailing.

Everything I've ever read has told me how important it is to get a baby on a schedule as quickly as possible, that it's best for them to have regular nap times if possible.

Well, those experts have obviously never met Jordan.

I glance at my watch and hurry from the living room, tracing my fingers along the wall as I walk towards her nursery. She'd been a surprise baby, one I didn't think I'd ever have, especially not after my first marriage ended five years ago.

But then I met Lawrence—and it's not like we were careful.

He swore to me he couldn't have kids, and I took him at his word. Why use birth control when the man you're married to said he can't get you pregnant?

When I brought Jordan home from the hospital, I worried people would talk, thinking that I'd cheated. But I wouldn't. Not on someone like Lawrence. He always was the catch in the relationship, with the fancy job and impressive title, and now I have to figure out how to make it work without him.

You know what I'm getting now that my husband has died?

Not much.

"It's better to keep everything separate," he'd said, and now I'm waiting to hear back from the lawyer about whether or not I'm the beneficiary on any of Lawrence's accounts or retirement savings.

So far? No news is bad news.

Although I'm not sure how I'm going to handle it, I'm glad I took a job as a bank teller before Jordan came into our lives. I'm going to need something to get me out of the house, some way to feel like myself again instead of just an extension of my child, some way to pay for the home help I so desperately need.

Lawrence had suggested that I get a job, in fact. He'd always wanted me to be independent, which is the reason he gave for never adding me to his accounts.

So you can stand on your own two feet, Charlotte, in case something ever happens to me.

"Well, something did happen, Lawrence," I mutter, finally turning into Jordan's room and clicking on the overhead light.

She's right where I left her, on her back in her crib, swaddled up in one of those ridiculously expensive sleep sacks the store clerks promise will ensure a good night's sleep. Spoiler: they don't.

Even though her face is screwed up and she's still crying, for a moment, I don't move. I'm content to take in how perfect this scene is.

The room is light pink, the crib made from white oak. Her sheets are striped and match the curtains. A bookshelf on one wall is loaded with books, and there are dozens of stuffed animals scattered on the hardwood floor.

Standing here like this, staring at my girl... I could easily forget everything bad that's happened. But then she sucks in a deep breath, really filling her lungs, and lets loose another scream, tearing me from my thoughts.

"Hey Jordy," I say, crossing the room to her and pulling her from her crib. Her body is warm, and I snuggle into her. "I'm not sure you even slept. Are you hungry?"

I turn and lean on the crib as I rub her back. This level of crying probably means she's hungry. That, or wet, but I'd bet anything she needs a bottle.

As much as I'd love to breastfeed, some things just aren't possible.

I move quickly to check her diaper—dry, like I thought—then coo to her as I kiss her forehead. This makes her stop crying, and I allow myself to grin before carrying her out of her room.

This is how grief works. For me, at least. It's a passenger I can't seem to get rid of. Sometimes it rides in the front seat with me, ballsy enough to reach out and yank the steering wheel, even going so far as to try to drive us into a tree or a ditch. Other times it's quiet, in the backseat sleeping, maybe.

But as soon as I remember my grief, as soon as I do more than glance at it out of the corner of my eye, it's back, stretching itself awake and climbing up between the front seats, shoving me out of the way, grabbing the steering wheel and leering at me.

Lawrence.

I see him when I look at Jordan. Yes, her eyes are blue and his were brown. Sure, her hair looks more like mine than his, thick and brown with an enviable amount of curl even though she's only six weeks old. Still, looking at her makes me think of my husband. Lawrence is gone, but every single time I look at her, he fills my thoughts.

I carry her into the kitchen and hold her tight with one arm while I reach for the container of formula. There are clean baby bottles on the counter, and I set the can of formula by them before carefully pulling off the lid.

I must jostle her, or maybe I'm moving too slowly, because she starts to cry again. Gritting my teeth, I shake my head and push Lawrence out of my mind. Jordan needs to eat.

I have to stop thinking about the dead and focus on the living.

The doorbell rings.

Jordan cries harder.

"Oh, you can wait," I mutter, scooping out some formula and carefully tipping it into the bottle. Half of it goes on the counter, and I swear before measuring out another half spoonful.

This time, I get it all in the bottle.

I drop the scoop into the container and grab the bottle before hitting the faucet to run water. Normally, I'd worry more about the temperature, but I just need to get food in her.

"Jordy, hang on one second," I say, trying to keep my voice light, like this is a fun joke I'm a part of.

The doorbell rings again.

She stops crying for a second. It's only a moment of blessed peace before she sucks in another big breath, screaming harder this time.

"I hear you at the door," I mutter, shifting her so I can hold the bottle and screw on the nipple with my free hand. "Probably someone with another dried-out chicken-and-rice casserole."

Doorbell.

"Nasty casserole," I mutter. "They can shove it right up their—"

The doorbell. Again.

"I'm coming!" I shove the nipple into Jordan's mouth, cutting her off mid-cry. Instantly, she begins to suck, and relief floods over me. I'd always heard that newborns were hard, but I had no idea how bone-tired I'd be, how often I'd cry, how dirty both the house and I'd be because all I do is take care of her. "Chill out—your casserole can wait!"

Once at the door, I pause and take a deep breath. Steel myself for whoever is standing out there, waiting to offer condolences, wanting to get a better look at the woman Lawrence decided was good enough to marry but not good enough to take care of after his death.

I smile but not fully. Don't want people to think I'm happy about Lawrence dying.

When I open the door, my smile slides off my face.

The woman standing on our front porch isn't carrying a casserole. She stares at me, her perfectly lipsticked mouth puckering as if I'm not what she expected. Her blonde hair is pushed slick behind her ears, and that, with her lithe body, makes her look like a ballerina.

I definitely don't know any ballerinas.

"Charlotte?" My name is a song when she says it like that.

"Yes. And you are?" It's the only thing to say when a random person shows up on your porch and knows your name.

"Sophie."

I glance down and take in her perfect manicure, the gold rings decorating her fingers, the gold bracelets jangling against each other.

"I hope I'm not interrupting anything," she says, letting go of my hand and looking down at the bundle in my arms.

I stiffen and pull Jordan closer to me. "Is there something I can do for you?" She knows my name.

And I have no idea who she is.

"It's more of what I can do for you." Sophie gestures behind her. Three suitcases are on the porch, all of them sleek and black, with gold accents.

My eyes flick back to her. "What do you—"

"I'm here to help. That's what you need, isn't it? It's why you posted the ad for help. I saw it, and here I am." The smile she gives me is megawatt. "Lawrence dying? Out of left field. He was so healthy, wasn't he? Always hitting the gym and eating right. And you with a little one! I'm so glad you were willing to put out an ad for help, but you can take it down now."

I don't respond. I *can't* respond.

"This is just so unexpected," I finally manage to say. "I put the ad up yesterday and didn't expect a response so quickly. I thought you were bringing a casserole." Even to my ears the words sound lame.

"A casserole? That's hardly what you need. Another casserole?" She frowns, taking me in.

There's a moment where we both stare at each other, then it's like something clicks for her. "I'm sorry, did Lawrence never tell you who I am?"

THREE

Sophie

"He didn't tell me anything about you," Charlotte says, obviously trying to be careful with her words so she doesn't offend me. "Who are you?"

"Oh, I'm Sophie." I smile at her as I say it, and her eyebrow arches, making it clear what she's thinking.

Madonna?

Beyoncé?

Adele?

They're all allowed to go by one name, but not me. She has no idea who I am.

Charlotte stares at me, and I take a step forward, then another, making it clear that I'm going to let myself into her house. No matter what she might think, I'm coming in.

"I didn't think anyone would respond to my ad so quickly," she says, opening the door wider.

I had a pretty good feeling that Charlotte's Southern manners would be so ingrained in her that she wouldn't have it in her to deny me entrance to her house, and I was right.

She continues as I approach her. "I figured it would be a few days until someone reached out, at the very least." She has her baby held tight in her arms, then finally steps to the side, letting me walk through the door. I'm carrying one suitcase and dragging another behind.

"Well, sometimes things work out the way we need them to, don't they? Grab that for me, would you?" I ask, jerking my chin through the door at the final suitcase.

For a moment, she doesn't move. I don't blame her; I wouldn't fetch someone's suitcase while holding my child, but then she surprises me. She shifts the baby to one arm, steps outside, and pulls my suitcase behind her. It thunks into the house, and she closes the door behind us.

Interesting. What else can I make her do? The possibilities are endless, and I fight back a smile while I look around the house.

Nice. This is nice. Not as nice as it could be, but I'm going to blame that on her being busy and not having time to keep it as clean as I'd like now that she's a widow. But she'll believe that's why I'm here, so she can finally relax about the place not being tidy.

"Those are all photos of Lawrence and me. And Jordan." She sounds nervous, but I don't turn around to look at her.

This place is not as nice as my house, but few are. My husband and I always worked, and since we didn't have children, it was easy to put the money towards the things we wanted.

A lovely home.

Fancy cars.

International trips.

Lots of jewelry.

I stare at the pictures on the wall. Some of them are crooked, but I don't move to adjust them. There's Lawrence and Charlotte, the two of them at the state fair clutching corn dogs.

And here they are on a hike.

It takes me until the end of the gallery wall to find photos of the baby.

Swaddled in pink in this one. Dressed with a bow on her head in that one. It's surprising how much hair is sticking out in every direction, and so dark.

I take in the selfie of Charlotte holding the baby but note the obvious.

Of all the photos of the baby, Lawrence isn't in a single one. Not like he had a lot of time to be in them, to be honest. He died shortly after they brought the baby home.

"How old is your baby?" I ask Charlotte.

"Six weeks."

"Oh, a little thing still. I love the infant stage. It's so nice."

Charlotte laughs. "It can be." A pause. "Why don't you come with us to the kitchen, Sophie? I was going to finish feeding Jordy, and you can tell me how you knew Lawrence."

Jordy?

She has got to be kidding me.

"I'm sorry, what did you say her name is?" I leave my suitcases behind and follow Charlotte down the hall to the kitchen.

"Jordan," Charlotte says, patting the baby to burp her. After a moment, she plunks her daughter down in a rocker. "I know, it's not a very common name, but Lawrence's... great-grandmother, I think, was named Jordan. It was important to him to keep the name going."

"Jordan was his great-aunt," I correct. I'm standing next to the baby while Charlotte rummages through a cupboard. "And it isn't *Jordy.*"

"What did you say?" She turns to me, a box of crackers in her hand.

"Nothing." I force myself to squat down and let the baby grab my finger. The movement feels stiff. Unnatural. Like when you stop playing an instrument and pick it up a decade later.

Your muscles think they know what notes to play, how to move to make gorgeous chords, but everything is rusty, and things come out not quite right.

Charlotte nods, but her eyes linger on my face. After a moment, she nods again, this time more to herself. I watch as she gets a plate from another cupboard. She spreads crackers on it, then hurries to the fridge and piles slices of cheese next to the crackers.

"Would you like some?" she asks, leaving the plate on the counter for me.

My hand feels like it's on autopilot as I reach out and take a cracker. Even as I eat, my eyes don't leave Charlotte.

She brandishes a burp cloth at her daughter's face "Come here, Jordy."

"Jordan," I say, automatically.

"Right, Jordan, but I call her Jordy." Charlotte moves deftly, wiping Jordan's face, then smiles at her before standing and looking at me. "Coffee? Tea?"

"Wine? Vodka?"

She laughs and grabs a wine glass out of the dishwasher. I recognize the label on the bottle as she pours me a glass of Chardonnay. I've been to that orchard half a dozen times and picked up more than that many cases of this exact wine.

"Thank you," I say, taking the glass from her and taking a sip. "It's been rough since he died."

"It has." She frowns. Corks the wine. I watch as she presses some buttons on a coffee maker, then leans against the counter and looks at me. "Were you at Lawrence's funeral?"

I take another sip of wine before shaking my head. "I wasn't able to make it in time. He died on... what? A Tuesday? And you had him buried that Friday?" I make sure to keep any accusation out of my voice.

"I did. Lawrence never wanted people to make a big deal out of his death. I knew the more time and effort I put into the funeral, the harder it would be for me to move on. I needed that closure. So did Jordy."

Jordan is just six weeks old. The only closure she needs at this age is to still have someone change her diaper, give her bottles, and rock her to sleep. Jordan doesn't miss Lawrence. Not a chance.

"Where was he buried?" I already know the answer to this question, but I want to watch her squirm.

"Cremated, actually. And I scattered his ashes here, in the backyard."

"No urn? Nothing for you or Jordan to visit when you miss him?"

She pours herself a cup of coffee, then stares at me again. "Sophie, I don't want to be rude, but these are strange questions for someone to ask me when they showed up uninvited at my house." A pause. "You said you were here to help, but I don't know who you are or why you're really here or—"

"Oh, Charlotte." I put my glass down on the kitchen island. The countertop should gleam and sparkle, but there are smears of peanut butter and jelly on it. At first glance, the kitchen is gorgeous: custom and professional, built for people who love to cook. But now that I'm in here and getting a better look at it, it's clear Charlotte can't keep the place clean.

She's going to let this place fall into ruin.

Plenty of women every single day lose their baby daddy, and most of them aren't left with such a great place to live, with nice clothes, with a BMW in the driveway. It pisses me off, if I'm being honest. Charlotte had everything handed to her and she's acting like the victim.

She has no right to act like that. Not like I do.

"I'm here to help." My voice drops a little bit. When I glance at the baby, I'm not surprised to see her eyes already closed. *Milk coma.* "When's the last time you folded laundry and didn't pull wrinkled clothes directly out of the dryer to wear?"

She doesn't respond, but I notice how she chews her lower lip.

"When's the last time you ate a fruit? Or vegetable?"

"Applesauce with breakfast," she tells me.

Poor thing, she almost sounds proud, like she should win a healthy eating award for scarfing down store-bought puréed apples.

"I can tell. It's smeared on the counter." I point, and she blushes. "Listen, I didn't come here to step on toes. I came here to help you. And, no offense, you obviously need it."

She swallows hard. It's difficult to know for sure since she's backlit by the large kitchen windows, but I'd swear there are tears welling up in her eyes.

Good. She's weak. Backed into a corner. There's no way she'll be able to turn down my help, not once she sees how much better I can make her life.

"I do need help," she says. Her voice is low. Embarrassed. "I wouldn't have placed the ad if I didn't. And if you can help me, I'd really appreciate it. There's just one question that you haven't answered. Who are you?"

I laugh, enjoying the note of panic in her voice. "Charlotte, aren't you funny?" When she doesn't respond, I pin her in place with a stare.

Her cheeks flush.

"I'm Lawrence's sister," I finally say.

Her mouth presses into a firm line.

She looks confused.

I bet I know why: he never told her he had a sister.

FOUR

NINE YEARS AGO

Her

"That's the chef," I whisper, leaning across the table to my boyfriend. My eyes are on the man walking towards us. He's tall, with thick dark hair, deep brown eyes, and the type of jaw that men pay good money to have.

My boyfriend chuckles. The two of us have been together for a few months now, and while I like to think that I'm getting used to the special treatment that I get when we're out together, that would be a lie. I don't think I'll ever get used to dinners like this.

"That's him. Louis Marton and I go way back. We played rugby together when we were in boarding school." Lawrence says it casually, dismissively, like it's nothing. But to me, it's everything.

Boarding school. Rugby. Friends who can speak a different language? Yeah, I haven't experienced any of that in my life. Ever.

Until now.

Lawrence turns away from me. "Louis, *mon ami. C'est ma copine et elle a très faim.*"

Louis's white coat is spotless. "*Ravi de te rencontrer. Tu vas adorer le dîner, je te le promets.*" He gives me a little bow, then turns back to my boyfriend, a wide smile already on his face.

I keep a smile on mine too, even though I don't understand anything the two of them are saying. Louis gestures wildly, pointing to different areas of his restaurant, and my boyfriend responds in kind, although he rests his hands on the table.

Collected. In control. That's the man I love.

As they speak, I look around the room. Never in my life did I think I'd have a meal at *Le Nid du Moineau. The Sparrow's Nest.* It's not only the hottest French restaurant this side of the Mississippi, but the prices?

Oof.

I glance down at my menu. With a little help from the internet, I was able to figure out exactly what I want to eat. Coq au vin. It doesn't hurt that I saw the recipe in a cooking magazine one day in a doctor's office. I even used Google translate to help me learn how to pronounce the name so when Louis asks me what I want to eat, I don't embarrass myself.

But the two of them are still talking.

Dinner service doesn't technically open for another hour, which explains why Louis's white coat is still pristine. We're the only patrons in the restaurant, and over the soft classical music, I can hear a low hum and clatter from the kitchen as his crew prepares for the rush of guests.

Our tablecloth is white, starched, and crisp. The table we're at only seats two and is in the very center of the restaurant on a small raised dais. A little internet sleuthing told me that it often remains empty during meals because Louis refuses to seat anyone there who isn't dressed well enough to be a centerpiece.

That explains the plunging emerald-green dress I have on. It clings to my curves, shows off the swell of my breasts, and has a slit right up my thigh. Lawrence is in a suit—custom-made, of course—with cufflinks that probably cost more than my first car.

We look like we could be on the cover of a magazine. More than that, we look worthy of sitting in the place of honor of this restaurant.

As thrilled as I am with how I look, this outfit is a far cry from the sweaters and blue jeans I normally wear. And don't even get me started on the stilettos. My feet ache, and I'm really hoping that some delicious food will take my mind off the pain.

"*C'est bon,*" Louis says, then gives me another small bow before turning and hurrying back to the kitchen.

I frown. "I thought he was going to take our order," I say, and my boyfriend shakes his head. The smile he gives me is pitying, like he can't believe I'd say something so silly.

"He did, my dear. We just wanted to catch up at first for a bit."

"Coq au vin?" My mouth waters. The pictures in the magazine had made the meal look amazing, and while I'd thought about trying to replicate it at home, there's no way I'd be able to. I'd love cooking lessons so I can get better in the kitchen, but at this point, I know I'd butcher the meal and be disappointed.

"Oh, no. Bœuf bourguignon."

My heart sinks. "I really wanted the coq au vin," I begin, but then I hear how whiny I sound and stop myself. He hates whiny. "I appreciate you ordering, but I'm not a fan of beef. You know this."

"Sure, but, darling, you and I both know that you don't know much about food and what's good. I was just looking out for you. Making sure you got something that you'd really enjoy."

"But coq au vin looks—"

"Enough." The word carries weight, and so does the look he levels at me. "You're having bœuf bourguignon."

"And you?"

"Colin à la bordelaise."

I fight to keep from screaming. I'm not an idiot. I swear, I'm not. But sometimes he acts like I should just know things, like I'm not on the same level as him. "And what is that?" I ask, my voice as sweet as possible.

"Fish."

"Ooh, sounds good. I love fish." I take a sip of my wine. It's only now that I notice he ordered me red and himself white. I hadn't thought much of it at the time, but he's always told me that red goes with beef, white with fish and chicken.

I wasn't ever going to get my coq au vin.

"It will be amazing. Louis is the best chef I've ever met."

"Incredible that he runs this entire place and doesn't speak English," I remark.

He's reaching for his wine but stills, his hand in the air. "Why would you say that?"

"To run such a successful restaurant and only speak French? It's amazing. He's so accomplished."

Lawrence frowns, his eyebrows crashing together. "We went to boarding school together, don't you remember? Of course Louis speaks fluent English."

"I know that," I lie, "but then why didn't you—" I begin, but cut myself off.

"Why didn't we what?"

Speak English so I could understand you two.

But I don't say that. I don't want him to think I'm ungrateful or that I'm questioning him. Still, it hurts a little that the two of them would rather chat in French when it's clear I don't understand a word of it.

"Nothing. I think I'm just hungry."

"You do get hangry." He nods and grabs his napkin before giving it a flip and laying it in his lap. "Don't forget your napkin, love."

"I wouldn't," I say, but that's not entirely the truth, is it? Growing up, we used paper towels for napkins. We rested our elbows on the table as we ate. We certainly didn't have multiple forks and spoons to choose from.

He's taught me so much, and I silently berate myself for not remembering to put my napkin on before he brought it up. But that's the only screw-up I'm going to make tonight. I eyeball my cutlery, silently reminding myself of the role of each.

When I look back up at him, he's smiling at me. When he looks at me like this, his face softens. There are crinkles by his eyes. It's like his entire body relaxes, and I feel myself relaxing in turn.

"You know," he says, picking up his wine and holding it out to me in cheers, "you've come a long way. I'm just so glad I found you when I did, when you were still young enough to be taught. I love you so much."

Warmth grows in me. I needed him, and not just because he makes me laugh, because he makes a ton of money, because he's great in bed. I needed him to better me, to pull me out of the wreckage of how I was raised and make me into someone worthy of sitting in the center of a restaurant.

And he's done just that. It hasn't always been easy, but it's been worth it.

FIVE

Charlotte

"I'm his baby sister, if you want to get technical, but whenever he'd call me that, I'd punch him in the arm," Sophie says, staring at me like she can't believe she has to spell it out for me like this.

I gape at her.

Lawrence and I were together for years, and I'd swear in a court of law that I never heard him mention a sister. Not once. Not when I brought Jordan home and made a list of everyone we needed to notify about her birth. Not when we were on our first date competing to see who had the bigger family.

Not when I checked his Facebook friends to make sure I didn't miss notifying anyone important about his funeral.

I'd know if he had a sister.

Right?

"I'm sorry, but he—"

"Never mentioned me?" Sophie sighs. If her hair wasn't slicked back from her face, I think she'd probably run her fingers through it, but instead she reaches up and lightly pats her temple. Embarrassment washes over her face, but she forces a smile. "I was afraid of that, honestly."

She grabs her wine and takes another sip. A moment later, she's pulled out a stool at the counter and sat down. I glance at Jordan, but she's still sleeping. When Sophie gestures for me to join her, I do just that.

"Why were you afraid of that? And why wouldn't he mention you?" My heart beats hard as I stare at her, looking for any similarities between her and Lawrence. I know genetics can be tricky and don't manifest in the same way.

Maybe their eyes? A small squint when she smiles? Or the shape of her nose?

It's just so hard to tell.

"Lawrence and I have always been competitive." She sighs and traces her finger around the rim of her glass. "Me being the younger sibling and also successful didn't always sit right with him. You know how men can be." She inclines her glass of wine at me, and I force myself to nod in agreement.

"Sure," I say, although I'm not quite following. Yes, men can be *like that*, but I never thought of Lawrence as very competitive. He was kind and supportive of other people and always willing to hand a beggar a dollar or so. That, and he was always the best of the best. He had no competition. Maybe it's because he was older than me that I looked up to him the way I did, but I don't think that's true. He really was that amazing.

But Sophie is making it sound like the two of them were in constant competition.

"What I mean is... I went into architecture." She spreads her hands wide and shrugs like that's going to explain everything.

But it doesn't.

"I'm sorry," I say. "I don't follow."

"Architecture? Lawrence's life purpose? He wanted to be an architect, but I was better at it. That's why he became an anesthesiologist. He couldn't handle the thought of the two of us competing, especially when he wasn't going to come out on top."

I never knew he wanted to be an architect. I thought he'd told me everything about him, but obviously not. Maybe it was a sore spot, which would explain why he never mentioned it—or his sister. "So he cut you off because you two had similar career aspirations?"

"The same career aspirations," she corrects. "And there's more, I'm sure of it, but that's where it all started." She levels her gaze at me as she takes another sip of wine. "Do you have siblings?"

I shake my head.

"Parents? Why isn't anyone here to help you with all of this?" She waves her arm, encompassing not only the kitchen but the rest of the mess in the house that she has no way of knowing exists, but I do.

"My parents are dead," I tell her. "I'm an only child."

"Close friends then?"

I shake my head. "Lawrence was my life," I whisper. It sounds pathetic, doesn't it? To be so swept up in a man that you give up every part of what makes you *you*? Of course, I never meant for it to happen that way, but that's Lawrence for you.

Magnetic. All-encompassing. When he focused on you, it felt like you were the center of the world. And his sense of humor? Second to none. He opened the world for me in a way I didn't know was possible, with dinner at fancy restaurants and trips I'd only ever dreamed of taking.

I know people tend to deify the dead, but Lawrence deserved it. Sure, he could be... well, demanding. If you didn't live up to his expectations, he would let you know about it. Not everyone could handle being married to someone like that. And there were times I knew I'd let him down. There were things we disagreed on.

But I wouldn't have traded being his wife for anything. He worked and traveled all the time, so when he was around, I was willing to drop everything just to be a part of his life. After my first marriage, being put on a pedestal felt nice, and I threw myself one hundred percent into the relationship.

"You must feel so alone." She moves quickly, putting her glass down and taking my hands in hers.

"I'm fine," I begin, but the expression on her face makes me fall silent.

Resolve sets her jaw, and she nods. "Well, you are now."

"Oh, really, you don't have to—"

"Oh, stop. Don't be silly. You need help. I miss my brother. And I have a niece!" She grins like it's the best gift she's ever received. "You think I'm going to turn my back on you two now that I'm here? Not a chance. I hate that I missed out for as long as I did, but you don't have to worry about being alone again. Aunt Sophie's here to help."

She's just so... sincere. Sophie and Lawrence don't seem anything alike, so is it possible this is really his sister? It still blows my mind that he wouldn't tell me he had a sibling in the first place, but what do I know about family dynamics?

I know they can be messy, sure. I know there are plenty of family members who go low or no contact with each other over trivial things, so why not over something like this?

Besides, I'm drowning. Never in my life did I think I'd end up a single mom. I loved Lawrence and honestly kept thinking that we could make our little family work. Now though: no Lawrence.

But Sophie's here.

"I could use help," I say. When I close my eyes, I can see the piles of laundry in the laundry room.

Thank goodness the bank has great insurance so I can cover adding Jordan and don't have to worry about that, but there are other things for me to worry about.

I have her signed up for daycare, but I already know the mess is going to pile up at home with me back to work full-time. That's why I put up an ad for help in the first place. Still, Sophie arrived with suitcases and looks like she's moving in. When I placed the ad, I assumed someone would come here for a few hours twice a week and then go home. It was never supposed to be an overnight position.

But I can hardly turn down her help, can I? She wants to help, and I need it, but I'm not comfortable with someone in the house all the time. What if she were to get bored? Poke around?

What if she found out the secrets I've been keeping?

No way can I do this all by myself. I honestly had no idea how much I relied on Lawrence. But is it worth the risk?

I swallow hard and take the plunge.

"I don't want you to feel put out," I tell her. "I can offer you the guest room if you want to stay here, and I'm happy to pay you what I was going to pay the right person who answered the ad—"

"Pay me?" She inhales sharply and leans back from me, lightly touching her chest like she's grasping for pearls. "Pay me for helping out family?"

"I just mean..."

"Not a chance." She leans forward again, closer this time, her hands back on mine. "Trust me, Charlotte—I don't need your money."

I eyeball the jewelry she's wearing and concede to myself that she's probably right.

"We both lost the man we love," she says. Her voice sounds thick, and she swallows hard, obviously fighting back tears. "But that doesn't mean we can't have a family. Lawrence would want this."

"He would." I stare at her bright-blue eyes. I take in her nose, her mouth. Her features aren't the same as Lawrence's, but close enough. Close enough that looking into them brings me some peace. "Thank you."

"Oh, honey, you don't need to thank me." She stands and lightly touches my shoulder before hurrying to Jordan and picking her up.

I hadn't even noticed my daughter fussing.

"If anything, I should be the one thanking you," she continues, tucking Jordan into her chest and swaying a little. "Being with you, with Jordan... it will help me heal after losing Lawrence."

I smile at her—I can't help myself. Just when I need someone to be on my side, to make sure I don't flounder after losing my husband, here comes Sophie, eager and willing to move in and help me.

"She looks so much like him, doesn't she?" she asks, and I feel my stomach clench.

Does she look like him?

"I think this is going to be a wonderful relationship," she says, ignoring my silence.

I nod, my throat tight. I can do this. I can let her into my house; I can use her to get back on my feet.

But I have to be careful. If she's going to live in this house with Jordan and me, I need to make sure she doesn't get too close.

I knew it was going to be challenging after Lawrence died.

But that didn't stop me from killing him.

SIX

Charlotte

I have the shower running full blast, but I'm not getting in it until I take some time to look up Sophie. Some might call it creeping; I call it doing my due diligence on the woman in my house. She'd showed me her ID and put my mind at ease, but now I want to know more about her.

A shiver races up my spine, and I turn to click on the fireplace. Lawrence always wanted to surround himself with the finest things, which is why there's a gas fireplace in the bathroom. Is it excessive? Yes. Do I love it anyway? Sure do.

I stand in front of it and navigate to Facebook. Surely Sophie will be Lawrence's friend, right? I know she said they had a pretty big falling-out, but something like that doesn't last forever. Siblings are blood, and that matters.

First, though, I do what she said and delete the ad for in-home help. She's right—it's silly to rely on strangers when I have family offering to help for free.

Now to get down to business. I take a deep breath and type.

But when I search for her with Lawrence's last name, she

doesn't pull up, even though I'm sure that's the name I saw on her ID. Is she married? I close my eyes and think. I don't remember seeing a ring, but not every married woman wears one.

Or she might be divorced. If I could just think straight, I'd be able to remember if she said anything about that. I'm exhausted, and I know my thoughts will be clearer after I've gotten some rest, but first I have to make sure I'm not making a mistake letting her move in.

I try Instagram.

No dice.

TikTok? She doesn't seem like a dance-in-front-of-the-camera type woman, but I check anyway.

Nope. Oh, LinkedIn. Easily the most boring of all social media sites, it might be the one she's—

Not on it.

What in the world? Everyone has some social media presence. It's wild to me to think that a grown woman—a professional—wouldn't have some online profile.

Is she hiding something?

Just as quickly as I have it, I push that thought away. Just because I have secrets doesn't mean everyone else does too.

"Fine," I mutter. "I'll have to find out more about you another way."

I put my phone down by the sink and step into the shower. Even though the hot water is luxurious, I speed-wash my hair and soap up, rinsing off as quickly as possible. In just ten minutes I'm in my PJs and wrapped in a fuzzy white robe that's cinched tight around my waist.

Something in the kitchen smells amazing, and I hurry down the stairs to see what Sophie is doing.

In the kitchen doorway, I pause. Jordan's bouncer is by the island, far enough away from the stove that there's no risk of it getting splashed with hot water or grease. She's not in it, and I bet she's in her room for a nap. My stomach tightens—*should I check on her?*—but no, she's fine.

Only a psychopath would come into my house and hurt my daughter after spending all day bonding with her. And Sophie... I do know she's not crazy.

She's not a danger to Jordan.

Sophie's at the stove. She obviously didn't hear me come down the stairs because her back is to me. As she stirs something, she hums, and I take another step forward to see if I can make out the tune.

Before I get close enough to do that, however, she stops and turns to me.

"There you are!" Her face lights up when she sees me, and I feel a momentary pang of remorse over trying to find her online. "Risotto is finished, and I just took the roast chicken out of the oven."

"Oh, wow. It smells amazing," I tell her, going to stand by the stove so I can see the risotto. "And looks even better. I've never had it, but—"

She gasps, putting her hand on her chest in mock outrage. "Did Lawrence not ever take you out for risotto?"

I force a smile. "Oh, you know your brother. We did go out when we were first dating, but then we got married and he became such a homebody when he was around. Since he traveled all the time for work, he loved staying in when he was off. I swear, getting him to run to the grocery store was a bit of a nightmare."

"Really? Growing up he always loved travel. The theater, cruises, trips abroad... he wasn't one to sit around and wait for life to happen to him."

I flush. "People change."

"Sure do." She pauses, like she's giving me a chance to speak, but when I don't, she forges ahead. "I'm happy to cook. I figured I'd have a hot meal on the table for you when you get home from work tomorrow. Jordan and I can run to the store if we need anything else, and that way you don't have to worry about what you're going to eat when you get off work."

I still don't answer. She's plating our food now, each movement deliberate. Her confidence in the kitchen—no, in the way she handles everything—is inspiring.

"Sophie."

"Hmm?" She raises an eyebrow but keeps working.

"I'm going to spend a few more days at home with Jordan. And then she'll be going to daycare."

"Oh?"

"Yeah, I just wanted a bit more time with her. It's been the plan all along." I pause to snatch a breath but don't let her get a word in edgewise. "Please understand that this isn't personal. I want her to have routine, and I don't want to make you feel like you have to do more than you want to just because you're Jordan's aunt."

"Are you sure that's the best idea?"

"Daycare?"

"Exactly."

Her question surprises me, and I pause for a moment, thinking. "Of course it is," I say slowly. "I'm planning on going back to work, but more than that, I want what's best for Jordan. She needs routine. Stimulation."

The nod she gives me is brisk. She takes a deep breath then slowly lets it out. "If you don't mind me asking, how much does it cost to send her to daycare?"

"It's three hundred a week," I say.

"And I know you work at the bank, but did you say how much you make?"

I shake my head. "I'm just a teller, so I'm not making a ton of money. It's enough for bills, but honestly, if I knew for sure that Lawrence had left me the house, I wouldn't be so worried." I pause, wondering how much to say to her, but then the words spill out of me. "I'm not the executor, but the lawyer won't tell me who it is."

"You're not the executor?" She frowns. "But you're his wife."

I turn away from her so she can't see the tears that spring to my eyes.

I naturally assumed I'd be the executor, that I'd be in charge of everything, that Jordan and I would be taken care of. But after Lawrence died, I called the lawyer to make sure everything was set up with his will and found out that not only was the house not left to me but also that I wasn't in charge of his estate. Of course, he wouldn't tell me who everything was left to, or who was in charge, and it's driving me nuts.

Who in the world would it be if not me? I barely have time to register that thought before it hits me.

His sister. The one I didn't know he had.

Is that why she's here? To handle his estate and kick me out of the house? Would she do that—waltz in here and remove me without a second thought? Is that why she came with suitcases, all ready to move in? And if that's what's happening, why wouldn't she tell me that she's the executor? There must be something for her to gain by hiding that truth from me.

My stomach twists. To hide the fear growing in me, I take a sip of my coffee, but it feels like it curdles in my mouth.

I know I'm on borrowed time here. Whether or not Sophie is the executor, I know I'm losing the house soon.

That means I have to get my ducks in a row as quickly as possible. I have to figure out where Jordan and I will go. Being able to save three hundred bucks a week by letting Sophie watch Jordan would be so helpful. Just two months of that and I'd have enough for first and last month's rent for a new apartment.

My mind is racing, and I realize she's still waiting for a

response. "No, I don't," I say, giving my head a shake to drive the point home. "He never said."

She taps one finger against her chin. "Hmm. He left you in a terrible position," she tells me. "I'm so sorry my brother did this to you. I want you to know that you can change your mind about daycare. No pressure, but I'm here if you want. It would be a great way for you to save some money."

"I think," I say slowly, carefully choosing each word so they're the least likely to offend, "that we can take it slow. I don't see a reason to leap right into you watching her all the time, especially when I'm sure you have a life you're going to want to get back to. I'm sorry, but I need to know you better, need to know you're not going to up and leave right when we're relying on you."

"I wouldn't—"

"Jordan needs routine. And she needs me."

She nods and smiles. "Of course she needs you, Charlotte. You're her mother. But you can't be the only thing in her life, no matter how much you might want it."

I don't know what to say in response, so she continues.

"You're going to have to learn to rely on other people. And you're going to have to learn to trust other people to take care of her. Because..." She sighs and trails off.

"Because what?" It's bait, the way she lets her voice trail off, and I take it, but I don't care.

"Her father already met with tragedy. It would be awful if something happened to you too."

SEVEN

Sophie

So Charlotte thinks she'll do a better job parenting Jordan than I would, does she?

It's laughable. She can't even put together a healthy meal without me here to do it for her and she actually believes she should be a mother?

How she convinced Lawrence to let her have a baby, I'll never know. But I'm here now and I'm ready to figure some things out, like whether or not she even deserves to be a mother.

And if she's the reason Lawrence is dead.

I turn and look at her, trying to gauge what's going through her mind. She's hungry—I've heard her stomach rumble no fewer than three times since she came down from her shower—but beyond that, her face is so calm, so placid, it's impossible for me to read her mind.

No problem. I'm not going anywhere until I learn everything there is to know about the woman Lawrence decided to marry.

"Well, we can figure out Jordan's schedule later, but right

now we should eat," I say, breaking the silence and turning from Charlotte. I reach out and turn up the right knob on the baby monitor I have set on the kitchen counter.

Charlotte inhales sharply. "Did you take the baby monitor from my room?" she asks. Her voice is level, but it's obvious she's seething on the inside.

"Oh yeah, I grabbed it when you were in the shower. I figured it would be a good idea for me to have it since I'm going to be taking care of Jordan." I glance over my shoulder at her and throw her an easy smile.

She doesn't return it.

"You came into my bedroom while I was showering?" Her face twists, and I feel a jolt of pleasure.

"Don't make it sound like I was breaking the law." I turn to her, two plates of food in my hands. "I knew that if Jordan needed sleep, I'd need the baby monitor, so you weren't the one getting up with her." I pause to let that soak in. Make her think I'm on her side. "I'm so sorry if I did anything to hurt you. I obviously overstepped."

Charlotte closes her eyes and takes a deep breath. "No, you're fine," she says, shaking her head like she's trying to clear dark thoughts. "I just... Not having Lawrence and trying to manage Jordan and—" Her voice breaks, and she pauses before speaking again. "I know I'm probably paranoid. I know I need to relax a little and let people help, but it's strange to do that, you know? That's not how I operate. I like being in control."

"I'll ask you next time before I do something like that." On the inside, I want to roll my eyes at how sensitive she's being. But instead I put the plate down and reach out to take her hands. "You just have to trust me, Charlotte. I'm here to help you."

"Of course. I know you are." She takes a deep breath and completely changes the subject, surprising me. "Hey, did you call the lawyer before you came here? After you found out that Lawrence died?"

Interesting. "Why would you ask something like that?"

Her face burns, and she looks down and to the side. She's terrible at hiding what she's thinking.

"Ahh, you think Lawrence might have left everything to me? Oh, Charlotte, don't you worry about that. We weren't close, remember? What, was he suddenly going to leave everything to his estranged sister instead of his wife? Not a chance."

"But then who?" she asks. "If not his wife and not his sister, then who?"

"That's the million-dollar question, isn't it? Literally." I pause like I'm really thinking it through even though I already know the answer. "You find that information, you find who was more important to Lawrence than either of us." I shrug and grab my plate to take it to the dining room.

"So it's not you?"

I'm halfway to the table and I turn in surprise. "Me?"

"You're not the beneficiary? Or the executor?"

"Oh, honey. Lawrence always did whatever he wanted, didn't he? I wish I had a better answer for you than that, but the truth of the matter is that he lived his life on his own terms." I stare at her. "You said he didn't leave you the house, but what about his accounts?"

She shakes her head.

"But you two had joint accounts, right? I mean, you are his wife."

"He wanted everything kept separate." She turns away from me and opens the fridge.

Of course he did. Lawrence knew how to protect himself. I put my plate on the table and turn back to the kitchen where Charlotte is leaning in the fridge.

"See anything else you want on the table?" I ask.

She jumps. Grabs a bottle of wine. Closes the door. "White sound good?"

"It's always the right answer." I walk over to the cupboard where she keeps the wine glasses and pull two out. When I turn back to hand them to her, however, I pause. "Something wrong?"

"Nooo." She drags out the word. "How did you know where I kept the wine glasses?"

"Good guess," I tell her, then grin.

She doesn't respond while she pours the wine. When the glasses are almost full to the top, she corks the bottle and places it back in the fridge.

"Oh, I wanted to ask you," I say. "I saw insulin in the fridge. Are you diabetic? Should I worry about what I'm feeding you?"

She freezes, then slowly closes the fridge door and turns to face me.

"Not me," she says. "Lawrence."

I frown. "Lawrence wasn't diabetic."

"He was," she says, and she almost sounds confident. "Maybe not when he was younger, but yeah, now he had to have insulin."

She's lying. "Weird."

Her confidence grows, and she nods. "You never know when you'll develop it. There's so much doctors and scientists are now learning about type one and type two and how to treat them."

"Well, we can throw out the insulin then," I tell her. "He doesn't need it any longer."

"You're right. I just... haven't thought about it."

We walk to the table in silence. I keep glancing over at her out the corner of my eye. Her jaw is tight, her gaze locked on our food.

She's lying, but that's fine.

I'm lying too.

EIGHT

EIGHT AND A HALF YEARS AGO

Her

The boat pulls away from shore, slicing through the water, whatever motor used to make it run as silent as the breeze riffling my hair.

When strong arms wrap around me, I turn away from watching the land recede and go up on my tiptoes to plant a kiss on Lawrence's jaw.

"You enjoying your day?"

"Loving it." I grin at him and smooth my hands down over my dress. It's one he picked out for me in the spring, a floral halter that swooshes around my knees when I walk. I adore it, especially when paired with my new espadrilles.

He plucks at the halter of my dress, and I swat his hand away.

"Sir. I know you're not trying to untie me when we're still in sight of shore," I say, but even though I'm faking outrage, I can't stop the smile from playing on my lips. "I'm a lady, you know."

"A lady who should have put on the bikini I bought her," Lawrence responds, his fingers still lightly resting on the back of my neck. "If you had, then me untying your dress wouldn't be such a big deal."

"Hmm." I reach up and take his hand. Squeezing it, I bring it to my lips to kiss. "Well, how about this? We get away from prying eyes and my bra and undies can act like a bikini."

He frowns, but the expression only lasts a moment before it's gone. "That'll do, my love. But don't keep me waiting for too long. I want something nice to look at while we're out here."

Lawrence plants a kiss on me, then pulls away, presumably to speak to the captain. When we started dating, I'd gotten the feeling he owned a yacht, but he'd laughed and told me that owning a boat was never on his to-do list.

So, instead, whenever we want to get out on the water, we rent one.

Well, he rents one. I've seen the bill for how much it costs to take this thing out for the day, and there's just no way. At least not until my business really gets up and running.

Which, by the way, is something he promised he'd help me with. Not that him giving me a career boost is why I'm with him, but I'm not going to lie and say that I'm not happy about having his help.

Overhead, a bird screams, and I turn to watch it fly by. We have the yacht rented for the entire weekend, and since it's only Friday afternoon, there's plenty of time for the two of us to connect, but I don't want to start this trip off on the wrong foot.

Sighing, I reach up and untie the halter of my dress. It feels wrong somehow to prance around in my underthings, but really? They offer just as much or more coverage than the bikinis he likes me to wear.

My dress falls silently around my feet, and I kick it out of the way. For a moment, I consider losing the shoes as well, but they're just enough of a platform to give me an instant butt lift.

Sure, I've been hitting the gym three times a week and even

have a personal trainer now, but what girl doesn't want a bit of help from time to time?

When I bend down and gather up my dress, there's a low whistle, and I whip around. My face burns. I hold the fabric to my chest.

Did the captain come out here to watch? No way would he, not when he has to know how quickly he'd be fired. And knowing Lawrence, he'd get all of his money back for the weekend.

But it's not some old man with a beard staring at me.

It's Lawrence.

He stalks towards me, his eyes dark pools. I can see the tic in his jaw as he gets closer to me. His hands clench into fists before he relaxes them.

"It's not a bikini," I say, already primed to apologize, but he stops me, pressing his finger to my lips to shut me up.

"You're gorgeous." His hand falls to my hip, and he grips me there before slowly tracing his fingers across my abs.

I suck in—I can't help it.

"With a little more time at the gym, you'll be perfect."

My cheeks flame brighter, but I'm no longer embarrassed. It's silly to crave his attention, his encouragement, but that's exactly what happens whenever he tells me I've done a good job. I lap it up like a dog.

"I appreciate you setting me up with your personal trainer. She does great work."

"She does, doesn't she?" He steps back from me. "Turn. Slowly."

I do, my teeth sinking into my lower lip as I fight back a smile. I'm sure there are hundreds of women who wouldn't want to be on display like this. They wouldn't want their bodies picked apart, but I'm working hard, and I know how much he appreciates it.

When I'm facing him again, he's no longer standing.

His eyes are locked on me, but he's kneeling.

My heart kicks into high gear.

"I love you," he says, his voice clear and crisp. It feels like all of my senses sharpen, and I stare at him, doing my best to make sense of what I'm seeing.

Is this really happening?

"You are the only one for me. My entire life, I've been looking for my perfect person, my perfect partner. You're it."

I'm far from perfect. But I don't tell him that. Every single day I strive to do better, to be better. I try to make good decisions with what I eat and drink. I park further from the store so I can get in my steps.

I'm not perfect yet, but I'm closer than I was when we first met.

"Will you do me the honor of my lifetime and marry me?"

For a moment, I can't speak. I can't breathe. I feel like time has stopped, like the entire world is holding its breath as I prepare myself to say the only thing I can.

Yes.

Lawrence opens the ring box, and the sun hits the diamond just right. It sparkles, and I gasp, reaching for it before I have the chance to answer him. No, it's not the ring I would have chosen, but he chose it.

For me.

That's what matters.

"Yes," I whisper, then I drag my eyes from the ring to his face. "Yes, of course I'll marry you!"

He stands and whoops, grabbing my hand so he can push the ring on my finger.

It fits.

Well, almost.

"Five more pounds and it'll fit perfect," he tells me. One hand cups my chin, lifting it to him so he can kiss me. "You can do it."

NINE

WEDNESDAY

Charlotte

I'm scrolling through my phone, Jordan in my arms, when Sophie joins us on the front porch.

I'm still in my PJs, old ones that are soft, with holes in them, and she's already dressed for the day, looking as impeccable as she did when she arrived yesterday. She's holding two steaming mugs of coffee and sets one down on the small table next to me.

"Sleep good?" I ask, taking in her smooth skin, the distinct lack of dark circles under her eyes, how shiny her hair is. The answer to my question is obvious before she speaks.

"Like a dream! That mattress is amazing. I felt like I was sleeping in a cloud. What about you?" She sits in the chair next to me and watches me over the top of her coffee as she takes a sip.

"Fine. Just fine," I lie. In reality, every creak the house made, every time it settled, it ripped me out of whatever tentative sleep I was in. By two this morning, I finally got up and came downstairs. I'm exhausted.

"You look tired," she says. "You know, motherhood doesn't agree with everyone. Have you seen a doctor about your skin?"

"I've thought about it," I admit, reaching up to touch the newest blemish that popped up overnight. "But it can be so tricky finding someone who will really take care of you and doesn't see you simply as a paycheck."

"I can give you the name of my derm," she tells me. "She's amazing. She won't admit it, but I'm pretty sure she's a dermatologist by day, model by night. She's only... oh, thirty, forty minutes from here."

I stiffen. "So close?"

"Yeah, I'd say her office is halfway between here and my house. Why?"

"I didn't know you were that close to us." I feel my throat tighten.

"I'm about an hour and a half away. Is that not okay? What's wrong with where I live?"

"You're close enough to visit on your lunch break but you and Lawrence never talked?"

"Oh, Charlotte." She sighs heavily. "You don't have siblings, right?" When I shake my head, she continues. "Then you can't understand what it's like. At this point, I think Lawrence and I could have lived next door to each other and still not seen much of the other. Now, if I'd have known getting to see Jordan was on the table, I would have made amends before it was too late."

That makes sense. We all have regrets, no matter how much we don't want to admit it. From what Sophie is saying, her relationship with Lawrence was a source of a lot of pain. Still, I wish she'd been in our lives before...

But do I? It would have been a lot harder to kill him and get away with it if she were poking around.

And what about my other secret? That one would have been impossible to keep.

"Tell me more about when you and Lawrence were kids," I begin, but just then my phone rings. I juggle Jordan as I answer it.

It's the lawyer. Without thinking about what I'm doing, I hand Jordan to Sophie and stand. In a few seconds, I'm on the other end of the porch, leaning over the railing, desperate to put a bit of space between the two of us so she doesn't overhear what I'm saying.

"Hello?"

"Mrs. Moore? This is John Price, at Price, Laite, and Smythe."

"Oh, hi. Yes, what can I do for you?" My heart beats faster, and I turn and casually lean against the railing.

"I'm returning your call from last week. I'm sorry I couldn't get to you sooner, but I was on vacation and needed some time to look into your request."

"Great." I pause. "What did you find?"

"Mrs. Moore, I know you're eager to settle the will. And I understand that it's frustrating to feel like you can't handle things after Lawrence's death, but you need to bear with me. You can't keep calling me every week, expecting to get a different answer."

"I'm sorry." I lower my voice and cover my mouth with my hand. "I don't mean to be a pain and push you, I really don't. It's just that things are up in the air right now with the house and the accounts, and we just had the baby, and—"

"And if I had better news, I'd have called you. Lawrence did not leave you the house. As we discussed, you're not on the title, and that means the house will pass to his estate."

"Right. And I applied to be the executor, but I'm still waiting to hear back, and I'm starting to wonder if—"

"There is someone more suited to running the estate." His words are becoming increasingly more and more clipped. "I'm sure you understand that."

"Who would be more suited to running the estate than me?" *I'm his wife.*

He launches into an explanation but I'm barely listening. Instead, I look up at Sophie.

Someone more suited.

Not only is she actually related to Lawrence, but just look at her. She's put together and definitely knows her way around spreadsheets and how to handle all of the bills that will arise.

And I'm... me.

Does she know? Did she lie to me? If so, why would she do that?

"—remember, though, that all the bills you incur relating to Lawrence's death can be reimbursed by the estate. Once the executor has come forward and set up the account, you can send the bills you paid to the estate. You'll get your money back."

I don't want my money back. I want the house.

I want it all.

"Mrs. Moore, did you hear me?"

I clear my throat. "Yes, of course. I just have another question." When I glance at Sophie, I'm not surprised to see that she's standing with Jordan now, slowly rocking her back and forth. There's a smile on her face, and Jordan looks perfectly content.

I should be happy that my baby feels safe enough with Sophie to sleep in her arms, but there's part of me envious that she's the one holding her right now.

"I'll answer it if I can."

"Who is set to inherit the house?"

A pause, and I immediately know that I pushed him too far, that I'm not going to get that information. He's already made it clear that I'm not getting the house, that I'm not going to be in charge of the estate, and I highly doubt that he's going to tell me about who is, no matter how much I ask.

"Like I've told you, if I were able to share that information with you, I would." His voice has taken on a firmer tone. Very no-nonsense. I'm being shut out. "I appreciate you understanding that there is some information I simply can't give you. The executor will be in touch with you when they're ready."

"Right. Of course." He's so diplomatic. If Sophie weren't right on the other side of the porch, I'd scream, but I don't want to draw attention to me. It's embarrassing that Lawrence didn't take care of me.

If I'd known he wasn't going to take care of me, would I have done what I did?

Not a question. I'm a mother. Mothers will do anything for their children.

Case in point: killing Lawrence.

The news would spin it like I'm a monster, I know they would, but that really couldn't be further from the truth. I'm a good mother, just one who was pushed to the edge. When your husband never wanted a child and doesn't love the one you're lucky enough to have... what do you do?

You take care of things, that's what.

"I'll be in touch if I need anything from you. If you don't hear from me, you will hear from Lawrence's executor. Have a good day, Mrs. Moore."

And he hangs up.

My face burns as I slip my phone into my pocket. I take a deep breath to try to calm my fluttering heart, then finally turn and smile at Sophie and Jordan.

The last thing I want is for Sophie to realize how mortified I am. How Lawrence didn't take care of me the way I deserved. She knows part of it but not the full extent, and not the fact that I'm desperate.

Because I have nothing.

The house. The car. Those are in Lawrence's name, as are

all his bank accounts. Thank goodness I still have a few thousand in my checking account. If not, I'd be totally screwed.

So I have a few thousand dollars. Clothes. Shoes. If it weren't for him, I wouldn't even have the jewelry I'm wearing. My engagement ring has half a dozen huge diamonds, and I glance down at it.

I could pawn my jewelry, I guess. I know the market for used stuff isn't nearly as strong as for something brand new, so the amount I get won't be as high as I'd like, but at least then I'd have some cash.

And Jordan. I do have her.

And she's worth the stress I'm under.

"All good?" Sophie smiles at me.

I expect her to bring me my baby, but when she doesn't, I approach the two of them. "Thanks for holding her while I was on that call," I say, reaching for Jordan.

Sophie hesitates. I see it on her face, that she doesn't want to give Jordan up. There's a pang of worry in the back of my head, but then Jordan is in my arms, and the expression I thought I saw on Sophie's face is gone. I lightly kiss Jordan's nose.

She's mine. All mine.

"Everything's fine," I lie. "Now, you were going to tell me what it was like growing up with Lawrence."

Her face brightens. "I can do that! I have the link to one of his online photo albums. They're mostly from after anesthesiology school. Want to see them?"

"I do." I ache to see them. Lawrence was larger than life, and he still is, even in death.

"Oh, how about this?" Her thumbs fly across her phone's screen. "What's your email? I can send you some so you have them."

I rattle off my email and pull my phone from my pocket, eagerly waiting for the *ding* from my email app. An email from

Sophie pops up, and my finger hovers over it to open it, but I don't tap it.

I'm staring at her email address, a flutter of excitement in my stomach.

Using it could be the perfect way to track her down online.

TEN

Sophie

With Charlotte on the porch eagerly looking at photos of Lawrence, I have some time to myself to look around her house without being interrupted.

There's no time to waste in the guest room, so I close the door behind me and hurry down the hall to Charlotte's bedroom. Right outside her door, I pause, listening for any sound that would tell me that she's come back inside.

But there's nothing.

"Okay, Charlotte," I mutter. "Let's see what secrets you've got hidden behind door number one."

When I turn the handle, though, it doesn't budge. I twist it from side to side, then pause, leaning my head against the door.

I pat the sides of my head, feeling for a bobby pin, but come up short.

Fine. That's fine. It's a minor setback, but not one that will keep me out of the game for very long. I'll find a key for the door or get my hands on a bobby pin and unlock it when she isn't around. Just because I can't get in right now doesn't mean I'm locked out for good.

I should have paid more attention when I went in yesterday to get the baby monitor, but I was too focused on Jordan. But that's okay because there are so many other places in the house to explore. Her bedroom wasn't locked yesterday, so she must have done it this morning when she got up. Maybe I made her nervous.

I'll just have to be more careful. The last thing I want is for her to try to make me leave before I have all the answers and information I came for.

I didn't notice any squeaky stairs when I came up here, but I still take careful steps as I work my way back down to the first floor. Sure, Charlotte could come into the house at any time, but I'd rather her not catch me in the act of snooping. As quietly as possible, I walk to the front door and peer out onto the porch.

She's just where I left her, Jordan in her arms, her eyes locked on her phone. I barely take in the small smile on her lips before I look back at her baby.

She should be mine.

Honestly, someone like Charlotte, who can barely survive as a single mom, doesn't deserve a child. It's insane to me that there are so many women every year who have babies they don't want or deserve, and I've never been a mother.

I don't know how long I stand here staring at the perfect curve of Jordan's forehead, the way her nose flips up at the end a little bit, before giving my head a shake and stepping away from the front door.

Yes, Jordan is perfect. And sure, I could spend hours of my time here watching her and drinking her in, but that won't get me any closer to the answers I came here to find. It was pure luck that Charlotte became desperate enough to put out an ad for help right at the time I decided to learn more about her.

I'm sure I could have talked my way in here without the ad, but her being desperate made my life that much easier.

That thought is on repeat as I walk into the family room. This place was a pit when I arrived yesterday, and today it isn't much better, but right now I don't care about that.

I walk over to the bookshelf in the corner of the room and trail my fingers over the spines.

Lots of poetry. That's Lawrence's doing, since I doubt Charlotte could recognize iambic pentameter if it bit her on the butt. Some travel books, which I can attribute to Lawrence as well, and then...

Smut. Well, it looks like I found Charlotte's contribution to the bookshelf.

There's a single photo album, and I carefully pull it out and flip through it. Even though I know it's crazy to think there would be any pictures of me in it, I still hold my breath as I look at each picture.

They're all of Charlotte. Of course she'd gift Lawrence a boudoir photo shoot. I barely look at the pages before closing it and shelving it.

Okay, so there's nothing damning on the bookshelf, but this house is huge and there are plenty of places for things to hide, I'm sure.

Like the insulin in the fridge. I don't care what Charlotte said, Lawrence hasn't ever needed insulin. No relatives have diabetes, and while I know these things can hit you out of left field, that's not what happened.

Lawrence was healthy when he died, and on the younger side of fifty. I wasn't privy to his medical report, of course, since Charlotte handled everything after his death, but I'm curious.

Fine. If I'm honest with myself about why I'm here, it's not just because I want to know more about Jordan. I want to get to know the baby and spend time with her. I want to make sure Charlotte is fit to be a mother, which I really don't think she is.

It's also because I want to find out who Lawrence married. And if she killed him.

ELEVEN

Charlotte

Sophie going to her room to freshen up after lunch gave me the perfect opportunity to look her up without having her peer over my shoulder to see what I'm doing.

There's a certain part of your brain that won't ever forget important things, I swear it. I'll never forget the way it felt to hold Jordan for the first time, or how it felt when Lawrence told me he loved me.

And just like those, I'm confident I'll never forget Sophie's email address.

Social media failed me last night, but I feel good about this.

I type it into Google to see what will pop up. Any websites linked to her address should come right up. For a moment, I hesitate, then click to search.

The first result is for her architect firm. *Stone Creek Design.* I tap the link and am immediately met with a glamor shot of Sophie.

There. On her left hand, a small gold band.

Well, that answers my question about whether or not she's married.

Or was.

"Holy cow," I whisper, flicking my finger to scroll. I don't know what I was expecting when she told me she was an architect, but it wasn't this. For some reason, I was expecting a cold aesthetic, with white marble and subway tile everywhere.

But that couldn't be further from the truth. The houses she's designed are homey, with wide front porches, exposed beams, and kitchens that are the heart of the home. I find my jaw dropping as I check out her floorplans and give my head a shake to clear it.

As much as I'd like to keep poking around, any answers I'm looking for about this woman won't be found on her perfectly curated website, I know that much. Back to the Google results. My finger hovers over the next result from Fast People Finder.

I click it.

The page loads immediately and is so filled with information that it's overwhelming. I take a deep breath and start at the top of the screen where it lists Sophie's name and age.

Her address is blurred out, and I frown, then flick my finger on the screen to scroll.

Next are associated addresses, phone numbers, and additional email addresses she might use. They're all blurred out as well, though, so I can't make note of them and use them to find out more about her unless I pay, and I'm not ready to go that far.

"Possible relatives," I whisper, touching the screen and scrolling so I can get a better look at what's written there. "Lawrence, obviously. That makes sense. And their parents— Lawrence told me their names."

"Whatcha doing?" Sophie's voice yanks me out of my thoughts, causing me to jump. I fumble the phone and it falls to the floor next to me.

Screen up.

She frowns and picks it up before I can grab it.

"Sophie, I—"

She's silent for a moment, then clears her throat. "If you want to know something about me, Charlotte, all you have to do is ask. I'm an open book." She hands my phone back to me and gives me a smile, but it doesn't reach her eyes.

My face burns. "I'm sorry—I just wanted to know more about you. Looking you up seemed like a good idea."

"Please just ask me next time." She sits next to me on the floor. "Now, what can I do to help you? Want to swap Jordan-watching duties and take turns cleaning?"

Instead of answering, I look around the room to see if it's really as bad as I thought.

The space itself? It's incredible. Huge floor-to-ceiling windows run the length of the room, providing an unobstructed view of the garden. There's a baby grand piano in the corner, music open on the bench. I think it looks great, homey and inviting, but even from here I can see the layer of dust on the lid.

I wince.

The coffee table has drink rings in the wood. There are stacks of books and baby toys on the floor. From my vantage point, I can see three of Jordan's onesies scattered around.

Is that a diaper under the coffee table? I shake my head.

It's a mess.

"Splitting up duties sounds great—" I say, but before I can finish the sentence, Sophie leans over and plucks Jordan from my arms.

I stare at her.

"Oh," she says, her mouth widening as she looks at me. "Did you want to hold Jordan first? I thought I deserved a turn with her since you've held her since lunch."

I didn't think it was a competition, who was going to hold her when, especially since I'm her mom, but I force a smile. "No, that's fine," I lie. I try to keep the smile on my face even though what I really want to do is pull Jordan back from her and snuggle her myself.

Sophie looks satisfied. She gives a little sigh and sinks back, pulling Jordan even closer. She looks like a natural. Some women do, and I've always been envious of how quickly they took to being a mother. I would die for Jordan, but there are times when I feel like I have to work hard to know what she needs.

"I'm surprised you never had children," I offer before I realize what I'm saying. Even as the words leave my lips, I'm surprised at myself, but Sophie doesn't seem bothered.

"Do I look like a natural?" She brushes her finger against Jordan's cheek. "I always wanted them more than anything."

"Me too."

"But some things just don't work out." She looks up at me, and I get the feeling she had to fight to drag her gaze away from my baby. "Was Lawrence happy when you made him a father?"

"He was over the moon," I tell her. "Lawrence was an amazing guy. I miss him so, so much." I can say those words a hundred, a thousand times, but they still won't come close to touching how terrible it is to be without him.

"I know. Me too." Sophie shifts to pull her phone from her pocket and then thumbs it on. "As you know, all of our baby pictures were lost in that fire when we were younger, and I sent you some of Lawrence from when he was older, but here's one of him as a teenager." She turns her phone for me to see.

I'm greedy to see pictures of him. I miss him so badly and don't feel like I had enough time with him. Even though I know he loved me, I can't help but feel envious of Sophie for having so many years with him.

Lawrence was... everything. He commanded a crowd in a way I've never seen before, and even when we were in a group of people, he managed to make me feel like I was the only person who mattered.

How many times did he take me to fancy restaurants, show me off, even take me to the theater and introduce me to the cast? Well, at least before we got married, and then he told me he'd rather be at home with me, enjoying me, not where everyone else could see me. But still, everyone loved Lawrence, and when I was with him, everyone loved me as well.

The photo she's showing me is of both of them, standing together, him in a tux, her in a prom dress. Lawrence's rolling his eyes like there was some dumb joke made and Sophie is cracking up, her head thrown back in laughter.

"You two had a great relationship before it all fell apart, didn't you?" I ask.

"We did." Her voice is thick, and she clears her throat before continuing. "We really did. This photo pretty much captures our relationship. Always laughing, always having fun."

"Until you weren't."

A nod. "Until we weren't."

"Was he in your wedding? Or did your relationship fall apart before that?"

"What?" There's a warning in the word, but I've already stepped in it, so I continue.

I clear my throat. "Your email address. I thought you were married before."

The glance she gives me is sharp. "I was. How do you know that?"

My cheeks burn. "I found your website," I finally admit. "And I saw that you were wearing a wedding band in one of the photos."

"Ahh, so you're a sleuth. Good to know—I'll have to watch myself around you." She laughs, then gives a little shrug like she's embarrassed. "You're right, I was married. Why do you ask?"

"You kept your maiden name? It's the same as Lawrence's last name."

"Oh, yes." She chuckles and the tightness in her face relaxes. "I know it's controversial to some people, believe me. My husband thought so at the time, but I didn't go through architecture school and work my butt off just to change my last name and only be known as someone's wife."

I wait a beat to see what else she's going to say. When she doesn't continue speaking, I rock forward to stand.

She moves just as quickly, adjusting Jordan so she can reach out and take me by the elbow and give me a bit of support.

"Careful. You're almost dead on your feet." Her eyes flick up and down my body, and she hums in the back of her throat. "You look rough, sweetie. Instead of cleaning, why don't you go take a nap while I watch Jordan?"

"I couldn't—"

"You could and you should," she says firmly. "When's the last time you had a solid nap?"

Tears well up in my eyes as she pushes the right button. I feel all alone, and here Sophie is, swooping in like a guardian angel. I can't turn down her help.

No matter what secrets I want to keep hidden.

"Jordan and I have this covered," she continues. "Snuggling? That's basically my specialty."

"Are you sure?" I'm trying not to sound too hopeful, but I already know I'm going to let her help me out. I saw myself in the mirror this morning. The dark circles under my eyes are too deep to hide with makeup.

"So sure."

I can't say no. I need a break. I need help.

"I just changed her," I say, relieved when she looks at me. "I know it's probably crazy of me to say this since you're family, but—"

"You don't want anyone else changing her?"

I nod, and she smiles.

"I totally understand. If there's a problem, I'll wake you up. Otherwise, enjoy your nap."

"Okay, but only a short one. It's what? A bit after one?" I glance at my watch to confirm. It feels strange to have my arms empty after being the only one taking care of Jordan for the past month since Lawrence died. To have something to do, I dust my hands on my pants. "I don't want to miss the entire afternoon, so I want to be up by three at the latest."

She smiles. "You'll feel so much better. Take it from someone who naps whenever she wants to."

That sounds amazing.

I groan, then bend down and plant a kiss on the top of Jordan's head. After I straighten back up, I place my hand lightly on Sophie's shoulder.

"I had no idea Lawrence had a sister, and I'm going to feel guilty about that for a long time," I say. "But I'm glad you're here."

She smiles in response, and I glance at my watch. "Okay, a nap really does sound good. I'll set my alarm for three—how does that sound?"

"Oh, don't set your alarm. They're the worst way to wake up, aren't they? I'd much rather be woken up by this sweet girl right here." She nuzzles Jordan and breathes in her scent.

"Okay." For a moment, I'm unsure whether or not I should do what she says, but then I shake my head to clear it. "Yeah. That sounds good actually. Thank you."

I smile again at Sophie, then turn and slowly walk upstairs.

This is good. Getting help. Trusting someone? This is good. It's what I should do so I can be the best possible mom for Jordan.

And if, for some reason, it turns out that I can't trust Sophie? Well, then I guess I'll have to do to her what I did to Lawrence.

TWELVE

EIGHT YEARS AGO

Never once did I think that I'd be married in a church. Not that I thought that I'd burst into flames upon entering it, but church was never really my thing. Even when my parents were still alive, we didn't go to service.

So it wasn't important to me to walk down the aisle in a white dress, but that was my boyfriend's—I'm sorry, my *fiancé's* —idea, and of course I went through with it.

Now I'm waiting in the bridal suite for someone to come get me. When I get nervous, I twirl my engagement ring, and that's what I'm doing, sending it spinning around and around. He was right—five pounds was perfect for the ring to fit like it had been made for me.

I'm alone since I don't have any close friends to come hang out with me while I get ready to say my vows, but that's okay. I keep telling myself that I don't need anyone, that the only person I need will be waiting for me at the end of the aisle, and my anxiety decreases.

As I twirl my ring, I pace back and forth, barely noticing the few bouquets that are in the room. They're all sunflowers, so bright that they hurt to look at, and while sunflowers aren't my favorite flower by any means, they are his.

I keep telling myself that I wish I'd had a bigger role in planning the wedding, but truth be told, I'd be happy wearing a trash bag if it meant marrying the love of my life. Never have I felt anything like this before, and even though I would have chosen different flowers—

The sound of the door opening behind me makes me whip around. I gasp, the soft sound leaving my lips before I can stop it.

"What are you doing here? You're not supposed to see me before I walk down the aisle!" I feel a flush creeping up my chest, my neck, to my cheeks. Thank goodness the makeup artist promised me she'd be back right before I took the long walk in case I needed a touch-up.

"I had to see you. Make sure you weren't going to back out." Lawrence's voice is honey and caramel, and it washes over me, calming me back down. "I'm sorry, I really didn't mean to upset you. You're just so beautiful."

I'm drawn to him like we're magnets, and in just a moment, I'm in his arms. Whatever cologne he has on smells amazing, and I take a deep breath to breathe him in.

"You're not mad?" he asks, then plants a kiss on the top of my head.

"No." I want to bury my face in his chest, but I'm mindful of my makeup. A touch-up is one thing. Her having to do an entirely new face full would be another. "I'm not; I was just surprised."

"Well, I knew you didn't have anyone in here with you, and I didn't want you to be all alone." His voice is soft and soothing. One hand presses against my lower back, keeping me tucked close against him. The other traces up and down my spine. It tickles, and I shift closer to him.

"I'll never be alone again," I tell him.

At that, Lawrence squeezes me closer and then releases me, stepping back and taking my hands so he can get a better look at me. "You are so gorgeous. Very soon you'll walk down that aisle. You'll be my wife. And then you know where we're going?"

I shake my head. That's one part of today he hasn't told me. I'm dying to know where our honeymoon is going to be, but he's been keeping it a secret. Even when I told him that I would need to know so I could pack appropriately, he'd laughed and told me he had it handled.

No way did I ever imagine that his way of handling it would mean ordering me all new clothes and having it carefully packed in new luggage. It's in the back of the limo we're taking to the airport after we say our vows.

No reception. He didn't really want to wait around after we were officially married, and I was fine with jetting off into our new life together.

"Do you want to know?" His voice is teasing.

"I do," I say, but I refuse to play into his hands. For three weeks straight, I tried to get information out of him, but he never budged. I think he enjoyed it, honestly, being the one to know all the information, the one to hold the cards while I fumbled about. And so, while I'm dying to know the plan for the day, I'm not playing that role any longer.

"You could beg me."

I laugh and shake my head. "Not a chance. You had your opportunity to tell me what we're doing, but you didn't. Now I'm content to wait and see where we end up."

"Do it."

"Do what?" I'm still laughing, but the sound falls from my lips when I catch a glimpse of his expression. "Beg you to tell me where we're going?"

"Yes."

"No." I frown at him and pull my hands back. "Not a

chance. You didn't want to tell me and that's fine, but I'm not ruining the surprise now. I'm all-in to be shocked."

For a moment, neither one of us says anything, then he glances down at the Patek Philippe on his wrist.

"In that case," Lawrence says, "I better go. I'm needed at the front of the church." He fingers a lock of hair by my face. "Make sure you pin this back or use some hairspray so it doesn't look out of place in our pictures," he tells me.

I want to lean into the warmth of his hand, but before I can, he's gone, quietly closing the door behind him. For a moment, I don't move, then I hurry to the mirror with my hairspray. I thought the bit of loose hair looked nice, softened up my look a little, but he's probably right.

I spritz it into place.

There.

Just like he wanted.

THIRTEEN

It's the silence of the house that wakes me up.

I don't slowly pop up ready to take on the day—I'm dragged out of my sleep like someone tied a rope around my waist and is pulling me up out of the water. I drooled—I always drool when I nap—and there's hair stuck to my cheek.

Groaning, I brush it away, then rub my eyes.

What time is it?

It's not bright enough out still to be three. Unless there's a storm and it's cloudy, but no. I would have heard it.

And the house is silent.

At first, my body wants to sink back down into sleep. It's been a long time since the house was this quiet, since I could just roll over and go back to sleep, but then it hits me what the lack of sound means.

"Jordan?" My voice breaks as I say my baby's name. I flip back the covers and stand up, then immediately sit back down when my blood pressure drops.

Why can't I hear Jordan?

Is she still napping? Or is she outside with Sophie? I stumble to the window and press my face up against it, but I can't see the patio from here.

What I do see is just how dark it's getting out there. I don't sleep with a watch on, so I lunge for my phone on my bedside table. The light of the screen is bright, and I blink at it for a moment before finally making out the numbers on the screen—4:27.

"What the hell?" My head pounds. Without thinking about what I'm doing, I slip my phone into the pocket of my pajama pants, then hurry out of my room. Jordan's nursery is two doors down, and I call her name as I rush into the room.

"Jordan? Are you here?" I flick on the light, my heart pounding in my chest. The nursery is empty, and my heart sinks.

Maybe something happened to her. Maybe she's sick and Sophie took her to the doctor... but no, she'd wake me up—I know she would. Sophie's on top of it—no way would she take Jordan without letting me know something was going on.

They have to be downstairs.

Even though I want to run, I force myself to slow down on the stairs. The last thing I need is to fall and get hurt in my hunt for my daughter. She's here—I know she is. The panic I feel is partly because I just woke up and my brain hasn't clicked online yet, and partly because I've never been apart from Jordan.

I still don't hear them. By now I should hear them, right?

"Jordan! Sophie!" My throat hurts as I call their names. I race through the living room, barely noting how the blocks have been picked up. The coffee table has been cleaned off. I see it, but it doesn't immediately click that Sophie must have been here for a while, cleaning and tidying.

"Jordan!"

Into the kitchen. The island gleams, all smears of peanut

butter and jelly wiped away. There's a huge vase of lilies in the middle of the island, and I slow down when I see it.

I definitely don't keep fresh flowers in the house; they're just one more thing I have to take care of. Is it possible someone dropped them off for me? A delayed funeral bouquet?

Or did Sophie bring them here?

I take a step closer to them, then hurry around them, my eyes scanning the leaves for a card tucked inside them.

Nothing.

I force myself to stop. Stand still. I plant my hands on the counter and take a deep breath. Hold it.

Let it out.

Sophie wouldn't clean up the house, bring in fresh flowers, then... what? Take my child? Do I really think that she'd do that? Is that what's driving me to run around the house like a crazy person?

Sophie?

No way would she.

That's something a psychopath would do, not someone who looks and dresses the way she does. She's not a psychopath. She's rich. Put together. She came into my life like the answer to a prayer, and I have to tell myself that I didn't totally screw up by trusting her.

But then where is Jordan?

I'm feeling calmer now but still worried as I walk into the foyer and step outside. The harsh heat of the day is fading, and I feel like I can actually breathe out here.

My eyes land on the Lexus in the driveway.

She's here. Sophie is here, which means Jordan has to be here, because I can't imagine she would take her away from me *—but then how did the flowers get on my kitchen counter?—*but obviously she came *back* or the flowers wouldn't be here, would they?

Unless she brought them with her when she came and hid

them in her car and then put them in the kitchen to distract me, to make me not catch on to what she's doing, to—

I groan and clench the sides of my head to try to stop my brain from working overtime. Every thought I have is a nightmare—what could have happened to Jordan? And what might happen in the future?

Thinking like that isn't going to get Jordan back.

I don't bother to slow down and put on shoes before hurrying around the side of the house. This neighborhood is gorgeous, even though the yards are small. Still, its beauty is overshadowed by the fear gripping my throat.

I let someone into my house. If Jordan is really missing, this is all on me.

The next-door neighbor is grilling, and while I normally love the scent of charcoal and burning meat, right now it makes me nauseous. I grab my stomach, resting my hand there, and lean forward, taking deep breaths through my nose.

In and out.

Don't throw up.

Finally, I force myself to straighten up. I'm *this close* to falling apart, but I have to hold it together for Jordan, and to do that, I have to find her. I call her name, then hurry around the side of the house to the backyard.

She's a baby, so it's not like she needed a play set right away, but I ordered one the day we came home from the hospital. It had felt so decadent, holding her and feeding her while clicking around online to order her the biggest and best play set. By the time Lawrence came home from work, the shipping notification was in my inbox, and I was excited.

He... hadn't been as excited. I remember now how tight his jaw had gotten, how he'd looked from me to her, then back to me, one eyebrow cocked, the question right there on his face.

"Care to explain?" he'd asked, in that way that let you know you screwed up.

"She had to have it," I explained, but even as I tried to convince him of that, I knew that wasn't what he was looking at me strangely for. It wasn't concern over the play set, no matter how much I've tried to convince myself it was.

The problem was that I was already thinking long-term, considering the future, and Lawrence wasn't.

"Jordan," I call, but her name is a whisper in my mouth. "Jordy!" Louder, this time, and I draw strength from the fact that I'm almost screaming her name now, that I'm not going to let something happen to her.

I fought for her.

I killed for her.

Just as I'm about to call her name again, there's a loud crash from the backyard.

And then I hear Jordan start crying.

FOURTEEN

Sophie

Charlotte's face is white as she tears around the side of the house. I see her out the corner of my eye. She looks terrified, her eyes wide, her arms pumping as she races towards us, but I don't stop cooing to Jordan.

I don't want this sweet baby to wake up, no matter how her mother is acting.

"Sophie." Charlotte skids to a stop next to me and turns, already reaching out for Jordan, ready to snatch her from me. "Give me Jordy."

I look at her, then back down at the baby in my arms. Her eyes are closed, her cheeks slightly flushed. I watch as her mouth works a bit, like she's going to wake up hungry, but my continued swaying must be enough to calm her back down because she stills, her mouth no longer moving.

"She just fell asleep," I tell her, my voice barely above a whisper. "I don't want to wake her up. Here. Be careful."

I move slowly, carefully handing Jordan over to her. I watch, critical, as she tucks her arms around the baby, pulling her in to her chest, her face finally relaxing.

"She was crying," Charlotte says and takes a step back. "I heard her."

I'm shaking my head before she finishes speaking. "She wasn't crying, Charlotte. I don't know what you heard, but she's been snoozing off and on for an hour or so."

"No, I heard..." Her voice trails off.

"The proof is in your arms," I tell her. "Look at Jordan. She was perfectly safe with me. And happy."

She swallows hard.

"Maybe I misheard," she finally says.

"Must have." I reach out and lightly brush Jordan's hair away from her forehead. "This little angel never made a peep. I bet you're still waking up from your nap. It can be hard to do when you're exhausted. I've always said that I feel stupid after I sleep really hard."

I smile at her.

She wants to believe me.

I see it written all over her face. This woman is desperate for help, and I should feel bad for lying to her, but I don't.

She takes a deep breath. "What have you been doing?"

"Oh, Jordan and I have been having a wonderful time together! We picked up the house. Ran to the store. I wasn't sure what kind of flowers were your favorite, but I thought that everyone likes lilies, so I'd grab you some of them. And..." I pause, my voice trailing off.

She'll be dying to know what I'm not telling her—I'm sure of it.

"And?"

"And I cleaned out your fridge and refilled it with fresh groceries. I don't want to step on your toes, but aren't casseroles the worst food ever after a funeral?"

Charlotte's shoulders drop as she visibly relaxes. "They're pretty terrible."

"The worst! When my parents died and everyone brought over casseroles, I'd thank them at the front door, then turn right around and throw them in the trash. And do you know which kind is the most disgusting?"

"Dried-out chicken and rice?" she offers.

"Dried-out chicken and rice!"

Charlotte's grin tells me everything I need to know: mainly that she's completely on my side now. She trusts me—I can feel it. Or, if nothing else, she wants to trust me, and that's half the battle.

"Oh, sorry. The last thing I want is to wake up our sleeping beauty. But it's been a wild afternoon, let me tell you. I don't know what her sleep schedule is like, but—"

"She doesn't have one." Her voice is tight, and she reaches up to angrily wipe away a tear.

"Oh dear." I reach out and squeeze her shoulder. "Oh dear, no wonder you slept as hard as you did. That's something I can help you with," I tell her as I slip my arm around her shoulder. Slowly, I turn her and start leading her to the house. "I'm pretty handy with out-of-control sleep schedules, if I do say so myself."

"Are you sure you're not a mom? You're so great with her." Her voice drips with admiration.

I have to catch my breath before I answer. "No, unfortunately. It didn't work out that way for me, no matter how much I wished it would. But I've gotten to help take care of kids and love on dozens of them. I'm an honorary aunt for a lot of my friends."

"So you're an architect as well as a child development expert?"

She fell for it. Of course she did—she's desperate.

I laugh. Hook, line, and sinker. "I read a lot. I know the theories, at least."

"I thought becoming a mom would mean knowing what to do. Like it would all be downloaded into my brain." She gives a shrug. "Obviously that didn't happen, and it certainly didn't happen with Lawrence."

I frown. This is interesting. "You're sure he really wanted to be a father?"

"Um." Shifting Jordan to one arm, Charlotte reaches up and wipes her tears with her other hand. "It's just that she was such a surprise." Her voice shakes, and she takes a deep breath to try to still it. When she speaks again, it's stronger. "I always thought he'd pick it up, that it would be more natural to him, but it wasn't."

"He hated it?"

She nods. "It cramped his style." Her voice is a whisper. "And I know Jordan is a peach now, but she used to scream and scream."

"Like you can't get a break from the sound," I offer, and from the expression on her face, I know I'm right.

"Exactly. You hear about it and think you're prepared, but actually experiencing it is totally different. I wasn't ready."

"Oh, Charlotte." I pull her into a hug before she can stop me. For a moment, her body is stiff, then she relaxes. "Honey, I'm so sorry. I love my brother, I really do, but he could be terrible."

"I loved him," she finally manages.

I pull back from her. There's a weight to her words, and I want to look her in the eyes while she speaks.

"I did. And I'm so glad I married him. I know he wasn't totally on board with a baby, but I really thought that having one would bring us closer together. It's stupid, but..."

"So many people believe that," I finish for her. "You're not the first person to have a child thinking it will positively affect your relationship."

"Well, it's not like I have a relationship to affect anyway now," she says, her words bitter.

"But you do," I tell her, waving my hand in the air. "I'm family. We have a relationship. And you having a baby isn't going to send me running for the hills, trust me. I would have killed to have a child." I pause for a moment to make sure that sinks in. "Admit it, Charlotte. You need me."

"I—"

"Charlotte, I want you to listen to me. I'm not going anywhere, do you understand? There's not a thing you can do to make me leave."

She freezes. I see it on her face, like she's not sure what to make of what I just said, but that doesn't matter because I mean it.

There's not a thing you can do to make me leave.

It's a promise. It's what someone who really cared about Charlotte would say to her.

Now the question remains: is she smart enough to take what I said for what it is?

A threat.

FIFTEEN

Charlotte

I hate the fact that breastfeeding wasn't ever on the cards for me, but I push that worry out of my head as I give Jordan her bottle. She's almost finished, her eyes already closing, her breathing slowing down.

Smoothly, so as not to jerk her and wake her back up, I put down the bottle and lift her to my shoulder. A few pats on her back and she burps, then I snuggle her close to my chest. I'm so enamored with her that I barely notice Sophie staring at me.

"Did you decide to bottle-feed so that Lawrence could help?" Sophie's question is so intrusive that it takes me a moment to snap back to reality and pay attention to her.

"Umm, yeah. And she had problems latching." I pull Jordan's blanket up around her face a little bit to ensure she isn't chilled. The heat is on, and the house is pretty cozy, but the last thing I want is for her to catch cold.

"That had to be hard."

"It was."

"Did you ever talk to someone from La Leche League? My

best friend saw them when her baby had problems latching, and they were able to help her figure it out. Her problem was inverted nipples." She stares at me. "Want me to take a look? I bet we can figure it out together."

That's quite literally the last thing I want her to do.

"You're too kind, but we don't have to talk about my boobs. They failed me, and that's all there is to it," I say. "I mean, sure, Lawrence loved them, but he's not here to enjoy them any longer."

Her face darkens. *Oh, crap.* I probably shouldn't have made that joke about her brother. I clear my throat. But before I can figure out what to say to smooth things over, she speaks up.

"Lawrence always loved boobs." The smile on her face is strained. "Like most men, I'd guess."

"Totally."

There's a shift in the air. It feels awkward now, and I don't know how to fix it.

"Well, cheers to you being in the dead husbands club." She holds her hand up like she's got a glass of champagne in it.

"I'll be in charge of snacks," I say, and she laughs. "It's a pretty crap club, if you don't mind me saying." What I don't tell her is that I was already in the club before I married Lawrence.

Now I'm doubly in the club. It's a dubious honor.

"Oh, the worst. Absolutely the worst. The only thing that could top it would be losing a child. That's a club I'd never want to be in."

The awkward feeling is back.

Suddenly, she laughs. The sound is abrupt and feels out of place, but I instantly feel my tense muscles loosen.

She covers her mouth with her hand, her eyes wide as she looks at me. "I'm sorry, I've always laughed at inappropriate times. It's just how I deal with stressful things, and this is probably the most stress I've ever been under. Losing Lawrence was harder than I thought it would be, but I can only imagine how terrible it is for you."

Her words wash over me, but I can't focus. Instead, I blink, and I'm back in the past.

Jordan screaming her head off, screaming like she was in pain, like she was covered with ants biting her, their mandibles gripping her soft skin so they could whip their bodies around to sting her.

Me, holding her. Sobbing. Silent tears running down my cheeks to land on her tight, red face.

And Lawrence.

"Figure out how to shut her up," he'd snapped, already reaching for his keys. "This is not what I signed up for." One arm in his jacket, then the other. He'd opened the door, then like he just had to deliver a parting shot, had turned back. "I told you this was a bad idea."

The door had slammed.

I take a deep breath. Lawrence is dead. Jordan isn't crying.

"Well, I'm glad you're here and Jordan and I aren't facing it alone." I shift position slowly to tuck my legs up under me. Jordan's sound asleep, and relief rushes through me when I realize I didn't wake her up. Ever since I became her mom, I've had to carefully tiptoe around, being careful not to set her off, to wake her up, to ruin the quiet.

And it's worked. I may not feel as loud and fun as I was in the past, but she's not screaming, and I'm going to take that as a win.

"Me too. I really want to thank you for letting me in." She smiles at me, then her gaze drops to Jordan. "And, of course, for letting me be around Lawrence's child. She's perfect, Charlotte. If you ever decide you don't want to be a mother any longer, just give me a call."

She laughs.

I don't. Instead, I clear my throat to break the uncomfortable silence growing between us.

"I'd never give her up." My voice is tight, and Sophie must immediately pick up on how uncomfortable she just made me.

"Oh, Charlotte, relax." She lightly touches me on the shoulder. "I was just teasing. But I do want to see if she's like her dad when she grows up. Lawrence was always a wild one."

I think about the man I loved, the man I married, and I frown. "A wild one?"

"You better believe it. He was always the life of the party." Her eyes light up, and she leans forward, obviously eager to talk about her brother. "I remember, when we were in high school, he threw this huge party and ended up jumping off the second story into the pool. Naked."

I laugh, then quickly cover my mouth like that will keep Jordan from waking up at the sound of my glee. "Lawrence?"

She grins and nods. "Yep. He went to college two years before me. It was really, really hard being left behind, but I already knew I wanted to follow him to the same school."

Strange. Are siblings always that close? I don't have time to worry about that thought because she continues.

"So when I got there as a freshman, he was a junior. I had instant friends because of him. They all took me into their fold because Lawrence loved me."

"That had to feel great."

"It did."

For a moment, she's silent, and I imagine her back in college, fresh-faced and eager to learn, excited to make new friends.

"It was a blast, honestly. We went to all the parties and had a massive group of friends. He could mimic all the teachers on campus to the point that other teachers wouldn't realize they were being pranked if he called them on the phone."

I never saw this side of Lawrence, and envy rises in me. Of

course, people mature as they grow up, but it's still disappointing to hear Sophie talk about her brother like this. People flocked to Lawrence, but not because he was doing keg stands or taking body shots. It was the fact that he was powerful, and that power made people think he could do something for them. Or maybe they just didn't want to get on his bad side.

Keep your enemies closer?

That's a terrible thing to think about the man I love, but I've had that thought before, and now it flits back, refusing to leave.

"Could he still command a room right before he died?" Her question yanks me back to the present.

"Sure could. People loved dinner parties with him. They loved hearing his stories." I'm playing up how much the two of us got out with other couples after we said our vows. In reality, I only went to a few dinner parties with Lawrence. He traveled all the time, and while I wanted to join him more, that wasn't what he wanted, especially after we got married. He became more... protective.

I questioned if he was embarrassed of me. When we went out to fancy dinners, we went out of town. When we booked a B&B, we went further than I would have expected.

I would have dropped everything to be with him, to be by his side, his arm looped around my waist. It wasn't that he didn't want me there with him. He told me he did but that I was for his eyes only. He always hated it when he thought he caught someone looking at me.

Even at the meat counter at the store, me talking to the guy slicing our ham or turkey for sandwiches was enough to put him on edge. It's because he loved me so much that he wanted to keep me for himself.

That's all it was. He loved me so much he didn't want to share me. Not with the meat guy, not with his friends.

Not even with a baby.

"I'm glad." And then she launches into a wild story about

what happened at convocation when Lawrence dyed his cap and gown hot pink. I'm laughing so hard my cheeks hurt, no longer worrying about waking the baby in my arms.

Even as we talk, I can't fight the guilt rising in me. Sophie is so earnest, so kind. And I really believe her when she said that she's happy being here with Jordan and me.

But there's the rub, and while I would love to be able to correct her on what she said so we can have a relationship without any lies or secrets between the two of us, I can't do that.

Because as much as I want to pretend like Jordan, Lawrence, and I were the perfect family unit without any problems, I can't. I'd love to look back on the memory of him excited about her coming home. Of him holding her, saying *dada* over and over again even though she's way too young to speak.

But I can't.

Lawrence looked great on paper. If my parents had been alive when we met, I'm sure he would have charmed both of them. But as charming as he was, as rich and focused on his career, as personable as he could be, that's not all Lawrence was.

He was controlling.

I walked on eggshells around him.

And he made it very, very clear that he didn't want a child.

So, in all honesty, he brought what happened on himself.

SIXTEEN

Her

The water in Bora Bora is so clear you can see straight through to the bottom. I stretch, working out my sore muscles from the long flight here, then sigh a little as my husband wraps his arms around me.

Relaxing into him feels good.

Turning to kiss him feels even better.

"My husband," I whisper into his mouth.

"My wife." Lawrence forks his hand through my hair and roughly pulls my head back to kiss me. I feel like my back is going to snap as he bends me back, but I don't fight him.

He likes being in control in all aspects of his life.

When he finally stops kissing me, I feel like gulping air. My hands on his shoulders, I pull myself up to stand in front of him.

He's appraising me. I can tell from the way he looks me up and down, his eyes in constant motion, drinking me in, judging me.

But there's nothing to judge. Not really. I've done all the things he's wanted. Joined the gym. Eaten clean. Any flab on my body has been tightened, replaced with muscle. I'm not set to take the ring at a Krav Maga competition by any means, but I look dang good in this little bikini.

"You did a wonderful job at the wedding," he tells me, and I flush with pleasure.

I never thought I'd be the type of woman who got excited when I pleased my man, but I have to admit that it feels good to know he's happy with me. I *like* it when he tells me I did a good job.

I was such a mess before I met him. And now look at me. I'm successful. I'm put together. When I meet clients, they don't judge me and find me lacking just because of my clothes or hairstyle.

But I'm still me. Even under the fresh makeup, the haircut, the name-brand clothes, I'm still me, and nobody can take that from me. He told me one time that he was going to refine me like gold. Polish me like a fine jewel.

And he did.

"I would do it all again for you," I tell him, and I mean it. There's literally nothing I wouldn't do for the man standing in front of me, and he knows it. All he has to do is tell me what would make him happy.

When he says to jump, I ask how high.

When he tells me I need to tighten and tone, I ask him what gym to use.

When he made me promise that it would only be him and me, just the two of us, that nothing and nobody would ever come between us, not even a child, I...

Well, I hesitated. I admit it.

But then I agreed.

"I'm glad to hear it, but I'm not one of those saps who believes in renewing their vows." Lawrence tucks my hair behind my ear. "I've always thought that was stupid."

"Me too," I agree, even though I'd always found it romantic.

It was one thing to find someone you wanted to marry, another entirely to decide, over and over, to stick with them. "It's you and me, and we don't need to prove anything to anyone."

"That we don't." He moves quickly, bending a bit to scoop me up. With one arm under my knees and the other behind my back, he lifts me from my feet and pulls me close to his chest.

I laugh.

When he's happy like this, when things are going his way and he's had a glass or two of champagne, he's at his most addictive. I've seen him grumpy from work, seen him tired and a bit despondent when things don't go his way, but he's never been more attractive.

"Please tell me we're going jet-skiing or something this afternoon," I tell him.

He shakes his head. "No way do I want you on one of those things. Can you imagine if something bad happened to you? I'd never be able to forgive myself for allowing you to get on it in the first place."

My heart sinks a bit, but I keep a smile on my face. "Okay. Well, stand-up paddle boarding then? That sounds just as fun without the risk of losing a limb."

"You're so sweet." He kisses my forehead. "I know this water looks clean and safe, but looks can be deceiving. You just officially became mine. Please don't put yourself in a situation where I might lose you."

He turns away from the water and starts walking towards our bungalow. With its thatched roof and open design, it doesn't look stable enough to stand up to the storms that I'm sure rip through this area. But inside it's pure luxury.

The thread count of the white sheets rivals what we have at home. When we arrived, I was happy to find a huge pile of fresh fruit on the kitchen counter. We even have a private pool right in front of the bungalow, and that's where my husband puts me, my feet in the water.

"This is where I want you," he tells me, slowly lowering himself to sit next to me. He slips his feet into the water and sighs.

I'm disappointed, but I bite my tongue. Really, I should be grateful that he wants to keep me safe. I'm sure there are thousands of husbands who don't worry about their wives like he thinks about me. So what if he wants me to stay out of the ocean? He knows more about that sort of thing and whether or not it's safe than I do.

I lean against him. We smell of sweet champagne and sunscreen. Underneath it all, a bit of his cologne. The scent is delightful, intoxicating. I breathe him in. Breathe him out.

Make a decision.

"Hey," I say, sitting up and taking his hand. When I squeeze it, he turns to look at me. "I don't want to come across as ungrateful about anything," I say, "but I'm a bit disappointed that we're not going to do things on our honeymoon."

"Disappointed?" He frowns. "Me keeping you safe is disappointing?"

"No! I don't mean it like that. You keeping me safe is wonderful. It's everything. But there was part of me that wanted adventure. You know, skiing or mountain climbing or surfing." I smile to lessen the blow.

He doesn't return it.

His hand feels like granite in mine.

"I'm sorry, I just don't know where this is coming from. We said our vows, and you promised to honor me."

"I did. It's just..." I let my voice trail off. Here I go, making a mess of things. Seems like that's all I'm good at right now. "You know what, you're right. I'm sorry for bringing it up."

He brings my hand to his mouth and kisses my fingers. "You are the only one I want. Ever. For the rest of my life. Don't think for a second that I'll do anything to endanger you or risk what we have."

"You're right." I'm kicking myself for even bringing this up. "I just want to be with you. What we do doesn't matter."

"You and me against the world," he tells me.

I think back to the contract I signed before the wedding and smile at him. "Just you and me," I agree.

SEVENTEEN

Sophie

It didn't take much convincing to get Charlotte to go to bed early, although I was prepared to slip her a little something to help her along the way if that's what it took. Even after her long rest, she was still exhausted and went to bed well before I did.

At the end of the day, I really needed some time alone. I'm used to plenty of time by myself, and she sure is a chatterbox. While I could go to bed too, that's not what I have in mind.

I pause outside her door, my hand resting on her doorknob. Her locking it after I took the baby monitor means she doesn't completely trust me. Fine. That's fine. I get it because I don't trust her.

I think about what it would be like to pick her lock, open her door, and walk into her room while she's sleeping. No doubt she passed right out and would snooze through me standing over her in her bed. She looks so innocent, doesn't she?

She looks like a wide-eyed naive girl swept up in a love story by a man. *I couldn't help myself,* I can hear her say when the truth of what she's done comes out. *You should have seen how he came on to me.*

But scaring her in the middle of the night is not my goal. Not tonight.

Tonight I want Jordan.

Charlotte took the baby monitor with her into her bedroom, of course, so when I open the nursery door, I do it as quietly as possible.

It only takes a moment for my eyes to adjust to the dark. Light from the hall streams in behind me, and I cast a shadow over the crib. Rather than going right to Jordan, however, which is what I want to do, I pause and look for a small light.

There. On the dresser by her crib. Quietly, taking my time, I walk across the nursery and reach the baby monitor. One click of the knob on the top, and the power light fades out.

Good. Now I can spend time with this sweet girl, and Charlotte will be none the wiser.

I walk back to the door and close it, then turn on the nursery light. It's on a dimmer switch, and I turn it as low as it will go before walking over to the crib.

My arms ache to hold her, and I think about picking her up right away, but I make myself wait. It's hell to stand here and stare at her, but that's what I do because I want to soak her in.

She's in a little sleep sack with polka dots all over it. Her arms are up by her head, her face turned to the side. As I watch, she stirs, then slowly blinks and looks around, searching for whatever woke her up.

"Hey, baby." I lean down and lift her, enjoying her soft heavy weight. She fits perfectly in my arms, and I carefully lower myself into the rocker and snuggle her even closer. "I'm sorry to wake you, but you looked like you needed snuggles. What a day, huh?"

She makes little baby noises. I close my eyes and take a deep breath, trying to keep from crying.

What is it about babies that is so perfect? It's how they smell, how they sound, the way they're so helpless and need you. I could hold her all night and not get a wink of sleep but still be happy when the sun streamed through the window.

I start rocking. Slowly, of course, because I'm not here to wake her up. I'm here to show her that she's loved and to take care of her. It's got to be hard, to be a single mother, but I've seen the way Charlotte looks at Jordan sometimes.

Like she's an alien she isn't sure how to handle.

Like she's an intrusion on her life.

I hate it.

She says she wants to be a mother more than anything in the world, she proclaims to love Jordan, but there's something about how she holds her sometimes, almost like she's afraid of breaking her.

Or maybe I'm making that up, but I don't think I am.

Jordan yawns, and I lightly touch her cheek. Her skin is so soft. Everything about her is perfect.

Without thinking about what I'm doing, I start to sing. I'm quiet, of course, because even though I turned off the baby monitor, I don't want to risk Charlotte overhearing me and coming in here.

This is my special time with Jordan.

We rock and sing for a while, then she falls back asleep. My right arm is starting to go numb, but there's no way I'm going to make her move. Not yet anyway. Not until I've had my fill.

Although, really, there's nothing stopping me from coming back in here every single night to hold her, is there? Charlotte won't have any idea I'm in here, and that means Jordan and I can spend time together. She likes it—I know she does.

It's obvious that she settles easier when I hold her. She looks more peaceful too. Maybe it's how Charlotte holds her, like she's afraid of her or not quite sure what to do, but it feels like my arms were made for this baby.

And don't babies deserve the best that life has to offer? Isn't that what every good parent wants for their child—for their baby to have a better life than they did?

Can Charlotte really give Jordan the life she deserves?

My mind races as I rock. Charlotte can barely keep her life together—I've seen that firsthand. She's not a great mom.

She's not worthy of Jordan.

But I am.

EIGHTEEN
TWO WEEKS LATER

Charlotte

For a moment, when I wake up, I completely forget that Sophie is in the house. The two of us have fallen into a comfortable routine. Still, even though it's lovely having her around, I want to be Jordan's mom, to be the one taking care of her.

I've seen the way Sophie looks at her, like she can't believe she's real. When she holds my baby, it's almost like she disappears, lost in her own thoughts.

It shouldn't bother me that she loves my baby, but you know what? It's starting to.

I hit the nursery at a run, then skid to a stop when I see Jordan in her crib. She's stirring, probably because I hit her door so hard it slammed into the wall, and guilt washes over me.

But how in the world was she still asleep? She's never slept through the night.

"Hey, baby," I coo, gently lifting her. Her diaper is damp. I change her quickly, then slip on my housecoat before sneaking past the guest room. It's only when I reach the top of the stairs and hear clattering in the kitchen that I realize Sophie is already awake.

Slowly, because I'm still tired, I carry Jordan downstairs. She's not crying yet, but she's going to start soon.

I walk into the kitchen and am immediately struck by how wonderful it looks. Sure, I'd already smelled breakfast and knew it would be amazing, but it looks even better. On the table is a pitcher of orange juice. There are more fresh flowers, two table settings, honey, fresh butter, a bowl of cut fruit.

Sophie's at the stove, and she must hear me walk into the room and stop because she turns around, the spatula she's using still in her hand. She's wearing my favorite apron, and I stiffen for a moment, then tell myself to get over it.

She has no way of knowing that Lawrence gave me that apron or how much I love it.

"I wondered if the smell of breakfast would get you up!" She waves the spatula at me, then turns back to the stove. I watch as she plates up two servings of biscuits and sausage gravy, then jerks her chin at the table for me to follow her. "Just so you know, I crept into the nursery around midnight and then again around three to give Jordan a sleepy, sneaky bottle. It sometimes works to help babies sleep a bit longer. And don't worry—I didn't change her. I know you were worried about that, but that means her diaper was probably soaked this morning."

Relief makes my shoulders sag, but then I stiffen. If Jordan had a bottle in the middle of the night, wouldn't she be soaking, not just damp, this morning? It's possible Sophie is lying to me, but what if she's not? What if last night was just a dry night? I decide not to press it. "Thank you. Really. For that and for breakfast. It smells great," I say.

"I'm glad. This was always my husband's favorite weekend breakfast, and I thought you needed a treat since you're going back to work today."

"*Was* your husband's favorite breakfast? I know you said you're not married now, but that sounds like he's... I'm sorry, if that's rude to ask." She's been here two weeks and we haven't talked about... except she did make that joke about the dead husbands club, didn't she? Although I didn't realize that meant she was in it with me.

"He's dead." She gives me a small smile.

"Oh, I'm sorry." I hesitate. "If you don't mind me asking, what happened? And how long ago was it?" I'll admit it, hearing that her husband is dead makes me feel a bit closer to her. Our similarities end there, however, because I highly doubt that she killed the man she loved.

"He had a bad heart," she says. "And it was actually fairly recently. Honestly, it's part of the reason I mustered up the courage to come here. I guess I'm just looking for connection. We're family, you and I."

I hardly think this woman has ever had to muster up the courage to do anything. From how put together she is, I can see her doing anything from running a boardroom to giving a TED talk. But I get it. And her calling me family warms me. I haven't had family in years, just Lawrence and Jordan.

"I'm glad you came." There's more I want to say to her, about how it was brave of her to show up on my doorstep, but I don't know how to do that without coming across as weird. Or desperate.

She nods and gestures for me to join her at the table. We both sit, and she takes a deep breath before lifting her coffee for a sip. Her makeup is as impeccable as the first day she showed up, but she looks really tired today. That thought only lasts a moment in my mind before I take a bite of biscuit, and any other thoughts I have fly out of my head.

Holy cow, this is good. Between this and the rest of the food she's made, I've probably put on five pounds since she arrived. It's so good, in fact, that I barely register Sophie speaking to me.

"No, there's no amount of time or space between you and a spouse that will make hearing that they're dead feel less... horrible." She takes a sip of coffee and looks at me. "How are you doing with Lawrence's death?"

I put my fork down, the sausage gravy turning to glue in my mouth. I have to force myself to swallow, then I take a sip of water while I organize my thoughts.

"I've been keeping so busy with Jordy and the house and people stopping by that I haven't really had time to process," I say, and as I speak, I realize how true that is. It seems silly, with Lawrence being gone almost two months already, for me to not have taken the time to really think about how I feel and handle my emotions, but I've been on autopilot. I tell her that, and she nods.

"You're in survival mode."

"Exactly." I take a small bite of biscuit before I speak again. "I miss him." Tears burn my eyes. "He never wanted to be a father, but I think he would have been so happy with Jordan. Seeing her grow up. Walking her down the aisle."

Her face tightens for a moment before it relaxes. "He didn't want to be a father?"

I shake my head. It's embarrassing to admit this to someone, even to his sister, but now that the cat's out of the bag, I might as well tell her the truth. "He never wanted to have to come second in a relationship, and he thought that kids would make that happen."

"Wow." She takes a sip of coffee. Then another. "It must have been quite a shock to him to find out you were pregnant."

This is where I have to be careful, or all of the truth will come out. And while I've already told Sophie more than I normally would about Lawrence, the last thing I want is for her to figure out the whole story.

She'd judge me. I know she would.

"He was terribly surprised when I brought Jordan home.

He knew, of course, how badly I wanted a baby, but I think he was able to keep his head in the sand about the entire thing and pretend it wasn't really happening."

"Was he a supportive partner?"

"When I brought Jordan home?"

"When you were pregnant."

I nod.

"Was he not there at the hospital with you when you had her? You keep saying that *you* brought her home."

Her eyes are locked on me. I'm hit with the feeling that she can read minds and that she's waiting for me to back myself into a corner with my lies, but no. There's no way. She's smart, that much is obvious. And she clearly wants to know as much about me as possible, but that doesn't mean that she's a mind reader, or that she's conniving. Women share pregnancy and birth stories. We have since the dawn of time, as a way to bond and connect with each other when the men were off clubbing animals over the head.

This is no different.

I'm just paranoid.

"He was working and couldn't get away. Jordan came so quickly, it was a surprise."

"Always working, Lawrence." Sophie gives me a smile and tilts her coffee mug towards me. I respond by picking mine up and lightly touching hers.

As I take a sip, she launches into a story about Lawrence from when they were younger. I'm listening but only barely because my mind keeps wandering back to the first day at home with Jordan.

You made your choice. He'd said that, and I'd lifted my chin. Stared him down.

Yes, I did. I wanted both of them.

He'd been... not angry. Lawrence held his anger in better than most men I know. But he'd slammed the bedroom door and taken a long shower. When he'd finally come back downstairs, he'd cooled off, but it was clear we were still not on the same page.

None of that mattered.

And since then, I've been able to mold my life into what I wanted it to be. It took a lot of tears and effort, but there are simply some things you can't control.

I stare at Sophie and wonder if she's had to learn that lesson.

NINETEEN

Charlotte

"Charlotte, Andy is looking for you." Michelle, my head teller, throws me a small salute, then disappears from the bathroom as quickly as she leaned her head in.

"Crap," I mutter, then turn my phone off and slip it deep into my pocket. Andy, the branch manager, has a very strict no-phone rule when we're working, but there's no way I can leave Jordan at daycare and not check my messages from time to time.

Sure, they know where I work, and if there was an emergency, they'd call the bank to let me know what was going on, but what if they sent an update text? Or just a photo of her taking a nap?

I may not be able to be with her all the time, but that doesn't mean I'm going to miss out on all the little important moments.

And then, of course, one thing led to another when I was on my phone, but that's something for me to worry about another day. I keep online stalking Sophie, or I try to, but haven't gotten anywhere. I'd really thought that I'd find something if I dug deeper, but so far—nothing.

She's clean. Perfect. I'm just worried because I want to keep Jordan as safe as possible. When I tell myself that, I can justify poking around online to find out more about her.

If I'm honest with myself, I'm jealous of her. She's so put together, so enviable. I want to be her. Barring that, because it would take a miracle to turn me into someone half as amazing as her, I want her around as much as possible.

I smooth my button-up shirt and make sure it's perfectly tucked in. If Andy has something to say to me, I'm not going to give him the opportunity to complain about how I look at the same time.

After I'm sure I look great and I've plastered a smile on my face, I leave the bathroom, fully intending to walk to his office. He's like any other manager and loves the power play of having employees come to him.

Just like a man, to make women do all the work.

But instead of making it across the lobby to his office, I walk straight into him.

"Oh, Andy," I say, holding up my hands to show that I didn't mean to plow full force into him. "Sorry, I was coming to your office and didn't see you there."

"Not a problem." He adjusts his tie, giving it a little wiggle as if I somehow knocked it out of position. He's just a few years older than me but acts like he's the reason this place runs as smoothly as it does, when in reality, he's only been here a few months. "We can head in there now so we have some privacy."

"You got it." I fight my nerves and keep a smile on my face as I walk with him. He takes long steps, and I adjust mine to keep up with him.

"First day back," he says as we walk into his office. I sit in a soft chair facing his desk, and he lowers himself into the leather computer chair behind it. "After you took, what? About two months off?"

I nod.

He clears his throat. "How are you feeling?"

The day only started three hours ago, and I have already popped into the bathroom to check my phone four times, but I don't tell him that my nerves are making it difficult for me to focus on my job. I also don't tell him that the last time I was in the bathroom, I wasn't just looking for texts or calls from the daycare.

It's my first day away from home. Away from Jordan. At least Sophie isn't in my house because she might be tempted to snoop, and if she snooped, she might find...

"I'm great," I lie.

Great. I'd rather lick rust than be at work right now, away from Jordan, surrounded by so many people who don't understand what I've been through.

"Good." He turns to look at his computer when his email pings. If I were the branch manager, no way would I check my email while chatting with someone, but Andy does. His fingers fly across his keyboard before he turns back to me.

"Everything okay?"

"It's fine." A pause. "I'm sure you want to know the reason I have for talking to you this morning."

I nod but don't say anything.

"You filled out the paperwork to add your baby to your insurance, but I don't have everything I need for HR to complete your request."

"Oh?" My stomach twists. Why isn't anything easy? Just for once in my life, I'd like for something to go smoothly, but that's not happening this morning. "What else do I need to get you? I brought you a copy of the birth certificate."

"Yeah, I don't know off the top of my head, but Janet in HR wants to talk to you."

I freeze. Everyone knows that getting HR involved in anything can result in problems. The only people who act like

HR are on your side are the vultures who work in that department.

"You got it." I reach up and press my fingers into my temple. Andy always gives me a headache; I just have to hope this doesn't turn into a migraine. Why couldn't the head teller have been the one to let me know I was missing some of Jordan's paperwork? I like her so much better than Andy.

"Good. Another thing, and this is uncomfortable, but I need to know." He takes a huge sip of coffee before speaking.

"What's going on? Does this have to do with my performance?"

He winces. "A little. I wouldn't normally say anything, but I know you've been through it. You've been going to the bathroom a lot, and I know it's only your first day back, but—"

I tune him out. My cheeks burn with embarrassment. This is not the type of conversation you want to have with a boss, much less a man. I stare at his face, watching him speak.

Then he stops.

"I'm... fine," I say, doing my best to answer in a way that will make sense with what he was saying. "I'm just having a hard time leaving my baby at daycare, you know?" My eyes burn, which is not intentional but is great timing. "And then there's the hormones and how bad my body hurts—"

"Just... try to keep it to a minimum." He holds his hands up between the two of us to stop me. The last thing he needs is for HR to think he was making me cry. "Can you do that?"

"I can," I sniff. "I'm so sorry—this is so hard. Losing Lawrence..." I let my voice trail off.

Andy nods, then reaches across the desk and lightly pats my hand. "I can imagine. Take what time you need now, then back to work, okay? Each day will be easier."

"I'm sure it will," I lie, then I stand and hurry out of his office.

It's only after I've shut his office door behind me that I feel like I can breathe again. I was holding my breath, trying to make myself as small as possible, trying to make sure he didn't focus on me and suddenly decide I'd done another thing he needed to talk to me about.

I glance around, then hurry back to the bathroom and pull out my phone.

There. A text from daycare, but it's nothing bad. It's Jordan, snoozing hard in someone's arms. She looks so peaceful, and the sight makes my heart break. Tears flow, and I angrily dab at them with a paper towel. When I've calmed down enough, I open my browser.

Just before Michelle leaned in to let me know that Andy was looking for me, I'd had an idea of where to find information on Sophie. Not social media, because she definitely doesn't have an account I can find, but voter records.

I don't give a crap who she voted for, but I am interested in knowing where she lives.

My heart beats faster when I find her. Lawrence is listed as an associate, as are two names I'm assuming are her parents.

But it's not the fact that I found her that gives me pause. It's where she lives.

Half an hour away.

Not an hour and a half, like she said. Why would she lie to me about that? Why would she want to move in when a half-hour drive to come help out with Jordan wouldn't be so bad?

Sweat pricks the back of my neck as I think about what other implications there are in how close she lives.

She'd acted like she'd never been to my house before when she first showed up.

But what if that was a lie?

TWENTY

THREE YEARS AGO

Her

One last time, I check the roast lamb in the oven.

Perfect. The crispy skin crackles as I run the blade of my knife across it, and my mouth waters when the scent hits me. The rosemary potatoes are ready, the slow-cooked lamb will rest for a few minutes before I carve it, and I have fresh bread just finishing baking in the second oven.

Dinner's ready and it's exactly what I wanted it to be. After all, it's not every year that you celebrate your fifth wedding anniversary. Lawrence promised me he'd be home on time, but I've noticed that he's been working later more and more.

I'm not worried yet, but I still check the time. Almost half past six, so he's only about twenty minutes late. Even though I didn't give him all the details of what I was making for dinner, he knows what today is. There's no way he'd be late on purpose, right?

Right. Not tonight anyway.

Still, my mind starts to race as I walk to the dining room and survey the table. Everything is ready—even the lighter is by my plate so I can easily light the cream taper candles. Everyone knows that candlelit dinners are the most romantic type, and while the two of us could have easily gone out for a meal to celebrate our anniversary, I wanted tonight to be really special, for me to have the opportunity to show him how much he means to me.

At half past six, I put the lamb back in the oven with the potatoes to keep it warm. The bread is out on the counter cooling, the compound butter already on the table. I pour myself a glass of wine and take a sip while I survey the space.

Is there anything else that needs to be done before he gets home?

Nothing.

All I can do right now is wait.

I wander from the kitchen to the front hall and peek out the window at the empty cul-de-sac. No cars are on the road, although every neighbor's house has lights on in the windows. Our front porch light is on to make our home look as friendly as possible.

My hand rests on the switch, but I don't turn it off.

At seven, I pull my phone from my pocket and fire off a text.

You okay? Can't wait to see you for dinner!

Lawrence doesn't like feeling rushed or checked up on. The one time I suggested adding the Find My Friend app to our phones so we could keep up with where the other person was, he got upset with me.

No, not upset. *Angry.* He accused me of checking up on him, of not trusting him, of trying to control him. I dropped it, of course. What he does and where he goes really isn't any of my business, but I think that him being an hour late is cause enough for me to start to worry, especially on our anniversary. Especially when I can guess what he's doing.

I won't call him, however. Not after the last time I did that to see when he'd be home and he lost it. He yelled at me for interrupting him and threatened to stay the night with a friend. My stomach twists when I think about how sick I'd felt at that threat.

I wander into the living room and turn on the local news in an effort to pass time. Before I can get settled in to see what's going on in the area, I hear the garage door raise.

I jump and turn off the TV. In the kitchen, I pull the lamb and potatoes out of the oven. They're a bit crispier than I like, but I'm not going to blame him to his face.

"Smells amazing in here!" his voice booms, filling the kitchen, and I jerk back from the sheet pan like it burned me.

Before I turn to him, I plaster a smile on my face.

"There's my beautiful wife." He pulls me to him, pressing his lips against mine, his hand slipping down my spine. It lingers on my lower back, the pressure there possessive.

"I missed you," I tell him. "Happy anniversary."

"Five years," he responds, and I feel a flutter in my stomach.

I shouldn't be surprised that he remembered, but happiness shoots through me.

"You were worried I forgot," he says, pulling back to get a better look at me. He raises an eyebrow as I fix my face into the picture of innocence. "You can admit it—I see it all over your face."

"Never," I say, but he's speaking again.

"I had to work late. You know how it is sometimes."

I nod, even though I choose my own hours. I work the ones I want, take off the ones I don't want to. No, I don't bring in as much money as he does, but I'm here to make dinner and keep the house clean, and that was part of the agreement when we got married.

"I wasn't mad. Or worried." I gesture behind me to the

dinner I spent all afternoon working on. "Why don't you go light the candles on the table, and I'll bring this out?"

"Sounds great, thanks."

Lawrence strolls out of the kitchen while I hurriedly plate the potatoes and lamb. At the last minute, I'd snapped some fresh green beans, and while they're not quite as al dente as we normally want, I still put some on each of our plates.

A few minutes later, I'm carrying the plates to the table. I put them down, then hold up a finger for him to wait. Back in the kitchen, I top off my wine and pour him a glass of whiskey. Two fingers. Two ice cubes. Just the way he likes it.

"Alright," I say, sitting down across from him and picking up my wine. "To us."

"To our perfect family," he says. "You're the only one I want to come home to. The only one I want warming my bed."

"We've got it made."

He takes a sip of his drink.

"You know Clarence at work?" When I nod, he continues. "His wife is pregnant. Twins. Can you imagine?" He pulls a face.

"That's awful," I say, but I have to force the words. I'd just taken a bite of lamb, and it's suddenly dry and tasteless in my mouth. "Is he excited?"

"Very. I'm so glad you agreed not to have children. What a nightmare. To go from doing whatever it is you want to do to changing diapers and making bottles and going to T-ball games?"

"Sounds terrible," I hear myself saying. "We have everything."

"Yes. We do." He puts his fork down and reaches across the table for my hand; I take his and smile as he links our fingers together. "Speaking of having everything, I have a surprise for you."

"You didn't have to get me anything!" I feign shock, but

honestly, I expected a gift. It's our fifth anniversary, after all. And while our life together isn't perfect, it's pretty close. After all, does anyone really love their spouse every second of every day?

I think not.

He shifts forward and pulls a small box out of his pocket.

I get more excited. Good things come in small boxes. *Shiny* things come in small boxes. Sapphires hopefully. He knows they're my favorite. Every time we go shopping, they're what I'm drawn to. More than emeralds, more than rubies, and especially more than diamonds.

"Happy anniversary, love." He hands me the box, and I take it, my hand shaking with excitement.

When I lift the lid, my heart sinks a little. "Diamonds?"

"Diamonds," he agrees, reaching out and plucking the necklace from the box. "I know you said before that diamonds weren't really your style, but come on—what else says love like diamonds?"

"Are they lab?" I ask, hope rising in me. Lab diamonds aren't blood diamonds, and maybe—

He shakes his head. "Not a chance. Nothing but the best for you. Put it on."

I don't hesitate. Instead, I lift the necklace and let it spin to catch the light, then clasp it around my neck. A glittering star made of diamonds hangs on my throat.

"Gorgeous." He lifts his whiskey and takes a sip, his eyes never leaving mine.

"Thank you," I tell him. "I love it. I got you something as well, but it's in the living room. I can go—" I'm halfway out of my seat when he stops me.

"Not now. Let's eat now, and you can get it later."

"Of course." I take a sip of wine. "By the way, I was thinking this weekend that we should get out of town. There's that cute little B&B on the coast of Maine we talked about going to, and—"

"I can't this weekend. Work travel."

"Of course. Another time then." *Work travel.* I know what those words mean. That's his little code, one I picked up on the first month we were married.

Work travel. Or, as I like to think of it: *cheating.*

TWENTY-ONE

Charlotte

Leaving Jordan at daycare so I can go to work makes me feel like the worst mom in the world. I wish I could stay home with her. It would be amazing to spend my day alternating between taking care of the house and my baby, but that just wasn't in the cards after Lawrence died.

My feet ache from being on them all day behind the teller line. Normally after work I'd do a little grocery shopping, but Sophie has made that task redundant. I feel a burst of gratitude towards her as I navigate past the discount store and pull into the daycare's parking lot.

It's not the nicest one in town unfortunately, but the staff there all seem to really love the kids. I know the building leaves a lot to be desired, and none of the other mothers who drive luxury vehicles would dare be caught dropping their kids off here, but not all of us are able to send our children to a nicer center.

If Lawrence were still alive, there's no way he'd want Jordan here. I can hear him now, pontificating about how our little family unit deserved the absolute best in everything.

Maybe, if he'd wanted to be a dad—

I push that thought from my mind. It's so easy for me to get angry at Lawrence even though he isn't here any longer. I wanted the perfect family with him, but what I had to give him wasn't enough, and I don't think I'll ever understand why.

He wanted me.

He just didn't want kids. That's all. End of discussion.

Heaving a sigh, I throw the car into park, kill the engine, and get out. It's not just my feet that hurt. My lower back aches like I've never experienced before in my life. It's funny, before Lawrence and I got together, I worked long hours every single day and it didn't affect me like this.

But I'm out of practice. I've lived long enough with the amazing comforts he provided me that having to be on my feet all day long is enough to make me want to go to bed by five.

Instead of pampering myself, I roll my shoulders back and head for the front door. It's not the nicest daycare, but I still have to knock and wait to be buzzed in. It's little things like that, the security measures like the cameras above the door, that make me feel perfectly safe leaving Jordan here.

I knock, then wave up at the camera. A moment later, Linda, the director, comes to the door. She's a shorter woman who's as wide as she is tall and is always smiling.

Except right now.

"Hi, Charlotte," she says, a furrow appearing between her brows. "Is everything okay?"

I stare at her. "Yeah, just... just here for pickup."

The furrow deepens. "You sent someone to come by already. Remember, you called this morning to give me a heads-up."

I freeze. I'm still smiling, but the expression feels stuck, like

I can't get my face to change. I take a deep breath and slowly let it out. It's only then that I feel like I can speak.

"I didn't send anyone by." My heart pounds so loudly I'm surprised she can't hear it.

She gasps, stepping back to press her hand to her chest. "Yes, you did. I wouldn't ever send a child home with someone who wasn't authorized to pick up."

"But I didn't authorize anyone."

"Your sister-in-law," she says, speaking quickly, like she's ripping off a Band-Aid and trying to get the words out before I can stop her. "She came by. Do you not remember?"

My... what? My mind races as I try to think through what she's saying. I understand all of her words, but them strung together like this they don't make any sense. I don't know who, I don't know what, all I know is that Jordan isn't here, and she's my entire world, and if she's gone, I don't know what I'll do—

"I don't have—" I begin, but then it hits me, and I close my eyes to take a deep breath. I want to scream. Throw up. But I have to hold it together in front of her. *Is it possible I called and don't remember?* "You know what, you're right. I forgot completely. It's this whole back-to-work thing that's making it difficult for me to think straight. I'm so sorry."

"Oh, phew."

The relief on her face is so obvious that I don't feel bad for lying to her. Linda would probably have a heart attack if she thought that she'd let Jordan leave with an unauthorized person, and I'm not going to do that to her. Still, my heart hammers in my chest. I thought Jordan was safe when I dropped her off, but clearly I was wrong.

"I was so scared just now, Charlotte! You know I'd never let any of our children out of sight without permission. That's my worst nightmare. It keeps me up when I should be sleeping."

"Don't worry about it," I say, slowly backing up. "This was on me, okay? Not you. You didn't do anything wrong."

As I'm trying to calm Linda down, however, my mind is racing. Sophie was here. She picked Jordan up without my permission and obviously wasn't going to tell me about it. She didn't even have the decency to text me and—

Maybe this is on me. I asked her to leave the house and she seemed more than happy to do that. She confessed the first week she was with me that she couldn't stay away from the office too long without her clients needing her. Errands, paying bills, drawing up blueprints, I don't care what she has to do, I only care that she isn't doing it in my house while I'm gone.

I'd worried at first about her making the long drive back to her place every day when I work, but that's not the case. It's not such a long drive after all. Shivers race up my spine at the thought.

What if I let her get too close? What if she found out the truth? Not about Lawrence but the other thing I did.

What if she took my baby?

My hands are cold as I get back in my car. I'm operating on autopilot as I make my way across town. I don't remember stopping at red lights or stop signs, but since no blue lights appear in my rearview mirror, I must follow all the traffic rules.

My mind is on overdrive, thinking about what I learned about Sophie. Why wouldn't she tell me she lived so close? We could have run into each other before this and never known it.

It's just weird, that's all. That, combined with the fact that Jordan was already picked up from daycare, makes me nervous. Sophie could take her home, and it would only be a short jaunt.

A chill makes the hairs on my arm stand up.

But no. She wouldn't do that. Nothing she's done should make me worried about her intentions with my daughter.

I reach up and press the button to open the garage door. Pull in. Press it again to lower it behind me. For a moment, I sit in the dark of the garage. I should hurry inside and try to find Jordan and Sophie, but I can't think straight right now.

What would I do if Jordan were really missing? They make movies about missing children, and half of the time they don't make it back. How in the world would I ever be able to find Jordan on my own?

But she's not missing. She's with Sophie. She's fine.

I take a deep breath and get out of the car.

I always leave the door from the garage into the kitchen unlocked, and I stop, leaning my forehead against it for a moment. It's cool, and resting helps me gather my thoughts.

As I stand there, I realize something. When I pulled into the driveway, there wasn't any other car outside. Sophie's car isn't here, and that means *Sophie* isn't here, and that means—

Jordan.

There's a burning inside me, fear and anger and horror all wrapped up together. I'm afraid it's going to consume me and I'll end up doing something stupid. Rather than letting it take over, I breathe slowly, forcing myself to calm down.

And then I hear it.

Someone's in the house.

Sophie's car wasn't parked out front, so who the hell is it?

TWENTY-TWO

Sophie

Charlotte slams the door and screams my name.

"Sophie! Hello!?"

She sounds absolutely terrified, and I can't help the smile that plays on my lips. There's the sound of her throwing her purse on the floor. I listen as she stomps into the kitchen then pauses.

"Hello?" Her voice is strained.

It's my time to shine.

"Charlotte?" I poke my head into the kitchen from the living room. "Are you okay?"

"Where is Jordan?" She races towards me, pushing past me in an effort to get into the room. Her hip bumps into me, but she doesn't slow down. "Jordan. Where is she?"

"Sleeping," I begin, and I'm going to tell her that it took a little while to get Jordan to go down for her nap so she needs to be quiet, but she isn't waiting around to hear what I have to say.

She races to the stairs. Tears up them. Honestly, she sounds like a herd of elephants running around, but at least she's stopped screaming for Jordan.

I stand still in the living room for a minute, then walk into the kitchen to start the dishes. There's always something to be done to keep a house looking as nice as possible, which is one thing Charlotte has obviously never learned.

I run the hot water and squirt some soap into it, letting it bubble up and fill the sink. Just another minute or so and Charlotte will be back downstairs wanting to talk.

I'm ready.

There are a lot of mothers who hate washing bottles, but I don't mind it. While I soap and rinse Jordan's bottles, I think about how wonderful it was to pick her up from daycare, to give her a kiss on her forehead and carefully click her car seat into place. Of course, I'd had to go buy a base that worked with the car seat she has, but I'm happy to buy whatever she needs.

I hear footsteps behind me, but I don't immediately turn around.

It's only after I finish washing the bottles, drain the sink, and rinse it clean of bubbles that I turn to look at Charlotte.

"Did you see Jordan? Isn't she sweet napping?" I dry my hands and lean against the counter. "How was your day at work?"

"How was... my day at work?"

"Yeah. First day back, and people can be tricky. So how was it?"

"Well. Work was fine." Her words are tight. She's pissed.

"Good! I'm glad. Do you want me to wash what you have on? I was going to start some laundry. Jordan spit up all over everything at daycare."

"No, I'm fine."

"Well, take a load off. Want a glass of wine? That's one benefit of not nursing, am I right?" I turn away from her but stop when she calls my name. Slowly, I turn back, the same smile still plastered on my face. "You okay?"

"You picked up Jordan from daycare," she says, each word slow and heavy. "And where the hell is your car?"

"Yeeeah, I did. And then I parked around the corner in the shade. I didn't want to block the garage so you could pull straight in when you got home." I stare at her. "Is something wrong?"

"I never asked you to do that."

She's right. She didn't.

"Yeah, you did. Charlotte, I know you're tired and over-worked, but I'm just trying to help." I pause to let that soak in. "Do you not remember asking me to pick her up?"

"Obviously not." She still sounds angry, but I can see the way her face is changing, a bit of doubt creeping in.

"Oh dear. You know, I thought you'd had a lot to drink last night."

She frowns. I've planted the seed of doubt and now she's questioning every decision she made. I should feel bad about doing this to her.

But I don't.

"But then how did you get into the house?"

"With the key you gave me," I say slowly.

She doesn't respond, and I walk over and slowly rub her back.

"I didn't..." she begins, but I shush her.

"Honey, you did. You told me that you put it in the side pocket of Jordan's diaper bag. I checked this morning before you left with her, and it was there. I just got her about... ooh, half an hour before you came home."

"Why would I ask you to pick her up?"

She has no idea what to believe.

"You didn't want to have to swing by there after work. You wanted to come straight home. I spent a lovely day at my office and going for a walk in the park. I took myself out for lunch and then got coffee this afternoon. Then I went to her daycare, picked Jordan up, and brought her home. She couldn't sleep at first, so I rocked her, then put her in her crib. I promise you, that's all that happened."

"But I didn't put you down as an approved pickup person. I know I didn't! So why would they let you take her?"

Probably because I called earlier and pretended to be you so I wouldn't have any problems picking her up.

"Linda made a mistake," I tell her, and her gaze snaps to mine. It's written clear as day on her face how badly she wants to believe me. All I have to do is sell it. "I hate to say that about someone, but that's clearly what happened here. She dropped the ball, but Jordan is okay. I promise you, she's as safe with me as she would be with anyone else."

She's breathing faster.

"Hey. Look at me." I wait until she does before continuing. "I'm so sorry you were scared. That was not my intention."

"I didn't know where she was! I thought something had happened to her." Tears shimmer in her eyes, but to her credit, she keeps them from falling.

I nod. "I can tell. But trust me, Charlotte, I would never hurt you or Jordan. I want to be a part of your lives any way that you're comfortable, and I'll do whatever it takes to make that happen. You're exhausted; when we're tired, we don't always think straight."

"I'm sorry I freaked out on you," she whispers.

I laugh and force myself to pull her into a hug. It's tight, probably tighter than it needs to be, but I don't let up.

"You don't need to apologize for a thing, okay? Trust me—you acted exactly how any mother would act in your situation. I'm not mad. Jordan is safe. She's here."

For now.

TWENTY-THREE

Charlotte

I haven't let Jordan out of my sight since she got up from her short nap. She took her bottle on my lap while Sophie and I ate the dinner she made—veggie burgers with sweet potato fries—then I gave her a bath.

Not that she needed one. She was clean and still smelled fresh, but I love spending time with her in the bathroom, singing to her and bathing her, knowing I'm the only one who gets to bond with her like that.

Then came a fresh diaper.

Little footie pajamas.

And rocking in the rocking chair.

Now I swaddle her, making sure it's not too tight or too loose. She's like Goldilocks, needing everything to be *just right* so she can get the best night's sleep ever. After I lay her down in her crib, I stand still for a moment, my hand on her chest, listening to her breathing get slower and slower until she falls asleep.

There.

That magic moment when she finally gives in to sleep is like a switch going off in my brain. I feel like I can relax, like the stress of the day is finally wearing off.

And what a day it's been. I still feel like an idiot for getting so upset over Sophie picking her up from daycare. She was obviously fine, and I acted like a fool, all because my brain wouldn't shut up. I didn't think I had too much to drink, but I might have. Or maybe it's exhaustion and stress. All of that could contribute to why I don't remember asking Sophie for help.

I brought this on myself.

But I swear I didn't call Linda this morning.

That thought eats at me until I pull my phone out and check. There, in black and white on my screen, is Linda's personal number. I called it before going to work and don't remember. My hand shakes, and I drop my phone like it's a snake. It lands on its back, the screen still lit up, Linda's name at the top of my recent calls.

Now I'm scared. I'm clearly forgetting things, but I can't worry about that right now. I need to make sure I can hear Jordan while I'm in the shower. The baby monitor is still in the kitchen, and I walk downstairs to get it for my shower, but first I crank the water to hot. Because of where the water heater is located, it takes forever for this bathroom's water to warm up.

I hate standing naked in the bathroom, shivering as I stick my arm under the spray from time to time to check how warm it's gotten. It's best to turn the water on as hot as possible, then gather up my pajamas and whatever else I need for a shower.

Tonight, that includes Jordan's baby monitor. No way can I hear her over the sound of the water running. I thought I could when I first brought her home, but even though my shower was short and cold, I didn't hear her scream.

By the time I got out and realized what was going on, she'd worked herself up so much that she'd thrown up all over her crib.

Never again. I'll never let her get that upset again, no matter what I have to do.

By the time I'm back upstairs with the baby monitor, I want to check in on her again. I'm not paranoid, I swear I'm not, but after the stress of thinking she was missing today, I just want to lay eyes on her and make sure she's fine.

I'm quiet as I creep down the hall. Waking her up right now would be awful. I'd feel bad, she'd be upset, and it would take forever to get her back to sleep.

It's how careful I am as I walk down the hall that means I don't step on a squeaky board. I don't kick my toe on the rug, or trip, or do any of that.

Which is why Sophie never hears me coming.

I'm not a snoop. I never have been. But her door is cracked, and I can hear her voice as clear as if she were in the hall with me. It's the first time I've heard her on the phone with anyone since arriving here, and then it hits me—she thinks I'm in the shower.

Here in the hall, the sound is so loud it's like a waterfall. More than a dull hum, it's almost overbearing, a clear sign that whoever was going to take a shower is more than occupied at the moment.

Did she wait until I was distracted to make a call?

That thought is silly, and I try to push it away, but it takes root. Ever since becoming a mother, I've become paranoid. I don't like it, but it is what it is.

That's why I slow down by her room. I should keep walking to Jordan's nursery. The door is *right there*, so close I just have to cross the hall and sidestep a few feet, but I'm drawn to the sound of Sophie's voice and can't help myself when I pause by the door, then listen as hard as I can.

"See, that's the thing," she says. "She has no idea."

She's not even trying to keep her voice low. But even though I can hear her perfectly well, I have no idea who she's talking to.

But I think it's about me.

Paranoid? Maybe.

I push that worry aside. My brain is working against me, which is something it's done since I was a little girl. I've always been worried about what people thought about me, about whether or not they were telling me the truth.

But Sophie hasn't done anything wrong since she's gotten here. I have to remember that and shut my brain up.

She laughs.

I take a deep breath. I have no way of knowing for sure if she's talking about me, but what if she is?

I'm breathing slow, holding each breath before letting it out. It's funny, when you're trying to hide from someone, how loud everything you do is. I don't think she'll hear me out here, but there's always the chance she will.

I reach out to push the door open but yank my hand back like it's been burned. She has no idea I'm out here. As long as the shower keeps running, she'll think I'm busy. Occupied. I just have to stay quiet.

Or you could talk to her like a normal human. But you're paranoid and always will be now.

She laughs again. The sound is like a troop of spiders skittering up the back of my neck.

"I don't know how long it will take, but you know me. I'm not a quitter. I won't stop until I get what I want."

What does she want?

She sounds so confident and in control, and the fact that she might be feeling that way about something to do with me—to do with Jordan—makes me nervous. I reach up and nibble a nail while I wait to hear what else she's going to say.

"Sure, I'll keep you updated. Like I said, this will be easy. She'll never see it coming."

Never see what coming?

I'm still in the hall trying to figure out what's going on when

I hear her tell the person on the phone goodbye. There's the sound of a drawer closing and then footsteps.

I leap back from the door, sure that I look guilty. There's no reason for me to hover outside of her room like this unless I was listening in, and I'm terrified she's going to take one look at me and know that I was snooping.

The door is opening.

I step back and turn as well, moving towards Jordan's room, like that's what I was doing all along. I'm just a mom, taking care of her baby, nothing to see here, nothing to worry about.

"Charlotte?"

I freeze. Turn back to her. "Oh, Sophie. Hi. I hope I didn't bother you."

She frowns. Are her cheeks more flushed than normal? "Of course you didn't. But what's going on?"

I look down at the baby monitor in my hand. "I... brought this up with me to have when I was showering, but it wasn't connecting to the one in Jordan's room. I was going to check it out. See what was going on."

She knows I'm lying. She has to. I feel like there's a band around my chest making it almost impossible for me to breathe. No way will she look at me and not tell that I'm lying. She has to know. She's—

"Weird. It was working fine earlier." She wrinkles her nose. "Did you check to make sure the cord was nice and tight in the back? Sometimes the plug pops out a bit."

"Does it?" I wiggle the cord and nod. "You know what, I think you're right. Thank you." I throw her what I think looks like a casual smile, then turn to go back to the bathroom.

"Hey, I thought you were in the shower. Everything okay?"

I turn back around. Take in the way she's standing in the door. How she's leaned against the doorframe.

Casual. Like she doesn't have a care in the world.

"Yeah, the water wasn't getting warm." I stare at her, daring her to call me out, then decide to take the plunge and ask her a question. She can't always be the one in control. Why can't I sometimes? "Who were you talking to? It sounded serious."

"My assistant," she answers without hesitation. "I've been working with a tricky client. They've been going back and forth between me and another architect, and I have to pull out all the stops to make sure they stay with me. The other architect... she's wily. But I don't want to lose this client." She pauses, her eyes searching mine. "Is everything okay? Did I say or do something to upset you?"

"No, not at all. Things are fine." I swallow hard. "Sounds like you have it under control."

She grins, and it feels like the ground shifts under me. "I always do."

TWENTY-FOUR
ONE YEAR AGO

Her

Two pink lines.

My hand shakes as I look down at the test. This... this wasn't supposed to happen. It was part of the deal, a huge part of our agreement. Not only that, but he'd told me he couldn't get me pregnant. Why would he say that unless it was a lie?

Unless he wanted to control me and make me jump through hoops to be with him? For a moment, when he told me the agreement he required, I'd thought about not doing what he wanted, but I was young and stupid and thought that I'd be able to change him.

Isn't that always how it is? We think we can change the person we love only to find out that no, they're stuck in their ways, *mired* in them, and now we are too.

The agreement was simple. So simple, in fact, that I barely had to think about it to agree to it. It was a no-brainer, and what was required of me was so easy, so basic, that no way was I going to disagree. Lawrence would do anything I want. Take me anywhere. Give me access to his accounts, to his credit cards and cars, and the only thing I had to do was keep taking my pill one time a day, every day. I had to prove to him, day in and day out, that I was willing to take the pill, that I was always thinking about him and the promise I made him.

Don't. Get. Pregnant.

That's it. How easy is that? There are millions of women all over the world who don't want kids or can't have kids and go their entire lives without peeing on a test, and yet, when faced with the simplest task of my life, I screwed it up.

He was so serious about it, we almost wrote it into our vows. He'd wanted to, honestly, but I'd thought about what it would be like to stand in front of his friends and family and read that out loud, and I couldn't do it.

So the night before the wedding, when most people would be staying up late giddy with nerves or having a sleepover with their best friend, the two of us were at the lawyer's office, filling out paperwork. I should have given it more gravitas, but I didn't. All because I was young and stupid.

In hindsight, I should have wondered *why me?* Why, when he could have had any woman in the world, looking the way he did, with his bank account as flush as it was?

I know now. I wonder how many women he offered this agreement, how many laughed in his face, unwilling to play his little game.

And then I came along, spellbound by how Lawrence talked to me, how he acted, how he treated me like I was his entire world. And I was! And, more importantly, he wanted me to stay that way forever.

Don't. Get. Pregnant.

And I haven't. For so, so long, I've done everything right. Even when I know I haven't forgotten a single pill, I still take a pregnancy test every month just to make sure I didn't miss anything, didn't screw up. He's that important to me, which is something I know a lot of people might not understand. And it's all been fine.

Until now. Tears burn my eyes, but I don't let them fall as I think back to my last period. Am I late? I'm so good about keeping up with it, about testing, that I must only be about six weeks along.

I don't realize I'm letting go of the test until it falls from my fingers and hits the bathroom floor. The tile is custom, heated so my bare feet won't get cold when I'm getting ready in the morning or just out of the shower in the evening, but a shiver rips through my body as I stare at it.

It landed right side up, and my stomach clenches as I stare at the lines. I'm a woman without many options of what to do next. Still, even though I know, deep in my heart, what needs to be done, I don't know if I have the stomach to do it.

I support women's rights to choose. But that's a hypothetical baby. It's someone else's problem, someone else's huge decision. Now that the decision is no longer a hypothetical one that a hypothetical woman on the other side of the world will have to make, now that it's staring me in the face, I don't know what I'm going to do.

As carefully as possible, like it's a bomb that could go off at any second and not just a pregnancy test from the store down the street, I pick it up with two fingers. I'd love to take a picture of the twin pink lines. Love to post it on social media so everyone can see what my future holds, but instead I slip it back into the box with the instructions.

Part of me wants to take another test. Just in case this one is faulty. There's no reason to, not when I know the truth. The nausea was my first clue. The test just solidifies what I already suspected.

Carefully, I search the bathroom, making sure that I haven't left any proof of the test ever existing in our house. The last thing I want to have happen is for him to come home, see the tiny corner of the test wrapper still on the floor by the trash, and know exactly what happened.

No, I have to get rid of all of the evidence.

Once I'm satisfied that it's all in the box, I wrap it up in a plastic Target bag from under the sink. My hands shake as I tie a knot, then another, then finally a third. It's not enough to simply throw it away in the kitchen trash.

And, sure, I could ask our housekeeper to take it with her when she leaves in an hour, but the longer it's in my home, the greater the chance that someone will find the proof of what I let happen.

Our housekeeper has never snooped before, but what if she started now? What if she got curious about why I'd tie three knots in a bag of trash? I can't see Helen picking them open, see her hunched over the bag in her driver's seat, but now that the thought has crossed my mind, it's a real fear that has taken root.

No, I have to get rid of this myself. If I don't, he might see it. Or Helen might see it and ask me where the test came from. She'd be excited, I know she would—the woman has four children and twelve grandchildren.

If I don't get it out of the house as soon as possible, I could lose everything. Or I'd cave and ask if we can keep it.

No, as much as I'd love to let someone else throw this away for me so I could pretend this didn't happen, as much as I'd love to sit back down with my book and escape into the land of a romance story where knights are worthy of the shining armor they wore, I stuff the bag into my purse and head for the garage.

I have to get rid of all of the evidence. I broke the contract, and my husband is the only one allowed to bend the rules.

If I do, I fear he'll kill me.

TWENTY-FIVE
FRIDAY

Charlotte

Lying to the head teller about having a migraine was easy enough, which meant that I was able to leave work well before the end of my scheduled shift. Had I gone to Andy, I don't know that I would have gotten off work that easy, so I got lucky. Michelle knows I have migraines, but I do a great job managing them.

A healthy diet with plenty of exercise and limited caffeine? Check.

Staying positive and focusing on the good things? Sounds woo-woo as hell, but desperation leads people to do whatever they can to avoid the crushing pain that comes with a migraine.

Avoiding stress? The thought makes me laugh.

Meds? Yep. Although how much they really help, I'm not sure. But when the option is a possible placebo or crushing pain that makes it impossible to do anything, the answer is clear.

I feel a little guilt as I drive away from my work. Michelle is great and does her best to take care of everyone on the team. When I told her I felt a migraine coming on, she told me not to worry about leaving early. Sure, lying to her was easy, but I still feel bad about it.

I could go pick Jordan up from daycare so she and I have a few precious hours together, but what I really want to do is get into the house without Sophie around. It's weird, to feel like a stranger in my own house, like I'm breaking into it, but that's exactly the thought that's running through my head. Sneaking around feels illegal, and the fear that she'll catch me and ask me what I'm doing is what's driving me to do this while I know she's gone.

I want some time alone without Sophie there, that's all. She's gone out of her way to be helpful since she moved in, but I haven't been able to do anything without her right around the corner. She's always just right there. Watching. Talking to me.

And talking on the phone. I snooped and possibly overheard something I took the wrong way. It wouldn't be an issue, but something about her is rubbing me wrong. I was grateful for her companionship at first, I'll admit that, but now she's holding Jordan more and more.

It shouldn't bother me, the fact that she wants to hold my baby and help out, but I thought her moving in would mean she'd take care of chores around the house, not that she'd want to take over snuggling my baby.

I thought she wanted one thing when she moved in, but she wanted something completely different. It's only when that thought runs through my head that I realize I'm chewing on my thumbnail.

Nerves. That's all it is.

In my neighborhood, I slow down, then pull up to my house. Sophie's car is nowhere to be seen, which doesn't surprise me. She told me this morning she was going to hit the gym and then wanted to spend the morning working on a new work proposal before hitting the grocery store.

Of course, she was more than happy to remind me that

she'd be picking Jordan up from daycare. I didn't argue. Did I really ask her to do that? I really don't remember, but then again, I've been sleep deprived for a while now. And if I didn't ask her to, how did she get a key to my house? The only way is if I gave her a copy.

I must have said something and forgotten. As much as I hate to admit it to myself, my memory isn't always reliable.

Even at work, or when talking to the funeral home, I don't remember all the things I've said. I have no real reason to believe that Sophie is lying to me.

But if that's true, why am I in the garage right now? Why am I sneaking around my house, heading straight for her room, like I have something to hide?

Probably because I don't know her. She's perfect. *Too perfect*, and my brain won't stop worrying about the conversation I overheard last night, even though she easily explained it away. She showed up here talking about her brother and how much she loved him, how much they cared for each other when they were younger.

But if they were so close when they were younger, why wouldn't Lawrence at least mention her? I would have understood him having a sister and not getting along with her now that they're adults. That's not out of the ordinary.

But he hid it from me.

He was everything to me, until Jordan took that spot. I inhaled him, drank him up the way some people do a fine wine. In little sips at first, like you can't quite believe what you're getting to enjoy, then faster and faster, downing it in big gulps. I wanted to swallow Lawrence up whole; I wanted to live inside him, stretching myself so his organs and bones shifted and made room for me.

I never wanted to leave him.

But he forced my hand.

He made me do what I did.

That thought is on repeat as I hurry up the stairs to Sophie's room. Outside it, in the hall, I pause, then take a deep breath and turn the knob to open the door.

Only the knob doesn't turn.

"Locked?" Frustration washes over me. I thought it would be easy to waltz in here, poke around, and find out what she was up to. Even though she'd seemed like the answer to my prayers when she first showed up, I'm beginning to think that maybe I need to get someone else to help.

Hire a real professional to help me.

I go up on my tiptoes and pat the top of the doorframe until I feel the little key there. They're on top of every doorframe in the house. I wish I could take credit for having the forethought to put them there, but Lawrence said they were there when he bought the place.

I never understood why you'd need one, but now I'm grateful they're here.

I press the little straight bit of metal in through the hole on the doorknob. It takes me a minute of jiggling it around until I hear a satisfying click. Before I forget, I put the key back where it was, then slowly open her door.

"What, were you expecting booby traps?" I mutter to myself, then to prove I'm not scared, I step fully into the room and turn on the light.

It... it looks fine. Clean. No exploding suitcases on the floor. No pile of dirty laundry in the corner, which is always what happens when I go stay with someone. It's awkward, isn't it, to be in someone's space and not know what to do with your dirty undies?

I only hesitate for a moment, then I walk to the closet and throw open the door. There's a small string hanging in front of me, and I yank it to turn on the light. Sophie's suitcases are in here, neatly stacked in the corner. She has a few pairs of shoes on the floor and hanging clothes on the bar.

"She really moved in." I'm not surprised, not really, not with how confident she acted when she first arrived at the house and what I thought I heard last night when I was snooping in the hall, but it's still strange to see someone's belongings put away in here. Yes, she's been here a few weeks now, but in my eyes she's still a guest.

I should have put my foot down. Put some ground rules in place. Anyone on the outside of this would think I was stupid and brought it on myself, but honestly, I was so grateful for help that I dropped the ball. Between taking care of Jordan and hiding the truth about what happened to Lawrence, my mind has been pulled in a dozen different directions.

And now look what's happened. She's moved in and I don't know how to get her to leave.

I stare at the suitcases for another moment, my mind racing. Lawrence and I never had people spend the night, no matter how many times I offered for him to have friends come visit us.

Controlling, some people might call him.

I preferred *focused*.

Until I saw him for who he really was.

I snap off the light and close the door, then walk to the dresser. Just like the closet, it's full of her clothes. They're neat and folded and perfectly fill the space, like she knew exactly how many to bring.

Strange though it is, there's nothing damning in here. Nothing that would give me pause. Her toiletries bag is on the floor by her bed, as if she didn't want to clutter up the bathroom.

After a quick poke through it, I can tell there's nothing out of the ordinary in there either.

I sit down on the bed as I think. It had felt so right, claiming to be sick so I could leave work early and come home to snoop through her things. Now that I'm here and doing it, though, I feel like a fool. I guess the best thing for me to do is either go get

Jordan or continue with the ruse that I really had a migraine. Either way, Sophie could come back at any moment, and I don't want her to catch me poking around in her room.

I heave a sigh and plant my hands on my thighs. Before I stand up, I have a thought.

What if she hid something under her mattress?

I remember Lawrence telling me one time that he always hid stuff under his mattress as a kid. Sophie's his sister, so maybe it's possible that she picked up the habit as well.

Without giving myself time to think it through, I drop to my knees by the bed and shove my hand between the mattress and the box spring.

It's tricky to push my hand between them with the full weight of the mattress pressing down, so I shift position and try to push it up with my other hand. My muscles scream as I shove, straining against the dead weight.

Nothing here.

I scoot to the left and try again, my muscles burning with the effort.

I really need to hit the gym.

Sweat beads on my forehead, and I drop the mattress so I can go to the other side of the bed. This is a long shot, and it's probably silly of me to spend my time doing this when I could dig through her suitcases and clothes, but now that the thought is in my mind, I can't get rid of it.

I have to know if there's something here.

Lawrence didn't tell me he had a sister.

He didn't tell me who to call if something terrible happened to him.

Why wouldn't he tell me about Sophie? Could their falling-out really have been that bad? Or was there something more to it?

I know you shouldn't think ill of the dead, but really... how well did I know my husband?

TWENTY-SIX

Sophie

Charlotte beat me home, and I feel a stirring of frustration at the idea that she's in the house without me.

Stupid, I know. It's not my house.

Yet.

I put down the bag of groceries I'm carrying and tuck my hair back behind my ears. Charlotte protested a lot when I first moved in and bought food, but now it seems like it's expected. She doesn't stop me from going to the grocery store and hasn't asked if she can help pay for food.

But that's fine. I'm not here for her.

I'm here for Jordan.

After I put the groceries away, I pause at the bottom of the stairs. No way did she not hear me banging around down here. It's impossible to put groceries away quietly, and I'm sure she heard the cupboards closing.

But then what is she doing up there?

Snooping. Trying to learn more about me.

Ice shoots up my spine at that thought.

Of course she would—she'd be stupid not to want to know as much about me as possible, especially since she's letting me live in her home. I hadn't been surprised the time I caught her checking out my website, but I thought we were past that by now.

We're in a good routine. I thought I had her trusting me. She has no idea I used her cell to call Linda so I could be on Jordan's approved pickup list. It was so easy to do. Charlotte had gone back up to her room, leaving her phone on the kitchen counter. I'd been lucky that her phone hadn't locked by the time she'd gotten far enough away for me to make the call.

Still, I'm quiet as I make my way to the second floor. Her bedroom door is open, but the light is off. I pause for a moment, then turn to look down the hall.

Jordan's nursery door is open.

And so is mine.

My footsteps are silent as I hurry down the hall. I locked this door when I left this morning—I know I did.

She picked the lock. She had to.

I don't like the thought of Charlotte poking around in my things. Not that she'd find anything that would tell her who I really am. I'm careful. I have to be.

I pause in the doorway and watch as Charlotte sits back on her heels. She's at the side of the bed, and I realize instantly what she was doing—looking for anything stashed under the mattress.

Honestly? I'm impressed. Charlotte comes across as such a pushover, and I'm surprised she'd go so far as to poke around in my space. I'm not afraid of her, of course, but it makes me look at her a little differently.

I've been busy trying to find out more about her. I guess she's doing the same, which means I have to make sure she doesn't find anything.

As I watch, she wipes her hair off her forehead and breathes heavily before standing up.

"What are you doing?"

Charlotte's head snaps up. At the same time, her cheeks redden.

"I thought I left something under the mattress," she blurts out. "And I wanted to get it before you noticed it."

Liar. I don't call her out though.

"I meant home from work. This is your house, Charlotte—you're allowed to be in here."

She blinks at me, then reaches up and lightly touches her temple. "I had a headache."

I frown. "A headache?"

"I get migraines, and I wasn't entirely sure if this was going to turn into one or not. I told my boss, and she said I should head home while I still could rather than risk not being able to drive."

Not true.

"And you thought digging around in my room was better than taking a nap?"

No response.

"You poor thing." I hurry to stand next to her so I can lay it on thick. "Can you walk? I'm serious, Charlotte, if you need to rest, you should be doing just that."

"You know how it is when something starts bugging you," she says, and I nod. "I didn't feel like I had a choice. I had to look."

"Sure, I get it. But trust me, it never crossed my mind to look under the mattress for anything you might have left there." That's a lie. I did it my first night here, but she'll never know that.

I loop my arm around her, then lead her to the doorway. "Your bed or downstairs?"

"Downstairs."

"You got it. We'll be careful on the stairs. Now, I know what it's like to have to take care of something *right now*, but I wish you'd asked for help."

It's a test, to see how much she trusts me, but Charlotte doesn't know that.

Instead of arguing, she nods. "It felt silly asking for help when I didn't even know if there was anything there."

"Everyone has secrets," I say, but she doesn't respond. We're on the first floor now, and I lead her into the living room. "Tylenol? Ibuprofen? Coffee? I don't get migraines, so I don't know what you need."

"Nothing." The smile she gives me is wan. "Really. I got lucky on this one. I have meds for it, but this was just a nasty headache. False alarm."

"Good to hear." I sit next to her. The cushion is firm. Uncomfortable. "So, what kind of things would you stash under a mattress? A journal? Got some deep, dark secrets you want to share?"

Her mouth tightens.

"Ahh, it is a journal." I smile at her. I'm enjoying this. "Let me guess, you looked for your journal but didn't find it, right? I can help you look. Missing a journal is a bad feeling."

"No." She sits up as she snaps the word, then forces herself to relax. "No, thank you. I don't want you to worry about a thing."

A pause and I can actually see her steel herself for what's coming next.

"Sophie, we need to talk about how much longer you're going to stay. I appreciate your help, but it's time we had a conversation."

"Of course we will, but not right now." I smile at her and lightly pat her knee before glancing at my watch. She might think she can get me to leave, but I've taken steps to ensure she can't. Make myself indispensable. Gaslight her into thinking she's forgetting things. It's cute that she suddenly thinks she's got the spine needed to make me leave. "I better get going if I'm going to go pick Jordan up from daycare."

She forces a smile when she looks at me, but I see right through it. I don't know what changed, but one thing is obvious.

She doesn't trust me.

She shouldn't.

TWENTY-SEVEN

Sophie Moore. Lawrence's sister. An architect. A widow. Just as successful in her own right as Lawrence was but not close to her brother. She's great with Jordan, but is it possible that she's too involved? Too interested in my child?

That thought eats at me.

I had no idea she existed and certainly didn't have contact info for her to call her when Lawrence died.

So how did she find out about his death? I didn't put an obit in the paper. They're expensive, and I've always thought they were a little tacky, if I'm being honest. But nobody bothered to call Sophie, obviously, or she would have been at the funeral. That's the part that doesn't make sense to me. She and Lawrence had a falling-out, but did she have one with the entire family? Why didn't *someone* let her know what had happened?

But obviously someone did. It may have taken a while for the news to get to her, but the only way she would know about what happened to Lawrence is because someone had to have told her.

Right?

And then she found my online ad for in-home help. Maybe she heard about Lawrence's death after his funeral and looked me up. Saw the ad. Decided she'd come and meet me. Meet Jordan. Help out.

She showed up at the perfect time, right when I needed her the most.

It was perfect.

Too perfect?

I'm tired and I know I'm not thinking straight, but my brain is on overdrive right now and I can't calm my thoughts. Ever since becoming a mom, I've felt like I'm hanging on by a thread. I honestly don't know how people do it when they have more than one child.

There have been times, as much as I hate to admit it, when I stare at Jordan while she's crying and I just... want to walk away. I wouldn't, of course. That's not who I am. That's not the kind of mother I want to be.

But those intrusive thoughts get into my mind and they're hard to get rid of.

Sophie is here to help. I should let her.

I press my fingers into my temples and think. The effects of sleep deprivation extend beyond exhaustion. They include depression, memory impairment, mood changes, and anxiety, among other delightful experiences.

Memory impairment. That explains why I didn't remember asking Sophie to pick Jordan up from daycare.

Anxiety. You mean like how my brain refuses to shut off? I think these intrusive thoughts count. Except maybe they're based on reality, and that terrifies me.

I'm getting more sleep now that Sophie is here, but I'm still tired. I still feel like I could curl up and sleep for a week straight, Rip Van Winkle style.

My feet eat up the floor as I pace back and forth between the kitchen and the living room.

I just want my baby. Holding Jordan will make me feel better.

I could have been the one to pick her up from daycare.

I *should* have been the one to pick her up from daycare.

My problem is that I let people take control. Killing Lawrence was the first time I've taken control over my own life, and—

No, that's not true. The first time I took control over my life was when I became a mother. Then I killed Lawrence, and then... I let Sophie in.

And I'm beginning to think that was a mistake. I see the way she looks at my daughter when she's holding her, like she's the most incredible thing she's ever seen.

Like she wants her.

No. No way. That would be crazy, for her to come into my house, go out of her way to take care of me and Jordan, and then what? Take my daughter?

"Yeah, right," I mutter to myself. "That's not something that happens in real life."

Or is it?

That's it. This weekend I'm sitting her down and we're talking. I wish I had a close friend who could take Jordan for me so she isn't in the house while we chat, but it will be fine. I'll get rid of Sophie. No longer will I have to worry about what she might be doing, or thinking, or if she wants my daughter.

That fear eats at me, and I walk into the kitchen and pour a glass of wine, taking a moment to peer into the fridge.

It hasn't been this full since Lawrence died, and I'm a bit overwhelmed. There's broccoli and carrots, a quiche, fish wrapped in butcher paper, and two dozen brown eggs. My eyes skim over the new cheese, the lunch meat, the salad and dressings, the jars of olives and fresh pickles.

I ignore the food. All I need is something to calm me, to take the edge off. Just something to quiet the little voice in my head. A single glass of wine will do that, will put my fears to rest.

Everything makes sense. Everything is fine. Sophie is here to help.

She wouldn't dare hurt Jordan.

But would she take her?

No. Not a chance. That's something you see on late-night television, something you read about in the paper and then quickly turn the page so you don't have to see the child's face smiling up at you.

Kidnapped.

Taken.

Abducted.

Those are some of the most terrifying words for a parent to consider, but that's not going to happen to Jordan.

I won't let it.

TWENTY-EIGHT

Her

It's been three weeks since the twin pink lines showed up and they've consumed every waking thought I have. I still haven't told Lawrence. It's not that I'm going to keep the baby; it's just that I want to enjoy as much time being pregnant as possible.

I want to pretend like I'm going to be a mom even though I know that will never happen. I've been going to Target more and more, slowly walking down the baby aisles, trailing my fingers over onesies and little socks.

Pink? Or blue?

Or maybe an explosion of colors in the closet. Maybe every color of the rainbow, then I could dress up my baby, and later my toddler could dress themselves however they wanted, and it wouldn't matter.

I just want a happy baby. I want to count their toes, boop their nose. I want to debate between breastfeeding and bottle feeding. I want burp cloths over my shoulder, diapers in my purse, crumbs scattered all over the car.

I want all the things my husband doesn't, and that's why the two of us are at such an impasse.

It doesn't matter that I'm going to bleed and put on weight I know will be hard to shed. I don't care about saggy, leaking breasts. Nothing about the future with a baby scares me.

Sleepless nights? Sign me up.

Rocking my baby for hours? I'm in.

Worrying over diaper rash and what cream to use? I'm the queen of research.

I've never wanted anything as badly as I want this baby. My entire life, I thought babies were kinda neat—something other women wanted, but that changed after saying my vows. More often than not, I was leaning towards wanting one. Now, though, that I'm faced with actually having a child, it's all I think about.

Sure, I've missed having close friends I can talk to about this, but if I'm being honest, it's probably good that I don't have them. The last thing I need is to run my mouth and spill the beans that I'm pregnant.

I tell one person, they tell another. Soon enough, word gets around in this small town, and not only does it make it back to my husband, but then there are hard questions to answer after the fact.

Women may still have the right to make hard choices, but that doesn't mean they won't be punished for them.

I'm in the diaper section, and I turn around to head back to the bottles. One more trip through the baby section. Just one more, just today, then I'll call my doctor and get this taken care of.

That's the smart thing to do. Not only that, it's the only thing for me to do. It would be easy to drag my feet even more than I already have, to delay and delay until it didn't matter that women have a choice because I didn't any longer.

And I could do it, I honestly think I could. By the time I start to really show, it will be cooling off. And I've always been a fan of leggings and oversized hoodies. Nobody would bat an eye if I were to constantly cover up.

Then what? Keep the baby? Sure, my husband might not notice me being pregnant, but he'd sure as hell notice if he came home from work one day and there was a baby in the house with me. I may be able to hide a lot of things, but that's not one of them.

My husband travels a lot for work, and he hasn't noticed the morning sickness. He isn't around to watch me nibble a dry piece of toast, to run to the bathroom when I smell eggs, to see how sick I've been. But he'll be back in two weeks from a conference in Toronto, and I have to have it taken care of by then.

It's dangerous to wait too long—I know that.

Every day I wait is another day I fall further in love. Another day I struggle to give up my baby. Another day I'm closer to being a mom and that much closer to losing my husband.

How can a woman be asked to choose between the family she's already created by getting married and the one she wants to create with her husband? How can she be forced to make that decision when being a mother is now the one thing she wants more than anything else?

Who cares that I was willing to ignore any thought of being a mother for my husband? The thing is: I didn't have to agree to what he asked of me. He wouldn't have gotten mad. If I wasn't willing to agree, to give him the one thing he wanted—not a baby but the freedom from having one—the two of us would have parted ways.

It wouldn't have been a big deal in the long run. Yes, I love him. And yes, I would miss the lifestyle I have now. It's hard to think about giving up the things you have, much easier to never have it in the first place.

But it's on me. I sigh and put back a three-pack of baby bottles. I agreed to never have children. I was young and stupid and thought my husband would be able to fulfill every dream and desire I had. It was crazy of me to rely on a man for that.

I didn't know myself well enough to be able to tell whether or not I'd really be happy being married and not having a large family. I was so swept up in his love, in his affection, that I thought it would all work out.

My hand finds my stomach. It's still perfectly flat. No sign of life inside. In fact, I haven't even been to the doctor to get an ultrasound. For all anyone knows, I'm not pregnant, never have been pregnant, never will be pregnant.

Every morning since I peed on the test, I wake up and, for a few minutes at least, I don't remember that I have a baby growing inside of me. It's easy to forget it, to go about my morning routine of peeing, brushing my teeth, and getting dressed.

Maybe my toothpaste smells stronger than it usually does, but I don't really pay attention. And maybe I wake up after sleeping an entire night and I'm still as tired as I was when I went to bed.

But it's easy to pretend neither of those things have anything to do with me being pregnant.

So I go about my day, at least for a little while, forgetting that I have a terrible decision that I'm going to have to make. I forget about what my future brings and the fact that I can't have my husband *and* a baby.

I remember eventually, of course. I'm not a monster who can forget all the time about having a child. But off and on throughout the day, I continue to forget. It slips my mind, feeling more like a dream than reality.

But I know the truth. Whenever I start to doubt if the baby inside of me is real, I think back to those two pink lines. The baby is real. I'm a mother.

A mother who has to decide between saving her child or her marriage.

TWENTY-NINE

Sophie

Jordan was happy to see me when I picked her up from daycare, I know she was. She doesn't have to speak for me to know she recognizes me and likes me. And why wouldn't she? I rock her. I sing to her. Every night after Charlotte has gone to bed, I sneak into her nursery and hold her.

Loving her is easy, even though that's not the main reason I came here. I came to see who Lawrence married, who was so important to him that he'd choose her over me. And I definitely think she had something to do with his death.

But then I saw Jordan. Since then, I haven't been able to shake the feeling that she should be mine.

Now we're on the way home from daycare, and I slow down as I pull into Charlotte's neighborhood. Without realizing what I'm doing, I tap the brake and pull over to the side of the road.

Huge trees line the road, their branches stretching to meet in the middle. It's getting late, but the sun is still out, and it shines through the leaves, dappling my car and the road. It's such an idyllic neighborhood. No wonder Lawrence wanted to live here.

And no wonder Charlotte seems willing to do whatever it takes to stay. I've heard her on the phone to the lawyer trying to work through who the house belongs to, what she's going to do for money since she isn't on the accounts, and who the executor might be.

And, sure, I could answer some of those questions for her, but I have no intention of doing that anytime soon. I like having her off-balance. I like picking up Jordan and making Charlotte question if she really asked me to do it for her.

She's just so easy to control.

In the backseat, Jordan hiccups, and I take my foot off the brake and slowly drive forward. Nobody speeds in this neighborhood. Everyone drives slowly and takes their time since there are so many kids running around.

It's a far cry from the house I live in.

I could live here.

I don't mean to have the thought. It's not conscious, not by a long shot, but now that it's in my mind, I allow myself to consider it. Sure, it's a bit of a haul from my office, but the house is gorgeous. The neighborhood is incredible.

And if I were to be a mom, I'd need a nice backyard.

I pull into the driveway, but I don't kill the engine or get out because I'm too busy thinking about what it would be like to pull up to this house and have it be *my* house.

To carry groceries in and stick them in *my* fridge.

To hold Jordan and know that she's *my* baby.

My baby.

She's my baby.

I know it.

THIRTY
SATURDAY

Charlotte

For the first time since Sophie arrived—willing to spend money on us, willing to help with Jordan, willing to give me enough breathing room that I finally can relax—I imagined what our lives would be like without her.

She'd appeared like the answer to a prayer. She'd said all the right things, done all the right things.

But then things started to get a little weird. Of course she loves Jordan; I can't see how anyone who met my daughter wouldn't be obsessed with her, but it almost feels like...

Like what?

Like she doesn't just love her. Like she *wants* her.

Cold creeps across my skin, and I rub my hands up and down my arms. I'm still in bed so I can think things through without having to talk to Sophie, but my ears are pricked for Jordan.

Even though I didn't get very much sleep, I feel more awake than I have in weeks. Sure, I'm tired in that way that every parent is tired—a feeling deep in your bones that settles in like frost, but I'm alert.

I can do this. On my own.

I make a decision.

Sophie needs to go. I'm putting my foot down because that's the long and short of it: she was really helpful for a while. And then she wasn't. I made the decision yesterday, and even though worry kept me up a lot of the night, I know I'm doing the right thing.

And then, when she leaves, I'll single parent until I find in-home help. I don't know how, not yet, but I'll figure it out. I'm smart. I'm focused. I'll come up with a plan that will allow me to do it. It'll be hard, but I'm not afraid of hard things. Look at what I've already done to get where I am. And this time, I'll fully vet anyone before they come near my daughter. No more blindly trusting strangers.

It's the morning, and gorgeous, a perfect Saturday that should be spent lazing around the house in my pajamas, snuggling with Jordan, maybe watching some trashy court TV since she can't understand what's going on and there's no risk of rotting her brain.

But instead of doing that, I dress quickly. I grab an apple and munch it while getting Jordan changed and dressed. Sophie must still be in bed since I haven't heard a peep from her. As much as I want to get her up and have the conversation now, it can wait until I've cleared my head a bit.

I'm taking Jordan on a walk. It's probably good for both of us. The air is cool but not biting. I have on a heavy coat, and Jordan is tucked into the stroller with half a dozen blankets wrapped around her to keep her warm.

This neighborhood is nice, and I always like walking around to look at everyone's gorgeous gardens. That's in the spring, and even though it's winter and plants are slumbering, there's still stuff to look at.

Like the new porch swing our next-door neighbor had installed over the summer. It's visible now thanks to the clematis twining up their banisters finally dying off in the cold.

Or the new birdbath someone across the street put in their little bird area. It's surrounded by half a dozen bird feeders, and I stop walking so Jordan and I can watch the birds flit around as they eat.

They're gorgeous—blue and red, black and gray. This morning is a fresh start with my mind. It's on my side. I'm not going to let it continue to bully me.

Lawrence never told me the truth of what his life was like before he and I met. If he had...

I shake my head to clear the thought, then reach down to adjust Jordan's blankets. The wind whips down the street, and I flip my collar up to protect the back of my neck.

If he had, what? Would I have said no to his proposal?

If I'd known what his parents' marriage had been like, I might have been able to infer what kind of a husband he'd be. His passion for being involved in my life—*call it like it is, it was control*—his long hours at the office, his disinterest in being a father...

His inability to keep a relationship with his sister. She said they had a falling-out over her career, but there's something about that that doesn't quite ring true to me.

Maybe, if I'd known him better, things would be different. I'd know better what makes him tick. Of course, if I knew him better, there's a chance we wouldn't be together, but he'd be alive. At the same time, however, I wouldn't have Jordan, and then life wouldn't be worth living, would it?

"What do you say—just one loop around the cul-de-sac?" I ask her, then start wheeling her away from the bird feeder. My pace is brisk, and it feels good to move my body.

In just a few minutes, though, I've completed the circuit of the cul-de-sac and am back in front of my house. It towers over me, even taller than the houses next to it. They're all two-story homes, but ours has an attic while the other houses on the street don't.

Just that little extra height makes the house look commanding. I stare up at it, taking in how gorgeous it is, how happy I thought I'd be here with Lawrence, and—

There's movement in an upstairs window.

I freeze. Did I really see it? Or is my mind playing tricks on me?

Movement in an upstairs window shouldn't worry me. After all, the room Sophie's been staying in is upstairs, and it's not like she's not allowed to be up there without my permission.

But the movement wasn't in her window.

It was in mine.

My breath catches in my throat, and I push Jordan towards the house. As I walk, I keep looking up at the second floor. There's no more movement that I see, but I also don't see the lip in the sidewalk.

My toe catches on it, and I tip forward. At the last second, I shove the stroller away from me so I don't take Jordan down with me. It teeters on its right side then straightens out before rolling into the grass.

Predictably, Jordan starts crying, but I don't have time to worry about that, not when I've just smacked into the sidewalk. Hissing a breath, I roll over onto my side and press my palms together.

They sting from the impact. I can feel little rocks embed in my skin. I'd barely had time to catch myself before I hit the ground, but I'll take any amount of pain over letting Jordan get hurt.

For a moment, I lie there, my hands pressed hard together, then I force myself to look at them.

"You have to know how bad you're bleeding," I mutter, then pull my hands apart.

They're skinned, which I already suspected, but there's no dripping blood. I was prepared for blood running down my wrists, for puddles of it on the sidewalk.

But it's not that bad.

"Weenie," I mutter, then stand and hurry to Jordan. I kneel next to her stroller, ignoring the cold of the ground seeping through my jeans. "Hey, baby. You're okay." I brush her hair from her forehead and slip her pacifier into her mouth. "Let's go inside where it's warm, okay? Mommy has something to do."

As quietly as possible, I get her in the house. The front door closes with a soft click, and I throw the lock for safety before carrying my baby upstairs. Leaving Jordan in her crib by herself isn't what I want to do, but I have to go down the hall and see what Sophie is doing in my room.

On my own.

I creep down the hall. My ears are pricked for any little sound coming from my room, but it's hard to hear anything over the sound of my heart pounding in my ears.

In my bedroom doorway, I pause, letting my eyes flick around the room. Sophie's standing at the foot of my bed.

What has she been doing?

I see the two closets, but they're both closed. The double dresser looks the same as it always has, which is mostly covered with my crap. There's a vase of dead flowers in the center of the dresser, the last ones that Lawrence gave me before...

Before he died.

And then I look at the four-poster king-size bed centered on the far wall. Over it hangs a gorgeous canvas print I had made of a photo of the two of us. I'd hired a professional photographer to take pictures of us after we started dating. Lawrence had been a little weird about it, but I took that to be because we hadn't been together very long.

Whatever he was feeling, he went along with the photos. And then, on our six-month anniversary, I gave him this oversized print of the two of us. We both look so happy. He has his arm around me, and I'm turned in to him.

My hand is on his chest, and I'm grinning up at him. He's looking at me, the laugh lines around his eyes softened as he relaxed.

Lawrence wasn't one to relax, and having photographic proof that he finally did for once in his life was amazing. I was giddy when I had it printed on a canvas. Giddier when I had it framed.

And the best part? His credit card paid for all of it.

But now, that gorgeous print of the two of us? The one I love so much? The one I sleep under every single night because it reminds me of the love Lawrence and I shared, no matter how it ended?

It's ruined.

There's a hole right through the middle of Lawrence's face.

And Sophie's the only one who could have done it.

I clear my throat, pushing down the rage I feel. "What the hell are you doing in here?"

THIRTY-ONE

Charlotte

Sophie looks feral, like she's a wild thing trapped and put on display in the zoo. She stares at me, her eyes wide, her mouth partway open, then glances past me to the door like she's expecting someone to walk in behind me and stop me from getting as angry as I feel.

But there's nobody to take the heat off her.

I repeat my question.

"What the hell are you doing in here?"

She stills. "I..."

It's clear she's digging around for a lie that she can throw in my face, something to keep me from losing it on her, but I'm not interested in giving her the time she needs to come up with something.

You shouldn't have let her stay.

I push that thought aside and focus on her. "Sophie. You're in my room. Tell me now what you're doing in here." I pause. "Don't make me call the cops and have you removed from my house."

She has to leave. I have to get her out of here.

Panic eats at me, but I try to look as calm as possible. No way do I want her knowing how upset I am because she'll try to spin it, try to gain control of the situation.

"I was just looking around!" The words explode from her, and while I don't think she's telling me the whole truth, I do think there's a kernel of honesty there. "I swear to you, I was just walking around the house, and then I saw the print of you and Lawrence."

My eyes flick to the print, and my blood boils even more. "Did you break the canvas?" I ask even though the answer is obvious.

She's creepy. You felt it and you let it get this far.

"I didn't mean to." She holds out her hands to me like she's trying to stop me from walking towards her. "I promise you—I didn't mean to do it. I was getting a closer look at it, and I fell."

"A closer look from on top of my bed?" My hands clench into fists, and I take a step closer to her. I want to fight her. I want to yank her hair and hold her down and make her scream and do all sorts of terrible things to her, but I have to stay calm.

For Jordan.

Get. Rid. Of. Her.

"I messed up. I'm so sorry." Her tone has changed from ready-to-fight to repentant, and I should calm down, but I don't think I can. "I only wanted to get a closer look. I screwed up."

"I'd say so." I take a deep breath. If I hadn't already decided that Sophie had to leave, this would be the final straw. Worry kept me awake a long time last night, but this is the right thing to do, no matter how helpful she was at the beginning.

"It was wrong of me," she says, her voice cutting across my thoughts. "I got carried away. I just miss my brother so much—you have to understand that. And that's a life-size picture of him, and I haven't seen him looking so happy, so healthy, in a while, and..."

She sniffs, then covers her face with both hands. I watch as her shoulders shake. She's crying hard, but that doesn't do anything to subdue the anger I'm feeling.

"I want you out of my house," I tell her.

That gets her attention. Her head snaps up, and I'm gratified to see the tear streaks on her cheeks. Her eyes grow wide, more tears already building up there, and she shakes her head.

"No, I'm sorry. Charlotte, I screwed up. You have to believe me that it was an accident, and it won't happen again." She pauses, then does her best to hit me right where she thinks it's going to hurt. "You need me. Jordan needs me."

She's right, but of course there's no way in hell I'd ever let her know that. I need someone around the house cooking and cleaning and taking care of my baby. Jordan needs someone stable in her life, and if I could trust Sophie with the truth of what I did, she could be that person.

And I did trust her, at least a little. Not about killing her brother, of course, and not about... the other thing. But maybe I was wrong to trust her at all.

"Out." I have to dig deep for the word, but it feels good to say. It feels good to be in control, to act like I really don't need this woman standing in front of me. Her help would be great. Her money would be amazing.

But this is a huge breach of trust, and I've never been someone that was good at going back in time and forgiving a person after they screwed me over. For Sophie to be here in my room is one thing. To know she was standing on my bed, stabbing her finger through the print I had made of Lawrence and me?

Yeah, that's not something I can easily get over.

She doesn't move.

"Sophie, I'm serious." I clear my throat and stare her down. "I want you out of my house. This is my house, not yours, and you're no longer welcome here."

Her face darkens. I'd always read that phrase in books and honestly thought it was a bit of a joke. How can someone's face darken? But that's exactly what happens.

Her eyes seem to narrow a bit. Her gaze is focused, locked in on me, and I see the way her jaw tightens. She looks like a predator ready to lunge at me, and I have to stop myself from taking a step back from her.

"You don't want to do this." Even her voice is darker than it was a moment ago. It's laced with something. Danger?

"Is that a threat?" No way can she look at me and tell that I'm shaking in my boots. I've never been great with confrontation. I hate fighting with people. Whenever I've had to in the past, I end up slinking away from the argument and then coming back later to handle things my way when the person thinks I've moved on.

But I don't want to do that right now. I stand tall. My jaw is tight. I'm not going to let my shoulders roll in and betray how I really feel. I just want her out. Sure, I could wait a few days, dig up some dirt on her, maybe find a way to make her want to leave, but the best thing for my mental health is to get her out ASAP.

"I wouldn't threaten you," I lie. "But I want you out of my house, and you have no reason to stay. No way would the police side with you wanting to stay if I went to them and told them that you were trespassing and I wanted you gone."

Cool. Calm. Collected. She can't tell that my stomach is tying itself in knots. She can't see the tears burning my eyes. My hands are still in fists, and I grip them so hard that my knuckles hurt, but I'm not releasing the pressure until I know she's gone.

"You need me. Jordan needs me. What, you think you can handle being a mom on your own? You can't. You saw the state of the house when I first arrived, and you can easily look around and see what I've done to help out. You're useless without me."

She's pushing every single button I have, but I refuse to back down.

"Maybe I'm not great at keeping my house picked up, but there's one way I'm not useless, and that's to Jordan. I'm her mother, Sophie. That's one thing nobody can take away from me. There might be a mess on the kitchen counters, and maybe the floor is dirty more often than not, but Jordan needs me, and I need her, and the best thing for the two of us right now is for you to leave us alone."

She doesn't respond. It's clear she's thinking of what to say. I watch her eyes flick around the room, as if she's looking for some sort of proof that she's indispensable, but there's nothing here that will allow her to take me down.

I should know. I've taken great pains to ensure that anything damning has been hidden.

THIRTY-TWO

Lawrence is home.

I'm in the kitchen chowing down on some microwaved nachos when I hear the garage door start to go up. I freeze, one chip halfway to my mouth as my mind races.

He wasn't supposed to be home until tomorrow. It is Friday, right? I thought he was going to spend one more night away from home so he could get up early and fly in before lunch.

That's how he's always done it. So why would he change it up now?

Hurrying, I dump the last remaining chips and slightly melted cheese into the trash. He hates it when I don't rinse my plate, but I skip that step and put it straight into the dishwasher. He hates it more when I eat junk.

How's my breath? I do the breath check where you breathe into your palm and give it a sniff, then wrinkle my nose. Not great, if I'm honest. I've been letting my snack cravings get the best of me today since I actually haven't wanted to throw up this afternoon. Pickles and nachos and cottage cheese and frozen taquitos... the combination makes my breath a little funky.

But I don't have time to worry about that. The garage door is lowering now, and I know that means he'll be sweeping into the house before long. I guess I could make a run for the second floor and brush my teeth before he comes in, but I know my husband, and I know what he likes.

He likes being greeted at the door when he gets home. He likes me in a little nightie as a welcome-home present.

I glance down at the faded flannel PJs I have on. They're not stylish, or cute, and I don't think I've worn them since we started dating, but they are super comfortable. And right now, when I'm not feeling my best, I just want to be comfortable.

My stomach churns, and I lean against the kitchen counter, trying my best to look casual. Normally, I'm thrilled to see him. Normally, I meet him at the door and jump into his arms, my nightie flapping around my bare butt, but right now the only strength I can muster allows me to stand completely still, a smile frozen on my face.

The door flies open, and he strides in. Tall, with thick brown hair and a bit of stubble, he looks the part of a leading actor in a romcom. His eyes flick around the kitchen, and I stiffen as I try to see it the way he does.

Normally, I'd have it all perfectly cleaned. I do my best to ensure he comes home to a spotless house. He told me once that the last thing he wants when he's back from a trip is to see a dust bunny or a spot on the kitchen counter.

And this place?

Not clean. Not yet.

"You're home early!" I say, my grin so wide it feels like it's going to split my cheeks.

"I missed you." He has his carry-on in his right hand, and he drops it to the floor before approaching me. His eyes are locked on my face, and I feel my heart pound.

I know it's the combined excitement and nerves over seeing him and not my baby moving that's making me feel sick to my stomach, but when we hug and he pulls me tight against his body, I can't help but worry that he'll feel a tiny bump there.

That he'll recognize it for what it is.

That he'll *know*.

"How are you?" he asks, but then he kisses me before I have a chance to respond. His hands are on my waist, then one slides up to the back of my neck, squeezing me and holding me in place.

I shouldn't have worried about him paying attention to anything but the thing he wants.

It takes a minute for him to let me go enough for me to step back from him and catch my breath. "I'm great," I whisper, making sure to keep my hands on him. One on his arm, one on his chest. It's better to keep contact with him like that than to accidentally cup my stomach.

I caught myself doing it the other day in the grocery store and had to stop. But the little girl walking by had been so cute with her perky pigtails and wide grin, and before I knew what was happening, I was holding my stomach, a stupid matching grin on my face.

What if someone had seen me? What if they'd put two and two together?

I know I should have taken care of it already, but I couldn't. Not yet. I have a little more time, even though just thinking like that makes me feel guilty.

"That's quite the outfit you have on," Lawrence says. "It's not what I'm used to, but I'm pretty sure I can still work with it."

I chuckle, some of the concern I had fading away. He's so focused on *me* that he's going to completely miss the secret I'm keeping from him. "I was a little chilly tonight and didn't want to turn up the heat. These PJs remind me of when we met."

He makes a noncommittal sound and kisses me again before pulling back.

"I've missed you," he tells me again, threading his fingers through my hair. "Did you miss me?"

I nod, my smile still on my face. I did miss him. That's the thing about my husband. Living without him is like living at a higher elevation. I can still breathe. I can still speak and sing and walk and dance, but I can't fully catch my breath. My lungs feel tight without him, colors are less vibrant; even birdsong sounds muted.

That's why I was so willing to sign a contract saying I'd never get pregnant. Because being without him means I'm still alive, but is life worth living when everything is dark, when it's quiet, when it's not as bold and exciting as it could be?

"I missed you," I tell him, stepping back from him to soak him in. His hair is as thick and dark as it was when we met. He's tan. And fit. And his deep brown eyes are mesmerizing. His gaze flicks up and down me, and then stops.

He takes a step forward, then another, closing the gap between us before I even realize he's moving. When his hand flicks out, the movement is so fast I don't realize what he's doing until his hand clamps down on my wrist.

"What are you doing?" His tone has changed completely, from rich and honeyed, full of love, to sharp and angular, the words like bullets as they leave his lips.

My eyes are locked on his face, and I have to drag them down to his hand to see what he's talking about. His fingers close tighter on my wrist, tight enough that I feel the bones shift against each other.

But as tight as he's holding me, he doesn't pull my hand away from my stomach. It's splayed out there, my fingers wide, protecting my baby.

And he knows the truth.

THIRTY-THREE

Charlotte

I never should have let Sophie into my house, and now I'll do whatever it takes to get her to leave.

"Out," I repeat, stabbing my finger through the air at her. "You. Out. Now."

"Charlotte, think about this." She holds her hands up between the two of us, but I'm not giving her the opportunity to weasel her way out of this one. "You need me. Jordan needs me."

Wrong thing to say. My anger is barely contained. I can feel it licking at the sides of my vision, making it really difficult for me to see straight. Even though I want to scream, I take a deep breath and try to speak as calmly and rationally as possible.

"I thought we did, but we don't. Jordan and I are fine on our own."

"You're really not..." she begins, and that's when I lose it.

"Get the hell out of my house right now, or I'm going to call the cops!" I scream the words, leaning forward as I do, my hands clenched into fists. All the anger and stress I've felt since

Lawrence died, all the fear over being abandoned with Jordan and the frustration that I did this to myself, all of it comes pouring out, directed at Sophie.

She takes a small step back.

"Now!" I roar and step out of the way, angrily flinging my arm out to the side to gesture into the hall.

There's a moment, maybe ten seconds, during which I don't think she's going to leave.

It could get ugly, I think, and I feel like every mama bear who has come before me. Every woman who has been willing to sacrifice everything they have to save their child.

But she bows her head and walks past me. She comes so close to me that the smell of her perfume wraps around me, and I take a deep, shuddering breath before going to stand in front of Jordan's nursery.

I watch as Sophie walks down the hall to the guest room. Like a sentry, I stand still, waiting for her to pack. It takes longer than I'd like since she'd unpacked completely when she moved in here, but in under half an hour, she reappears, peeping out the door to look at me.

"Will you help me with my bags?" Her voice is meeker than I've heard before.

I shake my head.

She nods, then takes her things downstairs. She needs a few trips to get everything in the front hall, then she turns to face me, her chin lifted high, a haughty expression on her face.

"You're going to regret this," she tells me, but I'm already speaking over her.

"No, I won't. I appreciate the good you did while you were here, but you've overstayed your welcome, and you know it. It's best if you move on. Go back home."

"Fine." Her eyes flick past me to the stairs, and I have a very good feeling I know what she wants to ask me, but the answer is no.

No, she can't see Jordan one more time before she leaves.

It takes all my self-control to stand still and silent as she takes her suitcases to her car. I watch as she loads it all up, then hops in. It's only when she pulls away from the house that I feel my shoulders start to relax.

She's gone.

I could overlook how overbearing she was. She came on strong at times, but I refuse to label her a *bitch* for that. But stabbing her finger through Lawrence's portrait? There's some deep-seated trauma there, and really the only option for her is good therapy.

I close the front door. Lock it. It's only when I've wandered back into the kitchen to throw away the most recent flowers that she bought that I realize how tightly I've been clenching my jaw.

My teeth hurt from me grinding them together. The pain extends up both sides of my head to my temples. When I press my fingers into them to try to relieve some of the pain, I'm not surprised that it doesn't help. A migraine is coming—and fast.

"I need a pill," I mutter, then hurry upstairs to my bathroom. I keep my migraine pills right by the sink, so I always know where they are. The thought of needing one and not being able to find it is terrifying.

Only the little orange prescription bottle isn't where I left it.

"What the hell?" I yank open the top drawer under the sink and take inventory. Hairbrush, hair ties, a small thing of dry shampoo.

No pills.

The next drawer then.

Or the next.

But my pills aren't in any of the three drawers. Panic grips me by the back of the neck, and I hurry into the bedroom, my eyes flicking around the space.

No pill bottle on my bedside table.

I drop to my knees.

Not under the bed.

Taking a deep breath, I force myself to slow down. To close my eyes and really try to picture where I last saw the bottle. I'd considered taking it to work with me in case I had a migraine there, but had I actually gone through with it?

Or was it just a thought I had?

"My purse," I mutter, then race downstairs. I must be too loud on the stairs, or maybe Jordan just has terrible timing, because she starts crying. It's quiet, at least for now, but I know how quickly she can ratchet it up and really get going.

I do my best to block her out and grab my purse from where it always hangs by the front door. When I dip my hand into it, however, my heart sinks.

No pills.

Jordan's crying harder now. It's not the desperate gasping cry she'll get right before she throws up, but that's not too far off.

I hesitate, my mind racing. I need those pills. I can continue to look for them in the house, but with her screaming getting worse and worse, I know what will happen. I'll be in a full-blown migraine and won't have anyone to help with her.

I don't want to do what I'm about to, but there's no other choice. In the kitchen, I make her a bottle. Some of the formula spills on the counter, and I swear, but I don't take the time to wipe it up. Instead, I grip the bottle in one hand and race upstairs.

Jordan's face is red as she wails. Without picking her up, I shove the nipple of the bottle in her mouth. I just need her to shut up. I need her to give me enough silence to think.

Miraculously, she starts sucking. The migraine is still coming, but I can breathe for a minute.

Silence is golden. Silence buys time.

I move quickly and get her out of the crib without her losing her bottle. Downstairs, I tuck her into her car seat and snap her safely into the car.

My hand shakes as I press the garage door button. It shakes even more when I turn, planting my hand on the back of the passenger's seat so I can back down the driveway.

This is dangerous.

That thought is on repeat as I slowly drive away from the house. I have to be careful. Focus on keeping it in the lines. If I drive extra slowly and extra careful, I can make it to the pharmacy—I know I can.

As long as Jordan stays quiet.

She does, and I could almost convince myself that this is going to pass without a problem. I smile and sit up straighter in my seat.

Yes, I think this was a false alarm. It was stress over Sophie, and then Jordan started crying, and really, I brought it all on myself.

I'm going to be fine. If I'm honest with myself, I feel better now than I did even when I woke up this morning. I'll still go to the pharmacy and get my pills just in case things don't work out the way I want them to, but this is all going to be fine.

I press down harder on the gas.

THIRTY-FOUR

Sophie

Charlotte may have grown the balls she needed to kick me out of the house, but there's no way I'm actually leaving. It had been so easy to follow her when she dropped Jordan off for daycare, so easy to prey on her tired mind and make her believe she'd really asked me for help. So easy to make a copy of her key.

Did she honestly think I would turn tail and walk away? That I'd give up on Jordan?

Not a chance. I'm not going anywhere.

I came here to learn more about who Lawrence married, but plans can change, and now I'm not leaving, not when I suspect the truth about who the baby really is.

Big words from someone currently sitting in the library parking lot so I can mooch off their Wi-Fi, I know, but I had to drive away for Charlotte to think that I'm actually doing what she told me to. She thinks she's big and strong right now, but as soon as I get my ducks in a row, I'm coming right back.

I should have taken more time to research her—that much is

clear. If I'd had more information on her before going to her house, I might not have had to move out, but honestly? I'd been dying to get here as soon as possible.

To meet her.

To learn as much about her as possible.

To see what Lawrence saw in her.

That's what I can't wrap my mind around. What was so special about her that he was willing to have a child with her?

If he were still alive, I'd ask him. I'd hound him until he didn't have a choice but to answer my question, but he's gone and all I can do is hope to piece it all together. Find out if she killed him. Find out where she got Jordan.

How she got Jordan.

The weather will be warm today, and I have no doubt Charlotte will want to take Jordan on another walk. As soon as she's out of the house I'll go back in. Dig up some dirt.

I push thoughts of her out of my mind and focus on my laptop. It connects easily, and I log into a website to check out the cameras I just set up in Charlotte's house.

In addition to the one I put on Lawrence's bedside table, there are ones in the kitchen, the living room, and in Jordan's nursery. Four internal cameras might be overkill, but I didn't want to miss a thing when it came to Charlotte. I chose those rooms because I think they're the best bet for me watching her.

Not that I think she's up to anything nefarious. She's not smart enough for that. But when I decided to up my snooping, I wanted to make sure she never caught me. The best way to do that was by installing cameras so I can keep an eye on her coming and going.

The website takes a moment to load, and I have to have a code sent to my phone to verify who I am, but soon enough I'm logged in. First I check the nursery, but neither Jordan nor Charlotte are in there. My heart beats faster at the thought of her taking her daughter out of the house and me not knowing about it.

I click through to the living room, then to the kitchen. The tension I've been holding in my shoulders only releases when I check the most recent recording from the outdoor camera and see her car back slowly out of the garage before pulling onto the road.

Good. If I knew where she was going, I'd have a better idea of how much time I have to poke around in her house, but since I don't know, I'll just have to move quickly.

And what will I find there? I don't know, but if it's important, I'll know it when I see it.

Charlotte's a piece of work, that much is for sure, but when I first arrived, I still wasn't sure if she was a murderer. That thought gives me pause, and I lift my hand to my mouth to chew my nail. At the last second, I stop myself and drop my hand back into my lap. No way would she hurt Jordan anyway.

Lawrence was fair game. I don't want to speak ill of the dead and say he deserved what he got, but he had it coming.

From the way she talks, she wanted a baby more than anything in this world. I may not like her, I may not trust her, but I honestly believe that Jordan is safe with her.

Still, she'd be better off with me.

I tried to ignore that thought the first time I had it, but now the idea has taken root. It grows every time I look at her, every time I hear her cry, and even though I'm kicked out of the house for now, no way am I leaving town. Not until I figure some things out.

How many times was I left alone with her? I could have taken her and been done with it, but that wasn't why I was there. Now, though, I'm kicking myself. This could all be over if I'd just taken Jordan earlier.

Hurried now, I press the start button, and my car hums to

life. Rather than backing out of my spot and driving straight to Charlotte's, however, I pause to think.

She knows my car. I have the advantage over her because she doesn't know I can watch her inside her house, but if my car is parked right out front, she'll know I'm there when she returns.

I press the button again to kill the engine. No, as much as I'd like to have my car on hand in case I need to make a speedy getaway, driving myself there isn't a smart choice. Charlotte's distracted and upset, but she's not stupid. If she were to catch my car there in her driveway or nearby—or worse, find me in her house—I have no doubt she'd lose it and probably call the police.

I'm shocked she hasn't yet. That tells me one thing—she's hiding something, something so big she doesn't want the cops involved.

Leaving my car here is the only option I have. My fingers fly across my phone screen as I call an Uber to take me to her house. I'll have them drop me off a few houses down, then walk up to it.

Without knowing where she's going, I don't know how long I'll have to poke around in her house. And without really knowing what I'm looking for, it would be easy to spend too much time there and get caught.

But this is still the best option. If she happens to come home before I've left, I'll have to do my best to slip out. There's no reason why I can't find my way out the back door while she's in the bedroom or nursery.

The cameras I placed around her house will help ensure I get out without getting caught. When I first came here, my goal was to learn more about her. To see what made her so special that Lawrence would marry her.

I want to know what was so special about her that he'd not only sleep with her but that he'd also give her Jordan.

It was easy to lie to Charlotte, to convince her that Lawrence was my brother.

But he was my husband.

THIRTY-FIVE

Charlotte

A dog runs in front of my car, and I swear, slamming on the brakes and jerking the wheel to the side. I catch some stray gravel and have a terrible mental image of the car turning over and over, but I drive a BMW 2 Gran Coupé, a car that might look speedy but, according to Lawrence, is the epitome of safe for a scattered driver.

The car shudders to a stop.

"You good, Jordy?" My voice is high and tight, even to my ears, and I turn around and pull myself back between the front seats to get a better look at my baby. Jordan's eyes are wide. But, miraculously, she's stopped crying.

"Okay. Focus." I sit back in my seat and grip the steering wheel tight enough to make the leather squeak. "I kicked her out. She's gone. I don't know what she wanted with me, but she's gone."

Just saying that should flood me with relief, but it doesn't. I still have a pounding headache, one that began the exact moment I saw Sophie standing in my bedroom. The gall of her to be in there! And for her to not only enter my bedroom, but then stand on the bed I shared with Lawrence and ruin the canvas I printed of the two of us?

It's infuriating.

I locked the door—I know I did. It's one thing for me to go into the guest room where she's staying, but after she took the baby monitor from my room her first night here, I'd thought I'd made it clear that my space was off-limits.

But she was more than happy to pick the lock and let herself in, wasn't she? Had she gone in there before to stare at his photo? The thought gives me chills.

I exhale hard and start driving again. The only good thing about living in this Podunk little town is that there's hardly any traffic on the road. I'd asked Lawrence—begged him actually—to move us to a bigger city. It wasn't enough just to be in a relationship with him; I wanted more.

I wanted excitement. I wanted bars and theaters and clubs. I wanted to feel like I was really living, to feel the breathing and movement of thousands of people around me, but that didn't happen.

Small town. Tucked away. Almost like he was embarrassed of me.

"Stop thinking like that," I mutter. Lawrence loved me. No way was he embarrassed of me. He wouldn't have been with me if he had been.

But he didn't take you on vacations, did he?

He got that ring on your finger and stopped taking you out, even to a nice restaurant.

And he didn't want to have a baby with you.

I want to pull over and cry, but instead I keep my eyes on the road. Jordan's still quiet, which is unusual. She's not great in the car and will often scream bloody murder. You know how a lot of mothers swear by car rides when their child gets fussy? Yeah, they don't work on Jordan. If anything, they rile her up even more, turning what could be a pleasant trip around town into a nightmare ride where I have to fight every intrusive thought and focus on not driving off a cliff.

"Just get to the pharmacy," I mutter, pressing down on the gas. I need to pick up my meds and then we can get right back home. If Sophie hadn't shown her true colors, I could have left Jordan with her, but that won't happen now.

All in all, I plan on being out of the house half an hour. Maybe forty minutes, tops. Then I'll go home, and Jordan and I will... what?

Yeah, what will I do? I don't have a ton of money. Lawrence didn't leave me flush with cash, so it's not like I can take her anywhere else to keep her away from Sophie.

But we'll be home, and we'll be safe, and that's the only thing that matters. I'll lock the doors. We'll be fine, no matter what Sophie tries to do.

I reach up with one hand and press down on my temple. This is what happens when I don't take my meds in time. I thought I'd been able to dodge it, but I feel that migraine coming on hard, and there's nothing that can stop it.

I press down harder on the gas.

My neck aches, and I reach up and massage it. It's stiff, like I slept on it wrong, but I didn't—I actually slept great last night for the first time since Lawrence died. Still, I rub it, my fingers digging into my flesh, searching for any relief.

I don't realize that I'm blinking and squinting until I put on my sunglasses. They're expensive, designed to help with light sensitivity and migraines, but they're not cutting it right now.

"Come on," I mutter, gripping the steering wheel tighter and leaning forward. I only have a few more miles to go and then I'll be at the pharmacy. It was wishful thinking to believe we'd be able to turn right around and go back home, but soon I have to get out of the car, get somewhere dark.

But I don't know what to do with Jordan.

As if on cue, she starts fussing. No, not fussing. *Screaming.*

She goes from zero to sixty, fast and furious, and her wails fill the car. They're like waves at the beach, one coming right after another without any break in between. They wash over me, each one stronger than the last, slowly dragging me under.

It feels like my head is in a vice. My lungs are tight, squeezed as if there's not enough oxygen in the car. I grip the steering wheel tight, tight, tighter, and start humming to myself to try to block out the sound of Jordan wailing.

It doesn't work. There's now an ice pick behind my eye, the stabbing so painful that I can barely breathe. I've had migraines for years and hated every single one. I've hated putting my life on hold, hating feeling like the day was taken from me while I rested, silent in the dark.

But this is worse.

I'd do anything to be in bed at home. Anything to be tucked under a blanket with the blinds drawn. I'd thought that was hell, thought that a migraine at home in my room was as bad as it could get, but I was so, so wrong.

Hell is hurtling down the road with a screaming baby in the backseat and a migraine coming at you hard and fast.

I should pull over. I know that. I have the thought and am aware enough to mull it over, to focus on it, to give it the weight it deserves.

That's what I'll do. Pull over.

But there are apple fields on both sides of the road, the trees twisted and gnarled, stretching their branches towards the sky, looking like skeletons.

Jordan keeps screaming.

I press down harder on the gas. After these fields there's... the library. There's the library, and as soon as I get there, I'll park the car. I'll figure out what to do when I'm not driving a two-ton death machine with my baby in the backseat.

She's still screaming.

Reaching up, I block one eye with my hand. I need darkness. I crave it, crave the relief it will give me. Just blocking one eye feels good; it gives me a reprieve, although it's not enough.

I switch my hand to my other eye.

She's still screaming. It's desperate, the cry of a baby who honestly believes they're never going to be picked up again. She sounds like I've abandoned her in the woods, leaving her at the base of a tree as an offering.

What I need to do is close both eyes. Just for a moment. Just long enough to black everything out and get a break, then I'll be able to open them again and I'll be able to drive. I'll get to the library and park and figure things out from there.

I take a deep breath.

Close my eyes.

Jordan's still screaming.

But, louder than her, the sound of a car horn.

THIRTY-SIX

Her

"You disobeyed me, and now you have to face the consequences."

My husband sits across from me at the dining-room table. There's a huge bouquet of flowers in the center of the table to welcome him home, but he shoved them to the side as soon as we sat down so he could look at me.

There's no place to hide. Behind him, our wedding portrait hangs on the wall. I'm thin in my dress, just as thin as I am now, just the way he likes me. And I still look at him like I am in the photo, like he's my whole world. Only now my world has gotten a little bigger thanks to the baby.

The baby.

My mind kept coming back to the baby while he was out of town. I knew it was dangerous to allow myself to imagine what it would be like to have a child of my own, but I did it anyway. And now he knows what I've done.

My husband... he's amazing. And he loves me. I've never once doubted that, not since the moment our eyes met across a coffee shop. It's so freaking cliché, how the two of us met, but it's the truth.

My life with him has always been a fairytale. Only now, when push comes to shove, when I have something that I want more than anything in this world, I'm going to lose everything.

"I didn't disobey you," I tell him. I have to fight to drag my eyes away from the portrait behind him. I want to stare at it, see the love on his face, but instead I force myself to look at the man sitting in front of me. There's a crease on his brow from frowning, and he has his arms crossed.

He couldn't look more different from the photo from our wedding if he tried. Love radiates from that picture.

But his face right now? There's no love. There's anger. There's frustration. A bit of disbelief that I would dare to go against him, that I would dare to do the one thing he didn't want me to do.

And hatred. It kills me to see that emotion on my husband's face, but I can't help but think that's what it is.

"You got pregnant. What would you call that if not disobeying me?"

"An accident." I lift my chin as I speak. It's a dare for him to get mad, to fight with me, but he doesn't rise to the bait, so I continue. "I think it was my antibiotics. They can mess with birth control, and I should have been more careful, but—"

"But you weren't." The words are heavy. Loud. "How long have you known?"

I didn't want him to ask this, but of course he was going to want to know the truth. I swallow hard.

"Four months."

"Four months?" He stands, slamming his hand on the table as he does. "Four months and you think you can go to the clinic now and get rid of it?" He turns away from me, his jaw working. "No," he mutters. "No, it's too late for you to do that. People will talk."

I feel like I'm outside of my body as I watch him. His words wash over me, but I can't respond, like this is a nightmare and I'm trapped in it. He's making decisions about my future, but all I can do is sit quietly and listen.

This isn't how it was supposed to go. I thought... well, I hadn't really thought that he'd suddenly change his mind on being a father. But I never once, not even in my nightmares, thought that it would go this badly.

And in my daydreams? In those he swept me into his arms and kissed me. He told me what a great gift I was giving him. He celebrated with me as I made him a dad.

"We can figure something out," I say, but he ignores me. His back is still to me, and I study the lines of it. It's obvious how tense he is, how he's holding all his muscles like he's about to snap.

"Nobody has to know," he finally says. He turns to look at me, then gives me a nod. I note how he's grinding his jaw, how his eyes bore into me, how every muscle in his body seems taut, like he's ready to fight. "I can fix this and make it so that nobody knows you went and did this to yourself."

"Nobody has to know?" My voice, in comparison to his, is small. My words are so quiet, and he's so still, that at first I don't think he heard me, but he gives his head a little shake and pins me in place with a stare.

I want to melt into the floor, but instead I lift my chin and stare him down.

"About what you did. Nobody has to know what you did. We can take care of it."

My hand presses into my stomach. I won't do it. I won't hurt my baby. I'll leave, I'll hide, I'll do anything to protect the little life growing in me.

"Take care of it?" He can't mean... no. He wouldn't. He's mad, and I get that, but there's no way he honestly thinks I'm going to be willing to just *take care of it*.

He walks around the table, but his eyes never leave my face. When he braces one hand on the table and leans over me, I have to tilt my head back, look up, to see him.

"I need you to understand something before I tell you what you're going to do. Do you hear me?"

I nod, my mouth dry.

"You don't have anything in your name. No money. No car. No property."

I nod again. I know, and I'd thought it seemed strange when we first got married, but I wasn't going to argue with him about how he set everything up. I was just so happy to be married, to be his wife, to finally have a family, and I've never wanted for anything, so why did it matter that I'm just an authorized user on his credit card? That I don't have my own bank account?

It never has.

But it does now.

"Do I need to spell it out for you?"

I shake my head. He's made his point. My parents are gone. No siblings. Any close friends I had, I'm ashamed to admit I dropped them as soon as he and I started dating. My mind is already racing as I work out the threat he's making, the future he's building for me without letting me be a part of it. I want him to stop talking so I don't have to have the memory of him actually *saying* this stuff to me, but he continues.

Even if he knew I wanted him to shut up, I don't think he would. We're past the point of it mattering what I want.

"I have a way for us to fix this, but you have to do exactly what I say. If you don't... you won't like what happens."

He's expecting me to nod again, to let him know I'm on the same page as he is, but I can't seem to move. Even though I don't respond, he obviously accepts my silence as agreement.

I couldn't respond to him if I wanted to. My spit is sour, and it feels like my throat is coated with sand. I know he wants compliance, that he demands it, but all I can do is sit and stare at him and hope that he's not going to say the thing I already know he will.

"I know how to handle this... baby." He sneers the word. "You're going to do what I say, then when this is all over, we're never going to mention it again. Understand?"

My mind races, but I force my tongue to move. "I understand."

THIRTY-SEVEN

Sophie

The first day Charlotte went back to work, I took her house key from Jordan's diaper bag and made a copy so I'd have easy access to her house. Once again, I'm glad I did, and I let myself in, quickly locking the door behind me.

After slipping the key back into my pocket, I stand still in the living room, taking a few deep breaths. This isn't the first time I've been in the house alone, but it feels different this time.

Charlotte is onto me. She's not smart enough to know the whole truth about me, but she did kick me out. That means I need to be careful. It also means I need to hurry up because I'm out of time.

I know exactly what room I want to search while she's out of the house. Rather than heading back up to her bedroom, which might house some secrets she wants to keep hidden but might not, I walk through the living room into the office.

I should have spent more time poking around when I was alone in the house and less time snuggling Jordan. But I never imagined that Charlotte would kick me out.

I thought I had more time, but I don't regret a second I spent holding Jordan.

I exhale hard and look around the room. It's clear this space was Lawrence's. What he needed an office here for, I'm not sure, but I'm not going to allow myself to worry about that too much right now. There will be time later for me to try to reason out his actions.

I flick on the light and stand in the door, soaking it all in. From the first second I lay eyes on the space, however, I can tell that something is wrong.

This is Lawrence's space, but Charlotte has been busy in here.

Cleaning. *Throwing things away.*

The huge desk across from me is fairly clean, with only a few stacks of paper on it. His reading glasses sit to the side of an empty coffee mug. The banker's lamp with its emerald-green shade is turned off.

But it's not his desk that is the most upsetting. It's the mess. Lawrence would never have boxes of his belongings stacked up against the wall. He's always been neat to a fault, and I know he wouldn't be the one storing boxes on the floor like that.

Rather than digging through them, however, I look at the bookcase behind them. It should be loaded with books, practically groaning with them, but there are multiple empty spaces.

Makes me wonder how Charlotte has decided what books stay and which ones have to go.

I walk slowly around the room, taking in the framed photos of Charlotte on the wall. The window looks out over the backyard, a nice-enough view, but there's nothing to see there, so I turn back into the office.

Even as I reach for a slim notebook on the shelf, I'm not entirely sure what I'm doing here. It's silly, that I'd question my actions right now when I've already lied and schemed to gain access to the house.

My eyes flick across the bookcases as I think. It was stupid of me to waste so much time in the house and not enter his office, but I've been wrapped up in Jordan. All I've wanted is to hold her, and when there wasn't a time limit on how long Charlotte would let me stay, I didn't have to worry about digging up dirt on her.

I got lazy. Complacent. And now I have to fix it.

She should be mine. If Lawrence hadn't died, would I ever have learned about Jordan? Would I ever have suspected the truth about who she really belongs to? Would I have known what I believe to be the truth about the baby if I hadn't had the chance to hold her myself?

The thought is unbidden, but once I have it, it starts growing, sending out runners and slowly taking over my mind. I want to rip it out and forget that I ever thought it, but I can't.

Instead of trying to force the thought from my mind, I focus on it, letting the thought grow more. With a sigh, I turn and lean against the desk. Doubt fills my mind as I think about what I'm trying to accomplish. Unless I find something damning here, maybe it's time for me to go. Sure, I came here angry, and I honestly still am.

I don't want to think about Lawrence with Charlotte. I knew he had affairs, but this is more than a one-night stand. He gave her everything I could never have. I'm envious of her for having my husband. And for having a child.

But that doesn't mean she's evil. It means she's lucky. Just like Lawrence was unlucky, Charlotte was lucky. Sure, the house isn't in her name, and she's going to struggle to make it as a single mom, but someone like her? Yeah, I wouldn't be too surprised if she didn't stay single for long.

She seems like the kind of woman eager to find another man if that means her life will be easier. No shame really. Not when I made such a hard decision and have regretted it ever since.

Sometimes, an easy life sounds like the best option.

A buzzing sound grabs my attention. It's not a wasp—I can tell that much. It sounds like it's vibrating like... a phone?

That's what it is. A phone.

I abandon the files I'm digging through and spin around, trying to place where the phone is. I probably don't have much time before whoever is calling hangs up, which means I need to find it as quickly as possible.

"Where are you? Come on," I mutter, opening drawers on the desk. Each one is loaded with paperwork and pens, empty envelopes and packs of sticky notes.

But no phone.

I stand up and walk around the desk, moving as quickly and quietly as possible. Just when I think I'm about to triangulate the phone's location, the vibrating stops.

"Dammit." I'm defeated and about to sit back down to continue my search through the financials when it starts vibrating again.

A second chance. Not very often you get one of those. This time I don't bother looking in the desk. My eyes flick to the stack of boxes against the wall. From looking at them, it seems like Charlotte started packing up the office and got tired halfway through.

I rip the first box open but am greeted with thick books. Moving quickly, I shove it on the floor and grab the second box.

Paperwork.

The next.

Files.

"Where the hell?" I ask, then finally see the phone. It's buzzing away on the shelf behind the boxes, still plugged into an outlet. I take a deep breath as I reach out and pick it up. Like my touch is toxic, it falls silent.

I hesitate, then carefully tap the screen to wake it back up. The home-screen photo is of Charlotte in a bikini, and I can't hide the curl to my lip. When I swipe to open the phone, a lock screen pops up. I don't have to unlock his phone to see who just called, but I want to know if I can. Without hesitating, I type in four digits and am not surprised to gain immediate access to his phone.

I wonder if Charlotte knew his PIN. Or if she kept trying over and over to access his phone. Maybe that's why it's plugged in here, so she could keep trying without the phone dying.

The thought that she never knew how to get into his phone makes me smile. First things first, I check his call history. Who just called?

Charlotte.

Her name is there in black and white as the two most recent calls. My hand grows sweaty, and I put the phone back down, then sit back on my haunches.

I don't know what little game she's playing by calling him, but I can't worry about that now. I have to focus on the task at hand: taking my daughter back.

THIRTY-EIGHT

Sophie

I'm up to my elbows in banking records when the doorbell rings. It's been a few minutes since Charlotte called Lawrence's phone, and I rock back on my heels, trying to sort through what's happening. No matter what I think, I can't get past the fact that she was calling him.

That makes no sense. No way can I wrap my mind around her calling him when she knows he's gone. Maybe she wanted to hear his voicemail one more time? But why right now? Nothing makes sense.

The doorbell rings again. My first instinct is to run for it, but I remind myself that there's no reason Charlotte would be ringing her own doorbell. She has a key. Heck, she has a garage door opener. So if it's not her at the door, then who is it?

A well-meaning neighbor? Most likely. I stand and wipe my hands on my jeans before walking over to the office window and carefully lifting a slat to look out. From here I can't see the front porch, but I can see the driveway, and the police car parked there makes my stomach lurch.

How would she know I'm in her house?

Because that's what it has to be, right? She somehow knows that I'm here and she called the cops to get me in trouble. She doesn't have cameras set up too, does she?

No.

I was so careful looking for them. I'd notice them—I'm sure of it. Sweat breaks out on my brow, and I angrily wipe it away before peeking back through the window.

The police car's lights aren't on, and that's a good sign, isn't it? Wouldn't they be on if they were here to arrest me? I'm not well-versed in cop etiquette, but I'm going to hope that the fact that the car is sitting there sans lights or siren is a good thing.

The doorbell rings again. This time, it's accompanied by pounding on the door. Just in case, you know, I can't hear the bell or anything.

Should I answer it? It's so ingrained in me to listen to the police and do what they say that I'm already out of the office and walking towards the front door before I realize what I'm doing.

As soon as it hits me that I'm about to open the door while actively committing a crime, I freeze.

But what if they're here because of something Charlotte did? I want dirt on her to ensure she can't kick me out of the house, and this could be it. If she did something terrible and they're looking to arrest her, they might tell me what's going on.

My heart has been hammering away since the doorbell rang the first time, but it feels like it kicks it up a gear as I consider that thought. Without taking time to weigh the pros and cons, I hurry to the front door and throw it open.

The officer is already turned away from me, clearly having given up on finding anyone at home. When he turns back to me, all the fear I had over the police being here because I did something wrong disappears.

The expression on his face is the same one doctors give you when they have bad news.

"Is everything okay?" I ask because that seems like the kind of thing you ask when there's a cop on your front porch. I'm nervous, and I brush some hair back from my face as I wait for him to respond.

"Are you related to Charlotte Moore?" His voice is low, which matches how broad his shoulders are. His brass badge glints in the light.

"I'm her..." I say, then pause as I fumble for a way to describe our relationship. Unable to come up with one, I simply nod.

"There's been an accident. She's unable to speak at the moment, but we found her ID with her address and came here to notify family. We tried calling her emergency contact, but Lawrence didn't pick up the phone."

Things click into place. It wasn't Charlotte calling Lawrence's phone, so I can get rid of that worry. But it's been replaced by another.

Now all I can think about is Jordan.

"Jordan." My voice is strangled. "Her daughter. She was with Charlotte. Is she okay? Did the baby get hurt?"

My knees feel like they're going to give out. I grip the doorframe and stare at him, willing him to hurry up and spit it out. The longer he holds back the information he knows, the worse this is for me. I don't know what I'll do if something is wrong with Jordan.

My mind jumps from disaster to disaster. What if the car seat wasn't attached correctly in the car? What if Jordan had been wearing a puffy coat? Everyone knows how dangerous puffy coats are with car seats, that the baby can accidentally slip from it and slide between the straps in an accident.

What if there was something hard in the car, something that could have turned into a projectile? Jordan could have been hit in the face. Or maybe she was holding something, a toy on her lap, a hard toy that isn't age-appropriate, one that Charlotte stupidly gave her just to keep her quiet when they drove to... wherever they were going.

But no, Charlotte adores Jordan, even though she's a terrible, sloppy mom. No way would she have put her in the car without her car seat. Right?

"The baby is fine. Rather than call DCFS, we're looking for family who can take her. Charlotte is on the way to the hospital, and I need someone to come take care of Jordan. Do you have a car? You can follow me."

"I don't." I start kicking myself for leaving it at the library, but it honestly seemed like the best option at the time. "It's parked at the library; I left it there—"

"The accident was right by the library. I'll take you to get the baby, and then you can get your car." He jerks his head towards his car, and I start walking in that direction, but he stops me. "You should lock the door."

"What? Right." I spin back and shut the front door. It takes me a minute to dig the key out of my pocket and lock up. I feel like I'm in a dream as I follow him to his car and buckle up.

The landscape slides past the window, and faster than I would have thought possible, we pull up to the accident.

Charlotte's car is crumpled around a tree. It's still steaming, something under the hood refusing to stop smoking. I gasp and cover my mouth as I get out of the car.

"She's okay, right? Charlotte?" My voice is muffled, but the officer must have been anticipating my question. He rests his hand on my shoulder and waits to speak until I've dragged my eyes away from the wreckage.

"She's going to be okay. She's on her way to the hospital. Do you understand?"

I nod.

"Good. Are you okay to take care of the baby?"

"Jordan. Of course I am." I stiffen, straightening my back a bit to try to pull it together. "Where is she?"

Her cry answers my question. Without saying anything else to him, I turn away and hurry to her.

A female officer is holding her, bouncing lightly on the balls of her feet, shushing softly. Her eyes flick over me, and she smiles. "You're here for the baby."

"I am." I don't hesitate as I reach out to take her. She's hot from crying, her cheeks wet with tears, and I pull her close to me before wiping them off. Barely realizing what I'm doing, I start rocking back and forth to try to calm her.

"Great. I'm going to get your information, and then you can go. Charlotte was taken to Mercy Hospital, so you'll want to go there to check up on her."

"Got it," I say, but I'm barely registering what she's saying to me. I'm looking at Jordan, at her perfect little nose, her sweet mouth that looks just like Lawrence's.

You're here for the baby.

Yes. She's right. Forget Lawrence and whatever Charlotte did to him. Forget him marrying her even though he was already married to me.

I'm here for the baby.

She's mine. I know she is.

THIRTY-NINE

Charlotte

The pain meds the doctor gave me are making it difficult for me to think a coherent thought, but at least my head no longer feels like it's going to explode. The migraine I had came on fast and furious, much faster than any I've had in the past, and I know who to blame.

Sophie.

It's her, the stress of her, the duplicity of her, that made me feel the way I did. No way would I have had that bad of a migraine if she hadn't been here, if she hadn't stabbed something through Lawrence's portrait.

Even as I focus on her, however, there's a thought in the back of my mind working its way forward. I'm forgetting something, that much is obvious, but I can't quite put my finger on what it is.

The thick haze surrounding my thoughts makes it difficult for me to focus on anything. I take a deep breath, doing everything I can to push the worry out of my mind, but it keeps resurfacing.

Jordan.

Her name hits me like a ton of bricks, and I stiffen, pulling my broken arm in towards my body. It's in a cast, snapped like a twig in three places, and although I'm sure it's going to hurt like hell in the morning, the insane amount of meds I'm on right now is keeping the pain at bay.

"My daughter," I say, stumbling over the words. If my tongue weren't so thick, if my brain weren't so foggy, I'd be able to speak more clearly. Make people understand me. As it is, the nurse in my room glances at me, one eyebrow lifted but no clear concern on her face.

"What's that, dear?"

"My daughter." I take a deep breath and speak as slowly as possible. It's like talking to a little kid, like trying to get your point across when you're speaking to someone who's drunk. "My daughter was in the car with me. Where is she now?"

"Oh, the officer was able to get in touch with your sister-in-law, and she came to pick her up. You don't have to worry about a thing, okay? Nobody wants to think about their child possibly with DCFS or with strangers, but your daughter—Jordan, is it? —is with family."

The smile she gives me is supposed to be comforting, but instead it makes ice slide down my spine. I shiver and pull my injured arm closer to me. She must not understand what I'm feeling because she gives me another big grin, then approaches me with a huge cup of water.

"I know it's overwhelming, Charlotte. You have to be so grateful to have her in your life. If your sister-in-law weren't here, then Jordan would be with someone she doesn't know. This is stressful, and I understand that, but things are going to be fine."

Then, before I can respond, she moves the cup closer to my mouth. I swear, this thing is the size of my head, and the water sloshes with every movement.

"Drink," she says. "You need to stay hydrated. No way will you get discharged if you're dehydrated and not doing well."

I drink, even though it makes me feel like a baby to have her shove the straw in my face like this. When she thinks I've had enough, she pulls the cup back and gives me a nod.

"Good girl. I'll put this right here in case you want more and go see about getting you out of here. From what the scans show, you got lucky. No internal injuries. No concussion. I'm sure the police will want to talk to you about what happened on the road, but right now I think you need to go home and rest. Let's see about making that happen."

"How will I get home?"

She smiles at me. She's plump, with a round face and thick dark hair pulled back into a bun. I'm sure some people might find her cheery and delightful, but the fact that she has all the information I want to know and isn't immediately telling me makes me hate her a little.

"Oh, darling, you don't have to worry about that! It's not like we're going to make you call an Uber or something. Can you imagine? A taxi after an accident like the one you had? You're so lucky." She pats the back of my hand. "Your sister-in-law is in the waiting room. She's been out there almost this whole time with your daughter."

"Sophie?" I ask, but she's already turned and flounced out of the room.

I sit back, still cradling my broken arm to my chest. Sophie's here with Jordan. I just kicked her out of the house, but now she's back.

How did they find her? Where was she? I kicked her out, but maybe she didn't leave.

My thoughts race, which is really hard when it feels like every thought has to trudge through molasses to make it to the front of my mind. Before I have a chance to worry too much about that, the doctor is in my room. He talks to me, signs paper-work, walks me out of the room.

My eyes are peeled for my baby. I should try harder to pay more attention to what he's saying to me, but all I can think about is getting Jordan back. Feeling her weight in my arms. Going home and being alone.

Only, we won't be alone, will we? No way will Sophie leave now, not when she has the perfect excuse for staying in the house. I can hear it now, her arguing her case in front of the doctor, him nodding as he listens.

And then we'll be right back where we were.

But then there's Jordan. Sleeping in Sophie's arms, wrapped up like a little pink burrito. I reach out to take my child, but my blue cast is bulky and hard, and I doubt anyone would be surprised that Sophie steps away from me.

She talks to the doctor while I stand there, useless. Even though I'm not participating in the conversation, I hear words that pertain to me.

Pharmacy.

Help.

Pain meds.

But I don't look away from Jordan. She looks so peaceful sleeping in Sophie's arms.

"The last thing she needs is to be left alone right now. That migraine came on hard and fast, according to her. She can't drive, not only because of the meds I have her on but also because of her arm." The doctor holds a clipboard in front of him like a weapon. Even though there's a sheet of paper on it with lots of writing, he doesn't glance at it while talking to Sophie.

I look down at my cast. I'm wrapped from my hand all the way up past my elbow.

"I'm going to take care of everything." That's Sophie, her voice firm yet sweet. It's the tone someone uses with an adult when they know they're about to get their way and they really want to seal the deal. "I'll swing by the pharmacy now to get her meds on the way home so we can stay on schedule. When does she come back to get her cast off?"

"I have all of that information here for you." He hands her some paperwork, and she tucks it into her purse before I have a chance to reach for it. "Let me know if there are any problems, but Charlotte is a model patient." He smiles at me.

I don't smile back.

"I want to ask you something," she tells him, stepping forward a bit to cut me out of the conversation. When she glances over at me, he nods, then puts his hand on her lower back to lead her away a few steps.

They want to talk without me. The thought enrages me, and I follow them, doing everything I can to be as quiet as possible.

"... the baby?" Sophie asks. She winces a little, as if the question was difficult for her. As if she doesn't love the thought of me being helpless and needing her.

"She'll need your help with everything, at least at first." He's lowered his voice but not enough, and I catch every word. "Cooking, cleaning, bathing, taking care of the baby? None of that will be easy for her. She has to learn how to operate with only one arm, and you'll have to be there for her."

"I could hire someone." The words burst out of me, but any excitement I felt over the hope that anyone other than Sophie would be in my house helping disappears when I see the expression on her face.

"That's an idea," the doctor begins, but she cuts him off.

"Charlotte, no. We're family. You don't have to worry about a thing." She pauses, and what she says next terrifies me.

"There's not a thing you can do to make me leave. Remember?"

FORTY

Her

My stomach is huge, and I keep bumping into everything in the house. You'd think by now I would have figured out where everything is and learned how to navigate the house because I haven't left it since Lawrence learned I was pregnant.

His rule, not mine.

I've been stuck in the house for months now, but who's counting? The days are going to pass no matter what I do. Every morning I wake up and orient myself in bed, thinking about my baby, reminding myself of what happened, what position I'm in, and how many days I've been pregnant.

I don't like trying to remember everything, but it really is my only option. I don't dare write this down in my journal. My memory has never been all that great, but it hasn't failed me with this.

For some things, like how many days I've been pregnant and when I first felt the baby move, I'm thankful I haven't forgotten.

For others, like the dark expression on Lawrence's face

when he found out I was pregnant and the terrifying calm he'd exuded when he told me his plan... I wish my memory would fail me.

I don't want to remember the way he looked at me, like I was the biggest disappointment in his life. Like he could never love me again after what I did.

And so, while some of the memories I have are horrible, keeping everything in my mind is the only option I have.

It's better than writing it all out where he can see it. Better than him knowing that the love I felt for him has drained away, leaving me feeling empty, more like a captive than an equal in this relationship. Better than him knowing that I'm counting down the days until I get to meet our son. Or daughter.

Because I don't know which one we've having. He takes me to the doctor, of course he does. But only in another town, and only after hours, when he can easily bribe the doctor to stay open later so that he'll see me, but nobody will know I'm a patient. When you have enough money, everything can be done off the books. Even having a baby.

I've never felt like someone I loved was so ashamed of me. I've never, not once in my life, felt like I was a problem someone needed to keep hidden, like letting someone know the truth of the situation I was in would be the worst thing in the world.

But that's how I feel. And even worse than the way he makes me feel is how removed I am from my own pregnancy. I'm there. I'm the one carrying our child. I'm the one who has to lie on my back, exposed to everyone, my stomach full and round, and wince as the tech squeezes ultrasound jelly on my bare skin.

I have to hiss in a breath when they perform internal checks. I have to lie there, my head turned away from the monitor, so I don't accidentally catch a glimpse of something I shouldn't see, while my husband stands by my side, his hands in his pockets, watching me more than the monitor to ensure I don't disobey him.

Any scans have been given straight to him. Any measurements? Well, I know them, since the tech says them out loud during my scans, but they're not doing me any good. And now I'm so close to popping, just a week away from what they tell me is my due date, but there's no nursery.

No baby clothes. No little socks. No baby meds tucked away under the sink, no bottles, no cute burp cloths, no tiny diapers. If anyone came to our home, they'd never know that I'm pregnant, never realize that there's a baby on the way. Just in case, though, I'm in flowy tops that hide my stomach. Nothing form-fitting, nothing tight that might give me away if a delivery person were to catch a glimpse of me.

The story? I'm in England, visiting family.

The reality? I'm trapped in my own hell, about to give birth, knowing full well that as soon as my baby is born, they will be whisked away, and I'll never see them. Then, once I've lost the baby weight and am back to shape, once nobody will be able to look at me and tell what I went through, only then will I be allowed to leave the house, to entertain, to have a life again.

That's what he says anyway. In my heart, I know the truth. I'll be alive. Technically, I'll have a life. He'll encourage me to go back to Pilates, to grab lunch with some of the wives from down the street. We're friendly but not friends, and none of them have ever asked me deep questions beyond how happy I am to be a wife and don't I feel lucky to have been chosen by him?

But I'll know the truth of what really happened.

As much as I still love my husband, I don't think I'll ever be able to forgive him. What he did to me—what he's doing to me— this is worse than anything I ever could have imagined.

And while he thinks that things will go back to normal, that the two of us will resume the life we had before I accidentally got pregnant, that this will be a blip in our past, some minor road bump we had to get over together, I know the truth.

I will never ever forgive him for taking my baby from me. Right now, I don't know what our future looks like. I don't know how I'm going to live without my child.

Or with the man who made me give them up.

He makes me so angry I could kill him.

I hum to myself as I flick a feather duster over the bookshelf. After it was decided that I would be at home until I had the baby, my husband put all the staff on leave, telling them that, since I was going to be spending a few months in England, that they weren't needed.

Of course, they're being paid while they're on break, and they'll come back full-time after the baby is born. Lawrence isn't a monster.

That being said, keeping the house clean and cooking is up to me. Since nobody else is in the house with me, I tend to blast '90s jams while I clean, and I've been eating a lot of spaghetti. Nobody's here to judge me besides him, and we're past the point of me caring about that.

I've got Sir Mix-a-Lot blaring on my Spotify and I sing along, flicking my wrist one last time across a stack of leather-bound books. There's a twinge in my back I can't quite seem to shake, and I straighten, pressing my hand into the small of my back to try to get it to release.

Something does, but it isn't my back. There's pressure, then a release, and liquid splashes down around my feet.

My baby.

Even though I know I shouldn't care if he's here or not, even though I know he doesn't really care about me or the baby, I can't help but reach for my phone. I want my husband. I want my baby.

But I can't have both. He's made that abundantly clear. My finger hovers above the green call button. If I have the baby here, by myself, without him, I won't have meds, but I can hold it after it's born. I can count toes and fingers and give my baby a kiss on the nose, and then—

A contraction rips through me and I scream, my finger hitting the call button.

He's going to know eventually.

I'm not allowed to keep this baby.

Better to give it up quickly. Get it over with.

Not fall in love.

FORTY-ONE

Charlotte

I never should have let her stay.
   Now I don't know how I'm going to get her to leave.

FORTY-TWO

Sophie

Charlotte looks dazed as I help her into the house, and I can't help but feel a jolt of glee shoot through me when I think about how helpless she is. I threw away the prescription bottle I found in her bathroom when I first got here. Triptan. Not that I knew it was for headaches, but it certainly worked out in my favor, didn't it?

Because now she needs me, and she can't argue with me sticking around to help.

Not that I want to help *her*, but if she can't take care of Jordan, I get to, and being a mother is the only thing in this world I've ever really wanted, even though most people would look at my life and think it was charmed. I loved being married, loved having that security. And travel? Yeah, sign me up.

I can't even count all the countries on my to-visit list. I've knocked half a dozen or so of them off the list already and really didn't have any desire to slow down. That is, of course, until real life hit.

I lost my husband.

He was still alive when I lost him. For the longest time, I didn't know he was even gone. He was in bed with me most of the time, although he did travel a lot for conferences. He stayed late at the office.

Or at what he called the office. How many other women were there? And I had to pretend to be okay with it because that meant I got to keep him, at least in some way.

At first I was in the dark, but now I know that the late nights, the early mornings, the weekends when he *went to work* to handle some things were so he could be around Charlotte.

So he could give her the baby I so desperately wanted. The child I was never allowed to have.

The child he stole from me.

Hi, I'm Sophie, and my husband is a bigamist. I tried to be okay with it because it meant I still got him at home some of the time, but in the end, I guess I wasn't as okay with it as I thought.

I've known from the moment I arrived at Charlotte's house who she was, that she had been cheating with my husband. I knew she was the other woman. The one, out of the dozen he had had, that he liked best. But more importantly, I knew he'd given her a baby.

It's impossible that Jordan is mine, isn't it? But I can't shake that feeling.

I could take her. I *should* take her. It would be the smart thing to do, but I want proof.

She should have been more careful. I showed up, pretending to answer the in-home help ad she'd placed, and had been surprised when she let me in.

More surprised when she trusted me with Jordan. Now is not the time to dwell on that, however. It's the time to take care of my husband's mistress.

"Why don't you sit on the sofa, and I'll get you a snack," I tell Charlotte, carefully plumping a pillow before guiding her to sit. "The doctor said your pain meds could cause an upset stomach, and that's the last thing we want." I check my watch and shrug. "Might as well give you another dose while we're at it."

She shakes her head. For the first time since we left the hospital, she speaks, and I'm surprised at how dry and quiet her voice is. "I don't want to take my meds."

I frown. "You need them," I tell her. *And I need you to take them so I can spend time with Jordan.* "Your doctor said you have to stay ahead of the pain, and it's not just your broken arm he's worried about. You slammed around in the car pretty hard when you hit the tree." I lower myself to the sofa next to her and wait for her response.

Tears fill her eyes. I see them, then look away, towards Jordan, to make sure she's okay. She's wide awake, her eyes bright, and she gurgles a little when I wiggle my fingers at her.

"I can't take care of Jordan if I'm on them." Charlotte stands up, the movement jerky, her cast arm swinging out to the side for leverage. It almost hits me in the face, and I scoot to the side, then stand as well, reaching out and looping my arm around her waist to keep her from falling.

"You can't be around Jordan at all if you fall and end up back in the hospital. Trust the doctor, Charlotte—letting me take care of you is the right idea for now. Think about when you brought her home from the hospital. Lawrence was there to help you, wasn't he?"

She nods slowly. "He was."

She doesn't sound convinced. Her lies are catching up with her.

"And I know it was probably really hard to sit back and let him handle a lot of the work, but you had to heal up. Having a baby is hard on the body."

"It is." She's still standing, but she hasn't taken a step towards Jordan, so I'm taking it as a win. "So hard—you have no idea."

I close my eyes. What she just said hurts, but I can't let her know that.

She sways against me, and my eyes fly open. I can see her legs are giving out, and I slowly lower her back to the sofa. Her head rolls back.

"Charlotte?" I lightly pat her on the cheek. What she needs is a good slap, but I'll show some restraint right now. I'd love to smack the shit out of her, but then she'd probably call the cops or go to a neighbor, and it would become a whole big thing. "Charlotte, you okay? You good?"

No response. She's breathing normally, just passed out.

"Well, I'll be." I stare at her, my heart hammering in my chest. For just a moment, I thought she'd died and, to be honest, it hadn't been that terrible of a thought. But the combination of the trauma to her body and the meds she's on have completely knocked her out.

I stand and watch her for a moment, waiting to see if this is a farce, if she's suddenly going to wake up. If I start poking around and she sits up, wide awake and alert, I'm going to feel like an idiot.

But she doesn't move. She makes a small whistling sound with each breath, probably because of the way her neck is turned, but I'm not about to shift her around to make it easier for her to breathe.

One, she'd probably wake up.

And two, I'm fine if she never wakes up.

When I'm confident she's not going to stir, I turn back to Jordan, but my eyes fall on Charlotte's purse. It's on the coffee table, the straps fallen down, the top halfway open. The officer who came to get me told me that they'd done their best to find all of her things that fell out of her purse during the accident, but there was no guarantee.

But I know for a fact her phone is in there. If they hadn't

found it, they wouldn't have been able to call Lawrence's phone.

Once that thought is in my head, I don't hesitate. I dig through her purse, pushing through gum wrappers, three tubes of lipstick, and a tampon to find her phone. After I pull it out, I settle down on the sofa next to her and try to unlock it.

But I have no idea what her PIN might be. For a moment, frustration bubbles in me, then I realize she probably has her fingerprint set up. I'm nervous as I reach out to take her hand and press her finger against the side of the phone, but when there's a soft click and the phone unlocks, I feel myself relax.

This could be interesting. Hopefully there are fewer bikini shots in here than there were in Lawrence's phone. I should have known he'd have half-naked photos of the woman he was sleeping with. He's been like that since we started dating as teens. Still, I didn't want to see them.

Let's see what you're hiding, I think, then settle back into the cushions. Even though it's just past lunchtime, I feel like I've been going all day long. I'm tired and the sofa is comfy, but my brain is too wired to sleep right now.

Not when I can snoop in her phone without worrying about her finding out.

But where do I start? I'm like a kid in a candy store, completely overwhelmed by all the choices. Well aware that I have a pretty unlimited amount of things to look through and a limited time to do it, I finally tap on her call log.

There are the two most recent calls to Lawrence. Every other call is to names I don't know, and I shake my head at wasting time looking through them. I'm not a part of Charlotte's life. I have no idea who she talks to, and I don't care to get to know her friends.

Her photos then.

I tap into them and start scrolling. Jordan. Jordan. Jordan, Jordan, *Jordan*. Almost every shot is of her daughter. In some of them she's sleeping. Others she's dressed with an ugly pink bow on her head. Some of them are selfies of Charlotte with Jordan snoozing on her chest.

I wrinkle my nose and keep flicking the screen, slowly going back in time.

Finally, Lawrence. My breath catches in my throat as I look at the photo. It's a recent shot, probably taken shortly before he died. He's standing in the backyard, turned part of the way away from the camera, staring at Jordan in a swing.

No, not staring. Glaring.

I know Lawrence. I know that expression on his face. He's not happy, or he wasn't in this shot.

Interesting.

Back I go, further and further, willing to torture myself to see shots from Jordan's birth. All newborn babies look like wet, wrinkly potatoes. We all know this, and yet we all want to see pictures of them, as if they're at all distinguishable from each other.

But there are none.

I glance over at Jordan. She's still watching me. Pretty soon she's going to get hungry or need a diaper change, but right now she's being a perfect angel.

I'm still scrolling through photos, but I've slowed down to make sure I don't miss a birth photo.

But they're not here. Frowning, I scroll faster, my finger flicking against the screen, sending days, then weeks, then months of photos flying past. Charlotte's in most of them, clad in a bikini, just like I knew she would be.

But she's not pregnant in a single one.

FORTY-THREE

Sophie

If Charlotte wasn't ever pregnant, who the hell does Jordan belong to?

Me. She belongs to me.

I marinate in that hope for a moment before shaking my head to clear the thought.

What if I just missed some photos? After I calmed down from flipping through the ones on her phone, I noticed a secure folder and tapped it, trying to get in, but was denied.

It required a PIN, which I didn't have, or to draw a certain unlock pattern, which I didn't have a shot at guessing.

Could her pregnancy photos be in there?

But if that's the case, why have them locked away? Why not keep them with the rest of your photos?

Something here isn't adding up, and the only way I'm going to get answers is to keep poking around.

I take a deep breath and glance around Charlotte's bedroom. She's still passed out on the sofa where I left her, and Jordan's sound asleep. When Charlotte caught me in her bedroom earlier, I had just stabbed my finger through Lawrence's perfect face.

Mature? No, not at all.

But it felt good.

The canvas print of the two of them is ruined, but I don't feel any remorse over what I did.

I'd seen it there and felt my breath catch. Then, without thinking about what I was doing, I'd climbed up on their bed.

I'd been looking for a scar, because that had turned into an easy way to date Lawrence's photos. When I found it, it was like something inside of me snapped.

It was there, right on his left cheek. From three years ago, right around the time he amped up his time with other women. I remember clearly how Lawrence got it, how he'd been up on the roof cleaning out gutters while I was in the kitchen going through his phone.

I'd had my concerns, but that day was the first time I'd acted on them to get the information I wanted. There had been little clues that something more serious than his usual flings was going on, like the fact that he no longer left his phone on the kitchen counter when he was in the shower, and how he locked his computer when he left the room. I was curious.

I had to know.

I'd just opened his texts and was starting to read them when he fell from the roof.

I'd screamed.

Called 911.

And, in the end, the only proof it had ever happened was a tiny scar from where he hit a stick just right as he landed.

It was one thing to see the scar because it was there in the photo. Pink and new, barely even a scar, if I'm honest. It has more of the look of fresh skin when you've been injured and just picked off the scab. Over time, that type of skin scars, but at first there's always a moment of hope that the blemish will disappear, that the only memory of the accident will be in some photos, a dark scab that disappears.

But this pink mark of skin on Lawrence never disappeared. It darkened, leather-like, a mark that would allow me to pick his cheek out of a million pictures of other cheeks.

I close my eyes. When I open them again, I look away from the print.

The bedroom boasts two closets, one at either end of the room. I don't give myself time to think about which one to open first and stride instead to the closest one. I swing the double doors open and reach in to flick the switch to turn on the light.

It's all Lawrence's things.

My heart hammers in my chest as I take in the sight of his clothes hanging on the racks, his shoes on the floor. Even though I haven't seen these exact clothes before, I know Lawrence's style so well that I could have easily chosen everything in this closet for him to wear.

It all screams him, from the brown leather loafers to the paisley ties, the crisp suit jackets to the drawer of gold cufflinks. Lawrence had money, loved money, and wanted people to know that he wasn't afraid to spend it.

I'm sure there isn't going to be some big surprise in here, but still I linger, my fingers tracing over the fabrics. I lean forward and smell the cologne he always wore, the scent familiar and dark.

It surprises me when I feel tears burn my eyes. I'd honestly thought that I'd locked all feelings of Lawrence so deep down in my heart that they wouldn't surface while here. It was the only way for me to handle coming face-to-face not only with his child but also the woman he apparently cared about enough to knock up.

But did he really knock her up? I'd thought that originally, but now I don't think he did.

Still, seeing these clothes is a slap in the face. It feels like

I've stepped into an alternate reality, one where Lawrence had a life that doesn't include me.

And I guess that's exactly what happened.

He had a life here. It never included me. I never would have known Charlotte or Jordan had I not come here of my own volition. He would have continued with his double life, and I would have been at home, wishing he loved me enough to want only me.

Part of this life is the same as the one I was part of back before... before everything fell apart. All these outfits are ones he'd wear in the world where I knew him. But the rest? It's all foreign.

My mind races as I close the closet door and walk across the bedroom to Charlotte's. This is where I think things are going to get interesting. As much as I'd love to spend some time in Lawrence's closet where everything feels familiar, Charlotte's closet is where I think I'll find dirt on her.

Well, if there is any. So far, she's squeaky clean, even though I do think she comes across as a bit of an idiot. To believe Lawrence would take care of her and then he left her nothing? It's laughable, at least to me. How stupid can the other woman be?

Although... he didn't leave her with nothing, did he? He left her with Jordan.

My face burns with frustration as I throw open her closet door. The switch is in the same location as in Lawrence's closet, and I flick it on, then step back and take it all in.

It's stuffed with clothes. The hangers are all crammed so close together that I don't know how she can get anything in or out of here without everything collapsing. Under the hanging clothes are dozens of pairs of shoes, all of them tossed together in a pile. It's dizzying, the pinks and sparkles and straps and leopard print.

Where Lawrence's closet was a lesson in control and design,

Charlotte's looks like a seven-year-old was in charge of not only selecting the clothes but putting them all in the closet. It's exhausting just looking in the space, and I trail my fingers across the fabrics for only a moment before turning the light back off and closing the door.

I don't have enough energy to dig through all of it if I'm being honest. I want to learn more about her, but I don't want to go crazy doing it.

No, best to keep looking, to try to find something that will be damning, something that will prove once and for all that Jordan is mine.

I know she is. I wasn't sure when I first arrived, but the more time I spend with her, the more convinced I am of the fact that she belongs to me.

She has to. I've never felt a deep connection with a baby like that before. After all, what's the saying? Ahh, yes.

Mother knows best.

FORTY-FOUR

Her

The pain ripping through my body feels like it's going to split me in half. I scream, arching my back the best I can, my hands twisted tight in the hospital sheets. Sweat plasters my bangs to my forehead, and the incessant beeping from the monitors I'm hooked up to makes me feel like I'm going insane.

"Again. Push again. You can do this." The doctor between my legs sounds calm, much calmer than I feel. If I look down, I can just see his cap over the mound of my stomach. To my right is a nurse. She keeps rubbing my arm and whispering to me, probably to make me feel less alone.

But nothing she can say or do will help. Not when Lawrence isn't here. He's supposed to be here feeding me ice chips and holding my hand. I want him letting me squeeze his hand until the bones rub together. I want him telling me that I'm doing a good job and that he's proud of me.

He drove me here, to a medical clinic in another town. It's after hours and nobody knows we're here. He's already told me his plan. To pay cash. To keep my baby from being reported.

Even knowing what he plans, I don't think I can stop him. The doctor himself let us in. I didn't miss how he opened the door for us, looked around the parking lot, then locked it. And Lawrence? He walked me in, one arm around my waist, that physical contact the most we've had since I told him I was pregnant. It was like the baby growing in me physically repulsed him. He'll give me a peck on the cheek. He'll lightly touch my arm as he walks by.

He's not a monster.

But he's also not going out of his way to show me that he loves me.

A scream rips through me, pushing the thought of Lawrence from my mind. Right now, there's only pain.

No regret over what happened, over me getting pregnant.

No regret over the fact that he can't be here with me even though I need him now more than ever.

No regret that my life has changed and I don't know if there's any way the two of us can find our way back to each other.

There's just pain, this all-consuming, searing pain that threatens to split me straight up the middle. It's lightning, burning and marking me, making it almost impossible for me to catch my breath.

Every muscle in my body contracts; sweat breaks out over my entire body. I feel like I'm being crushed, like every cell in me is crying out for help.

"You're doing great," the nurse says, and I want to scream at her for lying to me.

I'm not doing great. Nothing about this is *great*. It's physical and visceral and the most painful thing I've ever gone through in my life. It's not *great*. It's hell, a fresh hell that I can't even celebrate surviving, because when I do finally make it out, I won't have anyone waiting for me.

No child waiting for me to bundle them to my breast. No

husband pulling me into his arms and whispering into my hair to tell me that he's proud of me, that I did an incredible job, that I'm so much stronger than I ever thought I was.

No, there's just going to be me. An empty womb. Empty arms.

And a husband who might or might not love me.

And who I might or might not love in return.

"Again! You're almost there! I see hair!" The doctor sounds so excited. Even through the muffling of his mask, I hear the joy in his voice.

He's bringing life into this world.

And I want to die.

I scream, the sound ripping from me as I tear open, feeling like I'm turning myself inside out. There's a moment where I feel like I'm honestly going to die, then sweet relief, a falling sensation, like all my nerves have stopped firing and I can breathe.

Until the pain comes back.

It's duller now, and I lay my head back on the pillow. My breathing is heavy, and I feel like I'm gasping for breath, but I made it.

"The hard part is done," the nurse says, but I shake my head.

She's wrong.

The hard part, giving up my baby, hasn't even begun.

"Boy?" I ask. "Or girl?" I struggle to push up onto my elbows. I want to see what's going on. I want to see my baby. A quick glance at the door reassures me that my husband hasn't come into the room.

As soon as he does, any chance I might have had to hold my baby will be dashed.

But the door is shut.

The nurse doesn't look at me. She's squeezing my arm, suddenly tighter than before, her nails digging into my skin.

"Ouch," I say and try to pull away from her. "That hurts."

"Sorry," she says, letting up but not letting go. "Sorry, I didn't mean to hurt you. You did such a great job, you know. Such a great job. You can relax. Now everything's up to the doctor."

Her words wash over me in a wave, and I feel myself melt into the bed. *You can relax.* The relief I feel over her saying that is short lived, however, when another thought enters my mind. It bursts through the momentary peace I was feeling and leaves me shaking.

Up to the doctor?

I turn those words over and over in my mind, trying to make them make sense. Maybe if I look at them from a different direction I'll be able to piece together what the nurse was saying.

Everything's up to the doctor.

The beeping is getting louder and louder. I don't think anything in the room here has changed, but now that I'm no longer pushing and in pain, I can focus on what's going on around me.

There's movement at the foot of the bed, and I push myself up further, but the nurse stops me, her hand on my shoulder.

"I need you to push to deliver the placenta," she tells me. Her face is inches from mine. It's my entire world, like she needed to make sure I wasn't going to look away from her. "Can you do that?"

I nod.

She gives me a small smile, then squeezes my arm again. "Push."

I do, gritting my teeth and crying out as I follow her direction. It takes my mind off the strange feeling in the room, off the strange thing she said, off the way the doctor didn't hold my baby up, didn't pass them to me, didn't even tell me if I have a boy or a girl.

And then it hits me. I stop pushing, my entire body falling

flat on the bed as I realize what's going on in here, what's so wrong, what's making me feel like everything is falling apart.

I haven't heard my baby cry.

FORTY-FIVE

Charlotte

I feel like I'm coming out of the fog as I force myself awake.

My entire body hurts and I moan, shifting to the side and reaching for my blanket before I realize where I am.

The sofa. Not in my bed.

"Jordan?" I force my eyes open as I say my daughter's name. "Jordan?"

She's not here.

I feel sluggish, fighting through meds, but the realization that my daughter isn't here terrifies me.

Pain shoots through my good arm as I brace it on the cushion to push myself into a seated position.

"Jordan!"

No answering cry. No response from Sophie.

She took my baby.

I know she did.

FORTY-SIX

Charlotte screaming makes me race from the bedroom down the stairs to the living room.

She's where I left her, her eyes wide and slightly unfocused, her breathing fast and shallow.

"Jordan! Where is Jordan?" Her good hand is twisted into a claw as she reaches for me.

I stop, out of her reach, and stare at her. "She's in her crib," I say, my voice soft and soothing. "She's sleeping. She's fine."

Charlotte blinks at me. "Tell me the truth! Did you take her?"

I stare at her.

How did she know what I was thinking about doing?

"No. I didn't take her."

I force myself to step closer to her. Reaching behind her, I plump her pillow, then gently push her shoulder to help her lie back down. "Get some rest."

There's no response as she leans back against the sofa. Her

breathing slows, but the terror in her eyes is still there as she watches me walk around the living room.

I could take her now. If Charlotte would fall asleep, there's nothing stopping me from getting Jordan and leaving.

But not yet. Not until I've worked out the truth of what happened. I need to know everything.

I can't seem to sit and settle. My mind and body are in overdrive, and I walk around the living room as I think. Every so often I stop and examine a photo of Lawrence. Really drink him in. He's so happy in all these pictures, like he doesn't have a care in the world, and I hate that I haven't seen him like that in a while.

He wasn't this happy at home. It's like he saved up all of his happy to share with Charlotte and Jordan.

Although... there were times I'd see him this happy again. It was always when he was going to be coming here, always when he was on the cusp of a trip out of town, when he was going to get to shack up with her for a while.

I wonder what he said when Charlotte wanted a baby.

"What are you doing?" Charlotte's voice drags me out of my thoughts and centers me back in her house. I'm in her living room, not mine, looking at a photo of Lawrence, but I'm not the one who took it.

Under my feet are wide wood planks, not a soft fluffy rug I picked up at the farmer's market. The walls are pale blue, not the buttery yellow I used in the living room.

"Just looking at photos," I tell her as I put Lawrence back where he was.

She shifts. Her voice is low. Sleepy. "I was getting hungry, and I thought maybe..."

"I'll make you something." I glance at my watch as I walk towards the kitchen. "And I'll get you your next pain pill. I know you're not keen on taking them, but you have to remember what the doctor said—"

"No pain pills!" She cuts me off, her voice loud so it will carry into the kitchen. "I don't want to take them. I don't want to be... fuzzy."

"It'll make you fuzzy when I hold a pillow over your face so you can't breathe," I mutter to myself as I open the fridge. After pulling out the applesauce, I call out to her. "Okay, got it!"

She can't see me from where she's sitting on the sofa, which means she can't tell what I'm doing. I take a gorgeous teak tray from where it leans against the wall by the microwave and slam it on the counter.

Then: toast. It's expensive artisanal sourdough bread, the kind I love, and I slather a piece with butter to munch on while making the rest of her tray. No butter for her—it will upset her stomach.

And she doesn't deserve to enjoy her food as much as I am.

While that toasts, I tap a single painkiller from the orange bottle on the counter. For a moment, I consider the pill. It's small and white and looks totally harmless. I tap out a second. It's easy enough to use the flat side of a knife to break them down, then crush them into a powder. This stirs easily into a small bowl of applesauce I spoon out for her.

There. Dry toast, some lukewarm water, and drugged applesauce.

It's perfect.

I plaster a smile on my face as I carry the tray back into the living room. Jordan's upstairs and hasn't made a peep since I put her down for a nap. She'll need a diaper change soon but hadn't been wet when I put her down.

Is she dehydrated? Has Charlotte not given her enough bottles this morning? I'll have to pay attention to it and make sure she gets enough to eat.

"Here you go," I say, putting the tray on the coffee table. Part of me is worried that Charlotte won't eat the applesauce, but she dives right in, scraping every last bit from the bowl.

I smile and sit.

And wait.

It takes fifteen minutes, but she's soon snoozing on the sofa, her head back, her mouth open. For a moment, I study her, taking in the lines of her face, the sharp point of her chin, and try to imagine Lawrence waking up next to her in the morning.

It's too much, and I shake my head to clear the mental image, then leave the tray where it is and head upstairs.

Jordan needs me. I know she does, even though she hasn't made a peep. I can feel her, as if she's calling to me, desperate for me to hold her, to love her, to protect her.

I'm quiet as I walk into her nursery, but I must make just enough sound to wake her up. She shifts, already making little cooing noises, and I hurry to scoop her up.

"There, there," I say, patting her on the back. "You're okay—I'm here." She's warm from sleeping, her body soft and supple, and I snuggle her before I get a whiff of her diaper.

"I thought so," I tell her. "But that's no big deal. I've got you, Jordan."

Jordan. *Not Jordy.*

The changing table is perfectly stocked, I'll give Charlotte that. It's lovely that I don't have to search for diapers, wipes, or cream. I put Jordan on the changing table and hold my hand on her stomach while I grab what I need with the other hand.

All through high school, I babysat. While my friends were getting jobs at the ice cream parlor or coffee shop, I only wanted to babysit. There's just something so sweet and innocent and clean about a baby. They need your help and can't do anything on their own.

And the fact that this is Lawrence's baby...

I feel myself getting emotional over the thought that Jordan is part Lawrence's. It's amazing to know that I have his child right here with me, that he's living on through her.

Only—

I close my eyes. I looked through Charlotte's phone and didn't see a single maternity photo. Where were they? Don't most pregnant women spam their friends with pics of their growing bellies?

Don't they document every single time a pair of jeans won't fit? When their belly button finally pops like a Thanksgiving turkey timer?

So why not Charlotte?

Because Jordan is mine. I know it.

I mull that over as I unsnap Jordan's onesie, but my thoughts keep coming back to Lawrence.

He never wanted children. He told me that, over and over, really drilling it home. It could be possible that she got pregnant, and he got mad. That he didn't want to be reminded of her having a baby and he forced her to wear clothes that hid her belly. Maybe he didn't let her take pictures of it.

Or it could be that—

That I already know the truth. That mothers know their children even if they haven't spent time together, that there's no way to deny the fact that Jordan is mine.

FORTY-SEVEN

Sophie

Everything I thought I knew coming into this house has been turned upside down, and I don't know what to do or how to handle it.

"Jordan's my daughter," I whisper. I'm back in the kitchen, and I pour myself a big glass of wine and down it before saying the words again. Even the second time, they don't make any sense.

None of this does.

I've thought it for a while now, worried that she might be my daughter, that Charlotte somehow took her from me, but this is the first time I've allowed myself to say the words out loud. It's been eating at me, a worry I can't get rid of, but now that I've actually said it, it feels more real.

Did Lawrence take my baby from me and give her to the other woman he married? Would he do that? I know he wasn't someone to let you get away with anything if he thought you had wronged him. But to do that?

To take my child and give it to the woman he cheated on me with?

It's inconceivable.

At least by anyone who isn't completely crazy.

Charlotte has a lot to answer for. I have to know what she's planning, what she thought she was going to get away with. I have to pick through her brain and try to make all her lies make sense, but I really knocked her out with the meds I gave her.

Okay, maybe I went a little overboard with the meds I gave her earlier, but I really just wanted some time to think without hearing her chatter on. She'd have lost it if she knew what was going through my mind.

I take another huge gulp of wine.

Jordan is currently in a little swing in the living room. I can see her through the door, and I watch as she goes back and forth, back and forth. She'd been starving for a bottle after I changed her, but I barely remember making it. I was moving on autopilot, unable to concentrate on what was going on.

How many other lies has Charlotte been spinning?

Without thinking about what I'm doing, I finish the glass of wine and set it in the sink. Then, before I can stop myself, I walk back out to the living room and grab Charlotte's phone. It's easy to unlock this time—I know exactly how to place her finger against the sensor—and I immediately hop into her email.

A lot of hospitals send correspondence and bills via email now. I certainly didn't see any from her giving birth to Jordan when I was digging through the box of bills in Lawrence's office.

There might be something here.

Hospital.

I type the word into the search bar and... nothing.

Bill.

That brings up every single water, power, and gas bill Charlotte has ever paid, and I frown, using my finger to skip backwards through the emails as I look for something from the hospital.

Surely there will be something here.

But I can't find it. I think for a moment, then check for any folders she might have created to store her emails. Lawrence was always keen on that, always making folders and organizing his emails. He hated that I'd have over a thousand unread messages in my inbox.

But there's no folder like what I'm expecting. Nothing labeled *hospital* or *Jordan's birth*.

"Screw this," I say, getting up and walking back into Lawrence's office. I know it's a very millennial thing—to prefer working on a large screen versus a small one, but it's just tricky to find the information you want on a phone sometimes.

But a computer? That's my jam.

I turn it on, and it fires right up, which is another thing that reminds me of Lawrence. He was never one to skimp on the newest and best electronics, so I'm not surprised that the computer here is top of the line.

I click around in both his and Charlotte's email before giving up on finding something from the hospital. Maybe Lawrence paid for the birth in cash? I can see him doing something like that, especially if he were angry.

He'd want to make the problem go away, and for him, the best way to do that would be to throw money at it. It didn't always work, but it often did.

Was this one of those times? Or was I the only one he refused to let have a child?

I sigh and close the browser, then check out the apps. There are lots I recognize, and I have to fight to keep from clicking through to look at the photos and videos stored on the computer.

Torturing myself with shots of this little family wouldn't do any good. It would only hurt me.

My eyes flick across the bottom of the screen. Lawrence loved Macs, always loved having his most-used apps easily accessible right there.

Microsoft Word. Preview. Pages. *Photoshop.*

"That's interesting," I say and click it. It opens quickly, bringing up a blank screen, and I debate for a moment before clicking to open the most recent files.

Jordan.psd

My heart beats faster as I click on it to open it. Like everything else on the computer, it opens quickly, and it takes me a moment to realize what I'm looking at.

A birth certificate.

I squint, looking closer at it and using my mouse to drag it around. It looks... fine. Real. Just like you'd expect a birth certificate to look.

Why would it be saved as a Photoshop file? That's the part that doesn't make any sense. You want to scan a birth certificate into your computer to have easy access to it? Sure. I can see the case for that.

But why would you want to have it open in Photoshop?

"So you can edit it," I whisper. Every muscle in my body seems to freeze as I have that thought. It hits me out of left field, and even though I wasn't expecting something like that to cross my mind, once it does, I can't shake it.

I don't know a lot about Photoshop. I've used it, sure, but I prefer other programs, so I'm not the most confident as I click around. But as I do, I see one thing that's so damning I don't know how to look away.

The layers.

There are a dozen layers in this one file. Exported, all of the layers would flatten, and it would be impossible to tell what the original document looked like. But thanks to the layers still existing, I can click each one and hide or show it.

My hand trembles as I mouse over the layers and, one by one, hide them until only the original document is left.

It's a birth certificate, sure, just like I knew it would be, but it isn't Jordan's.

I hold my breath and slowly add the layers back. Each time I click a layer to add it, I do it a few times, looking to see where the change in the document is.

It doesn't matter where Lawrence and Charlotte got this original birth certificate. What matters is that they changed it to be Jordan's.

A few clicks to add layers back and someone else's birthday is in it. Their weight and height. Their parents' names. It's so easy to change it from the original certificate to this fake one that I can't believe it.

Would it hold up in court? Or at the hospital? I don't know. I don't know how stuff like this gets filed. I don't know what steps you have to take to ensure that a birth certificate is official, to make sure nobody copies it and changes it like this.

But I do know one thing.

Jordan doesn't have an official birth certificate from the hospital. She has... this.

And that, combined with the fact that there aren't any maternity pictures of Charlotte anywhere to be found, leaves me with one conclusion. Jordan isn't Charlotte's child.

I was right all along. My mother's intuition didn't fail me.

She's mine.

FORTY-EIGHT

Her

I jerk out of my sleep when I hear the front door open.

There's drool on my chin, and I hurriedly wipe it away. This always happens when I nap on the sofa: I wake up drooling and discombobulated. But as much as I would have preferred to nap in my bed, I didn't want to miss Lawrence coming back into the house.

"It's done." His voice is clear as he answers my question before I ask it, and I feel my throat close up.

I'm going to start sobbing again, which is all I've been doing since I made the decision. Sure enough, before I can speak, tears stream down my cheeks.

"Did you hear me? It's over. I fixed your mistake."

"I heard you." I gasp out the words as I force myself to stand. I'm dizzy, and I take a deep breath to try to steady myself.

"You pushed me to do this. I want you to understand that. What you made me do is on you. Thank goodness it will have a home where it's actually wanted."

I wanted it. But I don't say that.

Instead, I rush him. I'm unthinking as I reach for his face, my fingers flexed so I can dig into his skin, but he moves faster than I do, grabbing both of my wrists and twisting them down to my sides.

"You did this!" I scream the words at him, jerking left to right, but he doesn't release me. I kick him, my bare toes colliding with his shin. He barely winces while a hot pain shoots up my foot.

"I did nothing," he hisses. "*You* did this. And I fixed your mistake. Quit acting like a fool."

I hear what he's saying, but his words don't make any sense. Just a few hours ago I was pushing, dying to meet my baby, and now I'm empty.

Hollow.

My stomach is stretched, my skin marked, but there's no life in me anymore. My breasts ache and are so full I can't bear to touch them. My entire body hurts.

"I hate you." I quit fighting him and stare into his eyes to drive the point home. "I *hate* you. Do you hear me? You're disgusting. Despicable. The fact that I thought I loved you, that I slept with you—"

"You adored me, or you wouldn't have signed the contract." He squeezes my wrists one more time, then releases them and takes a step back. His body language is confident, like he's sure I won't try to attack him again, but his eyes are wary.

"Shove your contract," I say. My hands clench into fists. I keep thinking about what it would be like to press my fingers into his eyes, to press and press until they popped, until jelly ran from the sockets, until—

"The contract you were more than willing to sign. This is the life I promised you." He waves his hand to encompass the house.

The marble floors.

The original art.

The glaring lack of children's toys.

"I don't want this life." The words feel daring. Dangerous even. They hang in the air like a guillotine, and I watch his face to see how he's going to respond.

His expression doesn't change. "You don't get to make that decision."

"And what? You do? You've got to be kidding me." I cross my arms over my stomach. It feels instinctive, to protect the little bean growing inside, but there's nothing there. I'm deflated, and I feel the air whoosh out of my lungs at the thought.

"It's what I've always done. You've never had a problem with it before, so I don't know why you're starting now."

I stare at him, my emotions a confusing cocktail that I can't quite figure out.

I loved him once, right?

I think back to our wedding and how attentive he'd been. How he'd flown me to Bora Bora, how he'd taken me to incredible restaurants. I was obsessed with him.

"Did you ever love me?" I whisper. We're only standing a few feet from each other, but it feels like he's miles away from me.

"What?" While I was thinking about whether or not I'd ever loved him, he'd pulled his phone from his pocket and was looking at something.

"Did you ever love me?" My voice is louder now, and I get his attention. He clicks off his screen and shoves his phone in his pocket.

"Or did you love the idea of manipulating me?" I should let him answer, but I don't. "Did you love that I was young and stupid and didn't know how to stand up to you?"

"You're emotional. Hormonal." Lawrence exhales and scrubs his hand down his cheek. "Take a shower. Clean yourself up. We can talk later." With that, he turns and walks back out the front door, slamming it behind him.

My knees give out, and I sink to the floor. There's a spot on the tile in front of me. Honey from my tea this morning? It feels like forever ago that I was still pregnant, that I still hoped, just a little, that he would change his mind.

That he'd let me keep the baby.

Sure, I know the stats. I know that in North Carolina you can get your child back with enough effort. I think the time-frame is a month, one month during which a parent can change their mind.

Not that there wouldn't be hoops to jump through, of course. No judge would happily hand my child back to me after it looked like I'd abandoned them. But I could explain the situation I'm in, tell them how it was my only choice, but that sometimes new choices appear.

I'd fight. And I'd win.

If only I knew where my baby was.

That's what keeps rattling around in my mind. If I knew, I could do something. I could (*take my baby back*) yes, take them back. And as for Lawrence, I could (*kill him*) no, I couldn't do that, but I could leave him, right?

I could leave him.

Or kill him.

I could kill him.

But first I have to find out where he took my baby.

FORTY-NINE

Charlotte

The first thought I have as I come to on the sofa is that I never should have trusted Sophie. She drugged me—I'm sure she did. She put my meds in my food or in the water she gave me, and like an idiot I ate it all up, allowing her to knock me out.

It hurts, but I sit up, forcing myself into an upright position. The sudden movement sends bolts of pain shooting through my body. Not just in my head, but my arm and stomach. My back and hips.

The wreck did a number on me.

I could call out to Sophie and Jordan, but instead I stand, my legs unsteady. It takes me a minute to center my weight and feel like I'm not going to tip over, but I finally do, then take a few tentative steps away from the sofa.

What time is it? I glance down at my watch, but the face is fuzzy and it's difficult for me to make out the time. Rather than worrying about it, I decide to look for my baby.

Charlotte and Jordan are either here or they're not, and the idea that they might not be in the house is enough to give me chills. If Jordan is gone, if Sophie took her...

I'm not thinking straight enough to get her back, that much is sure. And I need help with her—anyone would be able to tell that much just looking at me. It's not like I can afford to hire someone, so what would happen with Jordan? Would the police let me have her back?

They'd have to, right? I'm her mother.

No, you're not.

I hate that little voice, the one that pops up when I'm least expecting it. I want it to shut up, want to fully be Jordan's mom, but the truth is undeniable. I didn't birth her. My blood doesn't run through her veins.

But I love her more than her biological mother does or ever did. You can't negate the fact that she's my daughter just because I didn't carry her for nine months and labor to give birth to her.

"My baby," I mutter as I stagger to the kitchen.

No Sophie. No Jordan.

Upstairs then, but when I stand at the bottom of the stairs and stare up them, I'm more daunted than I could have imagined.

"Jordan," I whisper, then sink back to my knees. My blood whooshes in my ears with every beat of my heart. I feel like I'm going to throw up. No way can I make it up the stairs. Instead, I crawl back to the sofa. There, I grab my phone and unlock it.

Or, rather, I try to.

I frown and type my PIN in again, but the screen jiggles.

I know my PIN. What the hell is this? Exhaling slowly, like that's going to keep me from blowing up, I carefully press my finger into the side of the phone, allowing it to read my fingerprint instead.

But it doesn't unlock, and it hits me what Sophie did. While I was sleeping, she used my finger to unlock my phone. But that wasn't enough for her, was it? No. She didn't just poke through my texts and photos.

She changed the PIN and fingerprint so that I can't unlock it.

I act without thinking, throwing the phone as hard as I can into the wall across from me. It shatters, the back flying off, bits of metal and plastic exposed before it even hits the floor.

And then it hits me: I could still have made an emergency call even with the phone locked. I could still have called 911.

"No," I whisper, then drop to my knees and crawl across the floor. Surely the phone is just in a few big pieces, and I can snap them back together. If I can do that, I can call the police. I can let them know there was a kidnapping.

All my fears over having the police involved have flown out the window now that Sophie is in control. I have to call for help, have to make sure the police know that Sophie is the bad person here. I can tell them my side of the story first and ensure that she'll never see the outside of jail again.

But the phone won't snap back together. I threw it harder than I meant to, or maybe it hit the wall just right, exactly on a weak spot, and that's what broke it into so many pieces. Whatever the reason, there's no way I can put it back together, no way I can call for help.

I sink back onto the floor, tears streaming down my face.

I'm at Sophie's mercy. And she's evil.

FIFTY

Sophie

I'm back upstairs, desperate to find something that will help me make sense of what's going on. Jordan might not want to take another nap right now, but she's dry and her stomach is full, and I'm hoping she'll snooze a little so I can poke around without having to take care of her.

If I don't find something that clears up all the questions racing through my mind, I think I'm going to go crazy.

Slowly, I spin in a circle, trying to look as critically as possible at every area of the bedroom. Surely I'm missing something, and I hope to God that it's not hidden in either of the closets because I don't have the energy to look more thoroughly through them.

I need something fast. I need to find something before Charlotte wakes back up or before Jordan needs me. Of course, the right thing to do would be to hire help for this woman. Put the in-home help ad back up for her. Walk away from it all. Go home and forget I ever met Charlotte.

But I can't forget Jordan.

Not when I know the truth. No, I don't have proof, but I *know* she's mine. Whatever I decide to do, I need to hurry. She'll call the cops if I take her—I know she will. I need irrefutable proof she's mine. Luckily, I have some time to spare as long as I keep Charlotte drugged.

Dropping to my knees, I look under the bed, but there's nothing there but a few errant dust bunnies. I lift the mattress and run my hand around its perimeter, taking my time so I can be as thorough as possible.

Nothing.

Back to the bedside tables. I pull out the drawer in Charlotte's and dig through her perfume, fuzzy socks, and Chapstick. After dumping it all out on the mattress, I tap the bottom of the drawer to see if it's a false bottom.

It's not.

The same treatment on Lawrence's bedside table yields nothing as well. I'm starting to sweat, and I lean out into the hall for a moment to make sure I don't miss Jordan crying.

And that's when it hits me. If Charlotte had a secret she wanted to keep from Lawrence, she sure as hell wouldn't keep it right under his nose in the bedroom. I know Lawrence. He didn't want kids.

He didn't even *like* kids.

It was shortly after Jordan was born that he died, but I'd be willing to bet whatever's in my wallet that he never set foot in her nursery. That's where I'd hide something if I wanted to keep it out of Lawrence's way.

And Charlotte is conniving, but she isn't stupid. She'll have figured out the same thing I did, that anything she wanted to keep secret from Lawrence should be as close to Jordan as possible.

There's a loud crash from downstairs and I freeze, listening. My ears are pricked for any additional sound, but nothing else comes.

Whatever Charlotte was doing, she stopped.

I hurry down the hall towards the nursery. Right before I step through the door, my phone rings. I fumble the phone and silence it, but don't answer.

The name on the screen is an accusation. I've dodged his calls since arriving here, but I can't talk to him right now. He'd ask too many questions. He'd push me until I cracked. He'd make me doubt myself—I know he would. No way can I talk to him right now. He'd want to know if I'm taking the pills he prescribed, but I won't. I'm not depressed.

I'm angry.

I slip my phone back into my pocket and enter the nursery. "Sorry, baby," I whisper, then turn on the overhead light. It's on a dimmer, and I turn it as low as possible while still making sure I can see my way around the space.

This feels right.

If something is hidden in this house, it's going to be in here. I just know it.

I tackle the nursery closet first, making sure to pull every piece of clothing out from the shelves to look behind them.

Nothing.

The bins of toys. The bookshelf. The bucket with diapers. Again and again I strike out, growing more and more frustrated all the time. Jordan starts fussing, and I stand up to put her pacifier back in her mouth.

My toe catches on the corner of the rug and I trip. It's only by catching the crib railing that I keep from falling completely over.

"Stupid trip hazard," I mutter, turning back to look at the rug. "Not at all safe with a baby in here." I slip the pacifier between Jordan's lips and turn back to look at the rug.

It's yellow and white, with flowers all over it and a fringed edge, the type of rug mothers buy for their nurseries when they don't think about keeping their child safe. A tired parent carrying a child could easily trip on this. And once a baby starts crawling, all of that fringe is going straight in their mouth.

She's so irresponsible.

Rage takes over, and I grab the rug, yanking it towards me and balling it up before tossing it in the corner of the room. I'm throwing it away. As soon as I go back downstairs, that stupid rug is going in the trash. It pisses me off that some people get to be parents when it's so painfully obvious that they're not ready.

And that they don't deserve it.

With that out of the way, I brush my hands on my jeans and turn back to Jordan, but something catches my eye.

I turn back slowly, my heart kicking into high gear.

"What in the world?" When I drop to my knees, I hit the floor hard, but I barely pay attention to the jolt of pain. I'm too busy staring at the small cut-out part of the plank of wood in front of me.

It looks like someone removed the top half an inch or so of the plank. The divot is about two inches long, and when I put my fingers in it, they fit perfectly.

It doesn't seem possible, but excitement makes my heart beat faster. I adjust my feet, leaning over the floor, then slowly pull back.

Nothing happens.

I wipe sweat off my forehead. Behind me, in her crib, Jordan starts to fuss again, but I ignore her. She's fine. She's safe. She might not like being left alone in her crib right now when she wants attention, but nothing is going to happen to her.

"I'm right here, Jordan," I mutter, then yank back harder on the plank.

My shoulders scream. They feel like they're going to separate at the joint, and I grit my teeth, pulling up harder, harder. For a moment, there's nothing, then I hear the high squeak of wood on wood and the entire thing shifts.

I brace myself on one hand and keep pulling with the other

until the plank is free. It's only raised a few inches now, and I yank it up, revealing a hole below the floorboards.

It's not big. At around six by eight inches, there certainly isn't enough room to hide something very large in the hole, but it's big enough to stash small items and keep them out of view.

I was right. Charlotte did have somewhere she hid things from Lawrence.

Jordan keeps crying.

Keeping my eye on the hole in the floor, I stand, then hurry to her side and grab her pacifier. It didn't work to calm her down for very long last time I used it, but I have to hope it will work a little bit longer now.

At least Charlotte is so out of it she's not likely to hear Jordan crying. I need time to look through what's stashed in the hole without her peering over my shoulder.

Jordan takes the pacifier, and I say a little prayer of thanks before kneeling over the hole again. This time, I pull out my phone and turn on the flashlight so I can get a better look inside.

I hold my breath as I angle the light into the hole, then slowly exhale as I see what's inside.

Papers. Lots of papers.

Without any time to waste, I reach in and grab them. It's a mix of different kinds of papers. Sticky notes, notecards, pieces of ruled writing paper.

And photos.

My eyes grow wide as I look at the photos. I'd been so frustrated that I couldn't find maternity photos of Charlotte when she was pregnant with Jordan. It's a judgmental thing to think, but she really struck me as the type of woman who would want everyone to see her belly.

She'd want them to comment on it and tell her how amazing she looked.

She'd even want them to touch it—I know she would.

Gross.

I flip through the photos, drinking her in. She looks amazing in all of them. Her hair is thick and shiny, which so often happens to pregnant woman. Her skin is clear, and her belly is basically flat. Whatever tiny little bump she has, she shows off by pressing her hand against it.

If someone had bothered to take professional shots of her, I have no doubt she could be on the cover of a magazine. But there's something about the pictures that feels off.

What is it?

"You got the baby you wanted," I mutter, flipping faster through the photos. "What more could you have asked for?"

I don't slow down until I've looked at every single photo. There's two dozen or so of them, and once I'm finished, I start back through them again, going slower this time.

One at a time, I look at a photo.

Move on to the next one.

"Pregnancy hormones were good to you," I tell her, flicking her face on the photo I'm currently looking at. "So many people age during pregnancy, but you look so young."

I freeze when I realize what I just said.

FIFTY-ONE

Sophie

I hold one of the photos I found in the nursery's floor up next to Charlotte to compare. She's passed out on the sofa again, her phone lying broken on the floor—she must've tried to access it and discovered the security settings had changed.

The woman sitting in front of me looks a lot older than the one in the photo, but is that really a surprise? She just lost the man she loved and has a baby she's taking care of on her own.

It stands to reason she'd have more lines on her face. That she would look more drawn, that there would be dark circles around her eyes. I'm ignoring how she looks from the accident. The bruising. The puffiness. But is being tired enough of an explanation for how different she looks from the photos I found under the floor in Jordan's nursery?

That's not even scratching the surface of *why* the photos were there. What purpose do they have being hidden out of the way where nobody can see them? Photos like this are supposed to be enjoyed. Shared.

I flip the photo around and look for a date on the back, but there's nothing there.

Because she's a liar, through and through. She wasn't pregnant with Jordan in these photos. She's done... something to get her hands on my baby.

My mind drifts back to the photoshopped birth certificate.

You don't change a birth certificate like that unless there's a really good reason.

Like the fact that you stole a child and need to pretend that they're yours.

Lawrence famously didn't want children. I should know.

But if he gave her my baby? Why would he do that? Why, when he didn't want kids, would he choose to give Charlotte my baby? That's the part of this that doesn't make sense, and if I figure out that piece of the puzzle, everything else will fall into place.

Did he think she'd be a better mother than me?

The thought is more painful than I ever could have imagined, and I refuse to focus on it. Or did he love her more than me, and so he agreed for her to have the one thing I was never allowed.

The thought twists my heart. Him cheating on me was one thing. I hated it, but I was able to survive it because I still got to enjoy Lawrence when he was home. But then he went and married Charlotte.

And he gave her a baby.

What's so special about her that she got the life I wanted?

"Don't get maudlin," I mutter to myself.

The longer I'm here, the more confused I become about what was going on in this house.

Nobody ever would have thought that Charlotte was a perfect mother. She not only needs help around the house and with the baby, but also probably a mental health counselor. It's clear she's not handling things well.

I should leave. Take Jordan and run.

But until I know exactly what Charlotte has been up to, until I know Lawrence's role in all of this, I don't think I have a choice but to stay.

I need more information than what I have, and the only way to get it is to keep poking around, keep looking. Keep Charlotte drugged and out of the way because no way do I think she'd tell me the truth about what happened with her and Lawrence and Jordan. Without hesitation, I hurry back up to the nursery and drop to my knees.

My hand dips into the hole in the floor, and I pull out more papers. It doesn't feel like I have a lot of time before either Jordan needs me or Sophie wakes up, but I'm not finished here. I shove the photos back where they belong and focus on the papers.

My hand shakes as I open the first piece of folded paper. It's a copy of a birth certificate—Jordan's fake one. I fold it back up and replace it in the hole. There's a handful of sticky notes that have lost most of their stickiness. Whatever was written on them in pen is so smudged that there isn't a chance in hell I could ever make it out.

The next thing is an index card with a woman's name and phone number written on it. Without realizing what I'm doing, I pull my phone from my pocket and thumb it on, then I stop myself.

I don't know who this person is or why Charlotte has their information. The absolute last thing I need to do is go in, guns blazing, and reach out to someone who has no idea that I even exist.

Besides what would I say? *I found your phone number in a hole in the floor in Charlotte's house? Why do you think that is?*

I turn my phone over and over in my hand.

Yeah, right.

I scoff, then unfold the last bit of paper from the hole. This is a newspaper clipping, so I doubt it's important to my search, but I raise my eyebrows as I carefully unfold it and see that I was halfway right. It's not just a newspaper clipping. It's an obituary from five years ago.

The man looking at me from the page is a stranger but familiar in a way. He has dark eyebrows and thick hair. He's staring at the camera with a bit of a smirk, which only makes him that much more attractive.

I might not have seen him before, but I can't help but draw a comparison to someone else both Charlotte and I knew.

Lawrence. The man isn't a dead ringer for him by any means, but he definitely has the same look going on that Lawrence did. If someone were to tell me that he and Lawrence were long-lost cousins, I honestly wouldn't have been surprised.

It's not just the fact that they have the same coloring. It's the expression on their faces, how they both hold their jaw, the way they both look like they're barely containing a laugh.

Interesting.

I take a deep breath and force myself to read the obit.

Halfway through, I have to stop.

I had fears over what I was going to find in the obit. Worries that things were more convoluted than I'd imagined.

But what I just read is much, much more concerning.

FIFTY-TWO

James Peters

James Conrad Peters, 39, went to be with the Lord on Sunday, June 27, 2020, at his home. A lifelong resident of Black River, North Carolina, he was the son of the late Anna Kay Peters and Peter Nathaniel Peters.

Born March 4, 1981, James loved his childhood in Black River. Growing up, he spent most of his spare time outside with friends, fishing and playing in the creek. As a teenager, he happily started working at the family pharmacy, sweeping, cleaning up aisles, and taking out the trash.

James graduated from Black River High School in 1999. After graduation, he continued his education at the University of North Carolina at Chapel Hill where he graduated with a degree in pre-pharmacy and then as a Doctor of Pharmacy. After finishing pharmacy school, he completed a two-year pharmacy residency.

Following his residency, James moved to Michigan for a few years before returning to North Carolina, having declared Michigan too cold. It was in North Carolina that he met his wife, Charlotte, and the entire trajectory of his life changed.

James loved spending time with his wife. He was a devoted husband who would have made a wonderful father. Not only was he willing to go above and beyond the call of duty for Charlotte but also for all of their friends. He was the person you called when you got a flat at 2 a.m. Not only would he come to help you change your tire, but he'd bring hot coffee for you to enjoy while he worked.

He was preceded in death by his parents, Peter Nathaniel Peters and Anna Kay Peters, as well as his in-laws, Mitchell and Diane Taylor.

Surviving James is his loving wife of five years, Charlotte Taylor Peters.

FIFTY-THREE

I drum my fingers on the steering wheel and stare up at the imposing brick building in front of me. Three stories tall, with window boxes on every floor, it looks like something out of a storybook, some magical school for kids who can move things with their minds.

My watch beeps, and I reach down to turn it off without looking at the face. That's my ten-minute warning, which means I need to get going if I'm going to make it to my appointment on time.

But I still don't move.

Getting out of the car feels like a Herculean task. I pat my pockets to double-check that I have my phone, wallet, and keys. They're all there, so really I don't have an excuse to sit here any longer.

I just don't want to go in.

My watch beeps again.

Eight minutes.

I move stiffly as I get out of the car and carefully close the door behind me. My eyes drift up the building to the top floor. That's where I'm headed. I'd know for sure exactly what window I'll be staring out of if I'd come to my appointment last week like I was supposed to, but I couldn't do it.

I'd canceled at the last minute, but Lawrence told me that wasn't a choice.

I had to go to therapy to deal with what happened.

No, to *get over* what happened, according to him.

But do you ever get over losing a child? I don't think that's possible. For just a moment, my heart had been outside of my body. My baby was a gift, something I had hoped and dreamed for, and all I was supposed to do was protect them.

Him. Her. I don't know... nobody will tell me anything.

I gave birth. There was no cry.

My baby was taken from me two days ago. Of course I'm not going to be fine.

Rolling my shoulders back, I force myself to the front steps. The handrail is cool under my touch, and it almost feels like it grounds me. For a moment, I'm confident, sure that I can do this, but as soon as I step inside, my confidence disappears.

There's an elevator, and I press the button for the third floor. It's smooth and starts off without a lurch, depositing me neatly at my destination much sooner than I would have liked.

My watch beeps again.

Four minutes.

By the time I walk to the door at the end of the hall, I feel like I'm melting. I stare at my therapist's name on the plaque and shimmy off my coat. Sweat pours down my back and beads on my forehead. Is it hot in here? Or am I just that nervous?

"Mrs. Moore?" The receptionist perks right up when I walk in. She swiftly moves a paper over what she was working on but not before I can tell it's a book of Sudoku puzzles. I used to love those, used to love how orderly it felt putting numbers in little boxes, but now it feels foolish to sit and waste my time on them.

"Yes. Hi. I'm here to see..." My voice trails off. There's a photo on her desk turned just to where I can see it. She must clock the expression on my face because she grabs the frame and turns it a bit so I can't see what's inside.

A baby. A sweet little baby wrapped in a yellow blanket.

My heart clenches.

The door behind her desk opens.

"Mrs. Moore," my therapist says. He steps out into the reception and gives me a huge smile.

Tall. Gangly. His arms are a bit too long for his body. His hair is sparse, and he has a gut. I take in his broken nose and the fact that he has a unibrow and give a little nod.

He looks exactly like the picture on his website, and for that I'm grateful. I didn't want to talk to someone pretty, didn't want to talk to anyone who had their life together. I wanted to work with someone who had dealt with pain like I have.

"Coffee? Water?" the receptionist asks as I walk past her to the office. I shake my head but don't look in her direction. Sure, she'll probably think I'm rude, but I can't see the photo of that baby again.

"I'm glad you came," my therapist tells me. While he speaks, he gestures for me to sit on a sofa, then settles himself in a chair across from me. There's a large wooden desk on the far wall of the room, and I feel a flash of gratitude that he didn't choose to sit there. "On the online form you filled out, you said that you experienced a loss and were struggling to get back to normal activities. Why don't you tell me what's been going on?"

I swallow hard, but my spit feels thick. Is it too late to ask for a water?

"I was pregnant," I finally say. "But I lost the baby."

He nods. There's an open notebook on his lap, but he

doesn't look at it or take notes. "That's horrible. When was that?"

I swallow hard because I'm not sure if I can tell him the truth. Instead of telling him that my stomach is still swollen but empty, that my breasts leak, that my arms ache for the child I had two days ago, I lie. "It's been a month."

"I'm sorry for your loss." He pauses, letting his words weigh down on me. They feel like they're pressing me into the sofa, they're so heavy. "Losing a pregnancy is a terrible thing, and many women—"

"I wasn't pregnant," I interrupt.

His eyebrows fly up. "You weren't?"

"No." I shake my head, trying to gather my thoughts. "I mean, I was pregnant obviously, or I wouldn't have had a baby to lose. But I wasn't pregnant when I lost my baby. I gave birth and then..."

When he speaks, his voice is kind. His compassion makes me feel like I'm going to cry. "Stillbirth?"

Not exactly. But I nod anyway.

"Yes. A stillbirth," I lie.

Stillbirths are acceptable. People understand them. They're terrible and shouldn't ever happen, but women all over the world experience them every year, so we know how to handle them.

We grieve. We compartmentalize. We support and bring casseroles, and talk about how this wasn't supposed to happen. Women are taken care of, they're loved and protected, and then when they're ready, they get to try again.

A stillbirth implies so much. That a baby is mourned. That they're supposed to be here and aren't. That a family is incomplete.

That the parents will try again.

"After a stillbirth, it's perfectly normal to feel—" he begins, but I tune him out.

It doesn't matter how I should feel, or what's normal, or what happens after you lose a baby during birth because that's not what happened, but I can't ever tell him the truth.

I didn't lose a baby.

My husband took my baby from me.

FIFTY-FOUR

Sophie

The fact that Charlotte's first husband died is eye-opening. I sit across from her, Jordan in my lap, watching for any sign that she's going to wake up soon.

Right now, while she's still passed out, is the perfect opportunity for me to get to really study her.

I want to see what it is that made Lawrence fall in love with her. Since coming here, I'd been questioning what it was about her that convinced him to have a baby with her. But now I know the truth. My question has changed: why would Lawrence take my baby and give it to her?

I look down at my lap. Jordan's sucking a bottle hard, her cheeks working hard at the nipple.

My eyes drift back to the woman sitting across from me. Well, *sitting* isn't the right word. She's slumped back, her neck at an uncomfortable angle, her legs splayed out in front of her.

There's a soft rattle as she breathes. While I don't know for sure, I don't think it's concerning. She's not going to die, not from this anyway, but it's a bit unnerving.

I almost get up to make sure she's okay, but then I settle back down. What if she were to die right now? No, I wouldn't get all the answers I wanted from her, but I wouldn't have to listen to her lies any longer.

I take in her broken arm, the bruising on her face. Honestly, I'm surprised she walked away from the accident. The doctor said it looked like she threw her arm up to protect herself at the last second, almost like her body knew what was going on even though she was very clearly out of it with a migraine.

Then, when the air bag went off, it slammed her hand back into her face. She broke her wrist, a bone in her hand, and her arm. It was a miracle she didn't crack her cheekbone, according to the doctor, but the bruising there is so intense that her face is puffy.

It's gotten worse since bringing her home. I should make her an ice pack. I could sit next to her, still with the baby on my lap, and hold an ice pack on her face.

She'd appreciate it, and if I worried about what she thought about me, I might do it.

But I don't care. The only thing that matters to me right now is figuring out the truth of what's going on here. I'm not sure how I'm going to do it, but at least I have more information than I did a minute ago.

Leaning my head back, I exhale hard and think through all the facts I've learned since getting here.

Fact one: Charlotte has been lying about her baby being hers.

Fact two: She was married before, and her husband is dead.

Face three: Lawrence is also dead.

Did she kill both of her husbands? And why kill Lawrence when he gave her my baby? It doesn't make sense.

I take a deep breath and try to reconcile facts two and three. The obituary didn't say how James died, just that he did. To die at thirty-nine is a shock for pretty much anyone.

"Unless he had cancer," I mutter, shifting the bundle on my lap so I can pull my phone from my pocket. "Or maybe there was an accident." Information like that doesn't always make the obituary. It's too dark, and families generally like to keep the sordid details out of the press.

Still, there might be something online. A family member or friend could have posted information on social media. I'm always amazed at the amount of personal information people are willing to share online.

Not me. That's the main reason I don't have any social media accounts.

Well, not any tied to my real name.

"James Peters obituary North Carolina," I mutter, my thumbs flying over my phone's keyboard. It's difficult to type without rocking the baby around too much in my arms, but I hit enter and wait for the results to load.

The first result is his obit in the local paper. The second is his obit from the funeral home. The third is on Facebook, posted by the local paper.

"Come on," I mutter, my thumb flicking up to go deeper into the search results. "There has to be something here."

The second page of results is where all hope goes to die. Everyone knows that there's never any good results on the second page, so I'm loath to click for more. I get lucky, though, since the last result on the first page is a Facebook post from someone with the last name Peters.

They must be a distant relative since they weren't mentioned in the obituary. After a moment, Isa Peters' post pops up on my screen.

She's cute, with a perky little nose and a smattering of freckles. A quick glance at her birthday tells me she was born about ten years after him.

A younger cousin perhaps?

In the end, it doesn't matter who the woman is, just that she might have more insight into what happened to James.

"Okay, Isa," I say, snuggling the baby closer to me as I sit back in the chair, "what do you have to say about the dead husband?"

We lost James last week. He was always so fun when our family would get together for dinner. He made me laugh and didn't care that I'm so much younger than him.

I'll never not miss him. James was like the big brother I never had. I know I won't ever see him again, and that kills me. But no matter what people say, I don't think he took his own life.

He wouldn't do that. He had too much to live for. James loved his life. He was into mountain biking, and his wife told me they were talking about starting a family.

That's it. That's the entire post. I click into the comments, but they're all people reaching out to tell her how sorry they are about James. I was hopeful, but there's nothing here that's helpful.

I take a deep breath and look back at Charlotte. She's in the same position she was in when I first sat down, and I almost feel guilty for the amount of meds I gave her. Who knows how long she'll be out?

But that's the least of my worries. So what if she sleeps the day away? Besides, she told the doctor the reason she was in an accident in the first place was because she had a migraine coming on and had lost control of her vehicle.

So, really, letting her sleep all afternoon is my gift to her.

I stand and stretch, shifting the baby in my arms as I do before slipping my phone back into my pocket. My mind is starting to race as I put things together.

Charlotte's first husband died, and it was apparently ruled a suicide. Now Lawrence is dead. Not that I know how he died, just that it was a medical problem, but it's obvious the police didn't think Charlotte had anything to do with it or she wouldn't be here right now. She'd be in jail.

I stare at her, trying to figure her out. Trying to decide what to do. My mind is racing, which makes it hard for me to focus, but there are a few questions that keep coming to the surface.

Isa didn't think James committed suicide. What if I'm right —that Charlotte had something to do with his death?

And, by proxy, what are the chances she had something to do with Lawrence's death? Is it possible she's the reason he's gone? How many men has she killed?

The more I consider it, the more possible it seems. I'm not ready to call the police and tell them that she murdered Lawrence, but what if she did? I think back to when I first got here and found the insulin in the refrigerator.

Lawrence didn't need insulin. He never did. She'd laughed and acted like she'd know better than me; of course the woman he loved would know better than his sister.

I don't disagree with that.

But what if the woman he loved wanted to kill him?

What then?

FIFTY-FIVE

Charlotte

The house is quiet when I wake up, but when I hold my breath and listen, I hear noise from the kitchen.

Relief washes over me when I realize Sophie is still in the house. Yes, I want her gone; I'd do anything to get her to leave, but as long as she's here, Jordan is still here.

It hurts to move, but I force myself to the edge of the sofa. A moment later and I'm on my feet, swaying and leaning forward to brace myself on the coffee table. It won't be easy making my way into the kitchen, but as much as I'd like to go to Jordan's nursery to check on her, there's no way I could navigate the stairs safely.

I'm dizzy, and my stomach aches. What I need is something to eat so I can think clearly again.

My mouth is dry, my skin feels tight. I'm dehydrated, and I know what happens when dehydration kicks in.

Migraines.

Before I can make my way to the kitchen, my knees give out and I sink back to the sofa.

Weak. Stupid. I can't even help my baby—except I did, didn't I? I took her in when Lawrence said she couldn't be with her mother.

"Sophie," I call, then wait. Knowing this woman, she's going to take her time coming to me. She's not going to rush to my side to help.

While I wait for her to join me in the living room, I look around for anything that could be used as a weapon. There are framed pictures across the room, and I could always break the glass in one and try to—

"You're awake." Sophie walks out of the kitchen carrying a mug of tea. She watches me over the rim as she blows on the liquid to cool it, and then takes a careful sip.

I have to try to remain calm. This woman is dangerous, and Jordan is currently strapped to her chest in an Ergobaby carrier. She wants my daughter—I know she does. That much has been clear from the first time she held Jordan. But why hasn't she taken her and run?

I nod but don't look away from her. "How long have I been out?"

"Hours." Another sip of tea.

My mouth hurts, it's so dry. I'd kill for the liquid in that mug, but I refuse to ask her for anything. Instead, I make to stand, but she appears in front of me, blocking me.

"No, no, sit back down. I don't want you to worry about a thing. The doctor called and wanted to make sure I knew to keep you on the first floor. You should be sitting as much as possible."

She's lying. But I'm afraid to let her know that I know the truth.

"The first floor?"

"So you don't fall in the middle of the night. The meds you're on are disorienting, as you can tell."

My mind races. She's too close. And she's watching me like

a hawk, making it impossible for me to think. "But I have to pee."

"By all means," she says, swinging her arm to the side and finally taking a step back. "Don't let me stop you. And then there are some questions I want to ask you."

I move slowly and take stock of my body as I do. As I walk down the hall, I can feel her eyes on me, so I take my time. I reach out and trail my fingers along the wall. Yes, I'm struggling, but I need her to think that I'm doing worse than I really am.

In the bathroom, I pee, then drink three glasses of water. When I splash cool water on my face, I inhale sharply. Every movement hurts, but there's one more thing I have to do. For Jordan. It takes me a minute to make my way into Lawrence's office, and the entire time I'm terrified Sophie is going to see me.

"Okay," I say when I've made my way back into the living room, "what did you want to ask me?" My heart hammers in my chest, both from the exertion of walking around and from nerves.

"Took you long enough," she scoffs.

When I don't rise to the bait, she continues. "You kicked me out. But I'd wager you need me more than you hate me."

"I can do this on my own."

"Really?" She laughs, and I wince. "You think you can take care of your baby with one arm? You can change her? Carry her up and down the stairs? You really believe you won't drop her? Hurt her?" A pause. "Possibly kill her?"

Anger flares in me, but I keep it hidden. "I wouldn't hurt her. I'd die before I let anything happen to her."

"Would you kill for her?"

The question hangs in the air between us.

"Every mother would kill for their child."

"Have you?"

"What the hell are you talking about?" I've been playing

defense this entire conversation, and I don't like it. "Are you asking me if I murdered someone?"

In response, she grins, and my stomach drops. It takes all my self-control to hide the impact she has on me.

"You're disgusting." It hurts, but I force myself to my feet. The water I drank helped, but I still need food. "You hear me? Sick. I kicked you out once, and I don't know how the hell you made your way back in here, but get out."

She doesn't move from her spot in the easy chair.

"Get out!" I scream at her. It feels good, to let out my rage, but Sophie doesn't react.

"Sit down before you hurt yourself."

I do. Only partly because I need to. But also because she has to see me as weak.

"I found your little cache of secret photos and notes in Jordan's nursery."

What? How?

My heart beats faster.

"And it's the weirdest thing," she says. "But when I looked through your phone—"

"And changed my PIN." My voice is flat.

She shrugs. "When I looked through your phone, I didn't see any pregnancy photos from the past year. It's like you weren't pregnant, but wouldn't that be weird? How would that be possible?"

I won't answer that.

"You and I know the kind of woman who loves to show off her baby bump. She pretty much shoves it in everyone's face, no matter what they're doing. Isn't that the point of social media? And let's be honest, Charlotte—you're the type of woman to make you being pregnant everyone else's problem, even if they didn't give a shit."

She waves her hand in the air. Her eyes are wide, her cheeks flushed.

This isn't just her being angry at me. This is personal.

"And another thing about the photos I found. You looked really, really young in them. Now, I know having a kid ages you, and you really don't look that great right now, but it's like night and day."

I refuse to respond to her.

"So tell me, Charlotte, the baby you were pregnant with in those photos... it wasn't Jordan, was it? She's not yours. You were pregnant a while ago, but it was another baby."

My mind races as I try to think this through, try to stay one step ahead of her.

"You were married to James when you were pregnant," she says. "Where's the baby, Charlotte? What did you do with it?" She pauses, then leans forward, resting her elbows on her knees. "Did he make you give it up?"

FIFTY-SIX

Her

It's been three days since Lawrence took my baby from me.

I'm by the living-room window, which is where I've been since I got up this morning. It's the same place I was yesterday, even when he came home from work. My husband and I don't speak, not when there isn't anything for me to say to him. My mind is on overdrive as I try to sort through what I did.

As I try to forgive myself.

I don't know the town my baby is in. It wouldn't have been smart for him to tell me because we both know what I would have done. Gone looking. Not stopped until I'd seen every baby in town, until I'd looked at every new mother, until I'd found her.

And even though there's no way for me to find her now, I can't help the desperation that grows in me the longer we're apart.

I made a mistake.

That thought won't do me any good, and it certainly won't undo what's been done, but it's on repeat in my head.

I tell myself I didn't have a choice, that it was my marriage or my child. However, part of me can't help but feel like I took the easy way out.

I stand, staring down at my empty wine glass. There's an indent in the sofa cushion from where I've sat by the window for hours today. My mouth is dry, fuzzy, and my head hurts, but I grab my wine glass to refill it.

In the kitchen, I stop and stare at the microwave clock—it's 2:48 in the afternoon. I blink at it, willing the numbers to make sense, because no way have I been sitting there not only all morning but half of the afternoon.

The numbers don't change.

Heaving a sigh, I put the wine glass on the counter. Grab the wine from the fridge. Refill it.

My phone pings as I'm drinking the last sip of wine straight from the bottle, and I pause, then drop the bottle into the recycling. The clatter is loud, and I wince.

My phone.

When I grab it, I pick it up upside down, and I have to focus to shift it around in my hand. Finally, I tap on the screen, thankful I set up a fingerprint so I don't have to worry about typing in my password just to check my message from a friend.

Just checking in. How are you? The flu really knocked you out, huh?

The flu, huh? That's the story he's told everyone?

I'm miserable, but I don't want to admit that. If I tell anyone that I'm struggling as much as I am, then they'll want to come check on me. Or it will turn into this whole thing where they tell me that I made the right decision, that there wasn't any other option, that not everyone gets to be a mother.

I'm great.

Lying through text is so easy, isn't it? There's no way for anyone to call you on your lie. No inflection, no pausing between words. No tears. My friend can't tell that I've been drinking since the sun came up. She can't tell that the only reason I can't cry right now is because I'm too dehydrated.

Need anything?

I stare at the text. I need a lot of things, but I can't tell her that. The best thing to do is stay home and deal with this myself. If anyone knew how badly I'm taking this, they'd be worried.

No thanks. I'm feeling better every day. :)

A wave of guilt hits me as I send the text. I hate lying to the people who care about me, but it's really the only option I feel like I have right now. What am I going to do, tell them the truth?

Tell them I had a perfectly healthy little baby and Lawrence took them from me? Admit that I don't even know if I had a son or a daughter? No. I can't do that.

And then the text comes through that tears me apart.

Luckily you have Lawrence. He'll take care of you while you're sick.

The words blur before my eyes. I can't look away from my phone screen as I reach out for my glass of wine.

Instead of grabbing it, I hit it with the side of my hand.

"Shit." I slip my phone into my pocket and lunge for the towel crumpled by the sink. It's crusty and hard, but I smack it down in the center of the spill and start wiping. The entire time, my mind is on overdrive.

Luckily you have Lawrence.

Luckily you have Lawrence.
Lawrence.
Lawrence.
Lawrence took my baby from me. I'll do anything to get them back.

FIFTY-SEVEN

Sophie

"I never meant to get pregnant." She lifts her jaw and stares at me, obviously daring me to push for more.

Triumph washes over me. "What happened to the baby, Charlotte? Your husband died and there wasn't any mention of the baby in his obit. What the hell did you do?" My heart pounds hard. Right here, this is the precipice of where everything either makes sense or falls apart.

I just need Charlotte to answer me, to clear a few things up, and then I can finally have peace.

She's crying now, and she reaches up to press a hand into her mouth, as if that's going to be enough to stop her from telling the truth. No matter how many lies I have to sort through, I'm not walking away from this conversation until I know exactly what happened.

"James never wanted to be a father," she says, and even though I feel a little tugging on my heartstrings, I do my best to ignore it. "He thought he wouldn't be good at it. His parents weren't involved. They treated him like crap, and he didn't want to continue the cycle. He thought that he'd screw every-thing up. I told him he'd be great at it, but he refused, even though all I've ever wanted was a baby. That was it! A baby. Just one. I could be happy with one, I know I could, but he wouldn't even give me that. And then I got pregnant."

I know what it's like to be married to a man who promises you the world and then balks when you tell him the one thing you really want out of life. I know that sinking feeling every single month when you get your period.

I know what it's like to sit on the floor of the bathroom and cry. And how terrible it feels to not be able to go to your spouse, the person who promised to love you in sickness and in health, because they don't care that you're not pregnant. In fact, they're *happy* that you're not pregnant, and you better not *try* to get pregnant without them knowing because that will destroy everything the two of you have built together.

Although... is it really worth having something that seems so wonderful when there's that lie between the two of you? When you want something bad enough to give up all good things in your life just to taste it for a moment, and he's willing to clip your wings so you can never fly?

How can that be worth it? How can *life* be worth it?

She's still talking, and I snap back to the present, pushing aside all the frustration I felt over never being allowed to have a child.

"—and after that, everything fell apart."

"How so?"

She shifts a little like she can't get comfortable, which I'm sure she can't, not when she was so banged up in the accident. Her mouth twists into a grimace, but she quickly relaxes her muscles, almost as if she doesn't want me to see she's in pain and offer her more meds.

"James was thrilled we weren't going to be parents and was unwilling to try again. But I fell apart. Do you know what it's like to finally get the thing you've wanted more than anything, only to have it ripped away from you?" Her face contorts, and she takes a deep breath. "Everyone worries about the mother's mental health. Nobody thinks twice about the father."

"He killed himself."

She inclines her head to me.

"Why would he do that if he were happy about not being a father?"

She doesn't respond, and I continue. "Isa doesn't think he did."

"Isa." There's a flash of emotion on her face before the mask slips back into place. "Isa thought James walked on water."

"And you didn't?"

"He had his moments. I loved him, don't get me wrong. But he could be very demanding. And when he didn't think things were going his way, he'd get mad."

"He hit you."

She's shaking her head before I finish speaking. "No, he never hit me. He wouldn't dare—I really don't think he would. But he could be manipulating and controlling in other ways. You know how men can get."

I do. Nobody wants to think they're in a bad relationship, especially when they love their spouse so much, but I do know how men can get. I know I have a tendency to put Lawrence on a pedestal even though he doesn't really deserve to be up there.

I know he wasn't perfect. I know he was controlling. He liked things to be perfect—that's part of what made him so dang good at his job. But it was his drive for perfection that could drive me nuts.

Still, I never once regretted marrying him. I told myself that having part of Lawrence was better than not having any of him. I didn't want to share him, but if that's what it took to keep him, I was willing to do that.

Charlotte will never know this, but she's just the most

recent of Lawrence's dalliances. Honestly, though, I never expected him to stick with one woman as long as he's stuck with her.

I close my eyes, trying to block the memory of that conversation I had with him, the one where he told me that *he had needs* and *I couldn't meet them.* The one where he decided that he could sleep around with other women as long as it never became serious.

I was fine with it, or I said that I was. It was all supposed to be short-term, nothing that really meant anything, nothing that would take him away from me longer than he was going to be gone for work trips.

But do you know what's not short-term?

Giving someone your child.

Lawrence promised me the women he slept with wouldn't ever take away from our relationship. He swore up and down that he had needs I couldn't fill, that some men needed more than others, that it wasn't fair of him to expect me to provide everything to him. When he was home, he was by my side, the model of the perfect husband. But when he was "traveling", he was with others. Mostly, he was with her.

"What was your baby's name?" I pull my phone from my pocket and thumb it on. *Obsessed* doesn't begin to explain how I feel right now. She has answers, and I want them. I know this has nothing to do with Jordan, but I can't help but push.

"I don't want to talk to you about this."

Ignoring her, I navigate to Isa's Facebook. Surely, since she was close enough with James to make a post about missing him, she would have made a post about him losing a baby.

Only, no matter how far back I scroll, there's nothing. Charlotte's lying. She has to be.

But why?

"What are you doing?" There's an edge to Charlotte's words, but I ignore her. "Tell me what you're doing."

Maybe in her photos? I click into Isa's albums and start looking for any photos of her with James and Charlotte. It takes a minute to go back far enough, but there they are with Isa at their wedding.

Coming forward, there are a few pictures of the three of them and then... nothing.

The photos stop a solid year before James died.

I look up at Charlotte. She's moved to the edge of the sofa and is staring at me like she'll be able to read my mind.

"Sophie. What are you looking for?"

"Anything about your baby." I click off my phone and slip it into my pocket. "But there isn't anything, Charlotte. No birth announcements. No nothing." I pause and think. "You already knew that, didn't you? That's why you didn't mention the baby in his obit. Because there was no record of the baby."

She's shaking her head, but I'm on a roll.

"No record of the baby being born," I say. "No record of it dying. Did you have it at home? Did you give birth in the bathroom and lose the baby there? Why can't I find anything about the baby online?"

"Because the baby wasn't born. I've told you that! Aren't you listening? I lost my baby at five months, and he didn't want to be reminded of it, so we didn't write an obit! We hadn't even told family yet—he wanted it to be a surprise!" She flings the words at me, but when she speaks again, she's calmed down. "Jordan is a gift. A blessing. My second chance."

"Jordan isn't even your daughter," I tell her, and as the words leave my mouth, I feel with certainty how true they are.

She looks like I slapped her. "What are you talking about? You're insane, you know that? You can't just—"

"She's mine. I had her with Lawrence, but he took her from me. And I'm taking her back."

FIFTY-EIGHT

Charlotte

My brain shorts out at what Sophie just said. She's sitting across from me, so cocky, like she's the one in control, but she has no idea how far I'm willing to go to keep Jordan for myself. There's no way Jordan is hers. I can't... I just can't wrap my mind around the implications of that.

"I didn't take maternity pictures," I tell her slowly, trying to make her see reason, "but that doesn't mean I'm not Jordan's mom. She's mine. I had her."

Sophie smirks. "And the photoshopped birth certificate?"

Thank goodness I already took care of that. "You really made yourself at home, didn't you?" I spit the words at her. "What part of my house didn't you go poking through?"

She ignores my question. "You know, I was angry at first that Lawrence would have a baby with you and not me. That's why I came here in the first place: to find out more about you, the woman he married on the side, and why he'd give you a baby." She pauses like there's something else she wants to say but keeps it to herself, continuing before I can get my thoughts in order. "I married him first, you know. Your marriage isn't legal. No wonder you're not on any of his accounts. No wonder he didn't leave you anything."

What? No. Lawrence wouldn't. Right? "You're not his wife."

She smirks. "Sure am. Where do you think he got the baby he gave you? You think someone just gave Jordan to him? He took her from me to punish me for getting pregnant."

No. *No.* This can't be. He told me he had a baby for me but that I couldn't ask questions about where he got her. He told me I could have her but that in return I had to let him go, that we were through, that he was moving on. Bile rises in the back of my throat.

I can't tell her any of this. Surely I can talk my way out of it.

"Lawrence and I wanted to have a child—"

"Bullshit. Lawrence never wanted children. Ever."

She's right.

What's worse, if she's really married to him, she knows she's right, and that means she'll pick up on all my lies.

"Somehow, you got Lawrence to give you my baby. Did he do it to shut you up? Was he tired of your nagging? And let me guess—then you photoshopped her birth certificate to make sure she'd be accepted by Lawrence and your friends. Only he didn't want you *and* a baby, did he?"

I see the moment everything starts to make sense for her, but I don't respond.

My silence must piss her off because she continues. "So you stole my baby—"

"Lawrence gave her to me," I correct, doubling down on what I've already told her. "He wanted a baby; he—"

"He never wanted one! But he took my baby to punish me." Sophie's voice is strangled. Her face is pale. She reaches up and lightly touches her throat like she's choking, but then her hands fall uselessly back into her lap. "He took my baby from me and gave her to you. What was she, a consolation prize when he ended things with you?"

I don't respond. Where Lawrence got Jordan is none of my business. Yes, he showed up with her and gave her to me. And yes, I was overjoyed. Less so when he told me that he was going to leave me, that he wasn't ready to be a father but he knew I wanted a child.

Jordan was a parting gift from Lawrence to me to ensure I let him go quietly, but at this point I don't care about that. How the hell Sophie put two and two together is beyond me, but she must know Lawrence better than I thought.

None of that matters. Lawrence. Sophie. Who cares?

All I care about is making sure I don't lose my baby.

FIFTY-NINE

Sophie

She took my baby.

She killed my husband.

Charlotte deserves to die, but I have to come out on top, I have to be in control, and right now I don't feel like I am. She keeps knocking me off-balance. Her answers for every question I have are making it difficult for me to find my footing.

Do I believe her that Lawrence wanted a child?

No, I don't, no matter how adamant she is about that.

But then why would he give her my baby? How did she talk him into it? What's so special about this woman that Lawrence would choose her over me to raise his child?

How could one man be so cruel? My brain races, desperate for some answer that makes sense, desperate to latch on to anything that will hurt less than the truth in front of me. Lawrence took Jordan and gave her to Charlotte because he loved her more than me.

"Where do we go from here? Lawrence gave Jordan to me.

He clearly thought I'd be a better mother than you." Charlotte's words are crisp, no longer slurred.

The meds aren't leaving her in as much of a haze as I thought they would.

"She's my baby." I sound petulant, like a child, but I can't help it.

Lawrence stole my child from me. And then he died.

And now I'm all alone.

"So, what did you think? That you'd come here and take my child from me?"

"She's mine," I answer automatically.

"Nobody would believe you. Do you have medical records? Any pictures of you pregnant?"

"A DNA test would prove that she's mine." My heart beats faster as I stare at this woman. Maybe it was stupid to come here, but after Lawrence died, I knew I couldn't let it go.

I'm going to take my baby back, and nothing can stop me, even if I have to get rid of Charlotte first.

SIXTY

SEVEN WEEKS AGO

Her

Dinner is silent except for the sound of cutlery against the dishes. I don't have an appetite—*haven't* had an appetite in weeks—but nothing keeps Lawrence from diving into his dinner every night with gusto.

As I watch him eat, my stomach twists.

He sighs and puts his fork down before patting his stomach. It's still as flat as it was the day we got married, thanks to his commitment to the gym and his dietary restrictions.

No gluten but not because he's celiac; he just thinks it makes him bloat.

Meat once a week.

Fish three times a week.

The rest of the time we eat vegetarian. I keep suggesting that we hire a chef because meal prep is taking up so much of my day, but as often as I do, he reminds me that I'm not working right now.

And as long as I'm not bringing in money, I need to find some way to be useful.

"Besides making dinner, what did you accomplish today?" His gaze bores into me. "Did you reach out to any clients and let them know you were coming back to work soon?"

How does he always seem to know what I'm thinking?

I shake my head. "No, I thought that one more week might be enough time."

"Seriously? What is it that you do all day?"

I want to scream at him.

Instead, I swallow the scream. "Laundry. Meal prep. I took all the bottles and glasses out of the bar today and dusted everything. It was tedious."

"But not as high stakes as my job."

I don't rise to the bait. "Few things are," I say with a smile.

"Are you taking meds?" His words come without a smile, and I feel mine slide off my face.

No, I'm not taking any meds. Yes, my therapist prescribed them, but I took one and immediately felt better. That's the thing Lawrence doesn't get. I don't want to feel better. I want my baby back, and taking meds to make me forget how much pain I'm in won't help me bring my baby home.

"Of course I am. They just take a while to start working. And sometimes you have to mess with the dosage a little bit to ensure you got it right."

"Good. It's been long enough. You need to pull yourself together. The baby is gone."

"We could try again," I begin, but even as I speak, I know the words are stupid and are only going to get me in trouble. "Never mind. Forget what I was saying."

"You. Signed. A. Contract," he grits out. "Or do you not remember doing that? What happened was an accident, but I'm not going to let it happen again."

It's only now that I realize how still he's been. How he's barely walked around since he got home, and when he did walk, how mechanical his movements were.

"You got snipped."

"It's called a vasectomy," he snaps. "And of course I did. You clearly can't be trusted to be reliable with your birth control, so I took matters into my own hands. I didn't want to, you know that. It's not something a man is supposed to do! You think I wanted to do anything that would make me less of a man? It's the woman's job to worry about having or not having babies, but I had to clean up your mess. You were supposed to take your pill every single day to prove to me that you wanted this. That I could trust you."

I can't wrap my mind around what he's saying. It's so insane that it's difficult for me to believe he's serious. Instead, I focus on what really matters.

"Where's my baby, Lawrence?" My hands twist into a knot in my lap. It's the one question I've wanted to ask him but I've been too afraid. Now, though, it feels like there's no going back, like the two of us are at a precipice. We might as well jump.

"What did you ask me?" His voice is low. His eyes glitter with anger.

"My baby. Where is it? I want to know."

"The baby is dead. Gone. Consider it to be medical waste." His words are weapons, and he aims them at my heart. "As far as I'm concerned, darling wife, there is no baby. Never was a baby."

His phone beeps, and he scowls at the screen. For a moment, I want to ask him what's wrong, but the dark expression he wears scares me. Whoever just texted him really pissed him off.

"Please," I beg, even though he hates begging. "I want to go to a grave or—"

He pushes back from the table, his hand instinctively going to his crotch because of the pain. After he grabs his wine, he downs it, then slams the glass back into place.

"Where are you going?" I stand, dropping my napkin onto

my uneaten food. Just standing makes me dizzy, and I know I should eat something, but nothing tastes good right now. Food turns to glue in my mouth, rocks in my stomach. I can't think of a single meal that wouldn't make me sick.

"Out." My husband stares at me. His eyes flick down to my plate of untouched food, and he gives his head a little shake. "You know, if you're not going to eat your meal, you might as well not cook the extra food. It's a waste."

Heartless. He's heartless, but how didn't I ever see it before? What's so wrong with me, so fundamentally naive, that I never once noticed the truth about how he treated me, how he acted towards people when he wanted something?

"Out?" The word is loaded, but I keep my voice calm. Level.

"Yes, out. Because I'd rather be anywhere than here with you watching you sit there like a lump, refusing to eat your food. When's the last time you put on makeup? When's the last time you went to the gym? God, you look like shit, you know that? You promised me, when we got married, that you wouldn't let yourself go."

That's not the only thing I promised him, but I'm impressed with his self-control to not bring it up right now.

"I'm trying," I begin, but he's already walking away from the table.

I watch as he grabs his coat from the chair back he threw it over. Angrily, he yanks it on and zips it up before turning to look at me.

"Clean this up. I thought your therapist was supposed to help, but if they're not, then find another one. I can't live like this."

And that's it. That's the last thing my husband says to me before he goes *out.*

But he's not going to a bar. He's not going to crash on a friend's sofa after drinking too many beers and talking about

how much I've changed since I lost the baby. No, I know
Lawrence, and I know that there's only one place on his mind
right now.

Her house. That's where he's going—I guarantee it.

The one he keeps running back to. The one who would
replace me, I'm sure of it.

I hesitate, then make up my mind. I've known for a long
time now that he cheats and that he chose someone else as my
replacement well before I'm gone, but I've never followed him
to see exactly where he goes, where this other woman lives.

That changes tonight.

SIXTY-ONE

Charlotte

My body is screaming for me to sleep, but I'm not taking my eyes off Sophie until I know my baby is safe.

What if Jordan really is her biological daughter? I'd been so excited to have a baby that I never really considered where she was coming from. And then, when Lawrence told me I was finally going to be a mother, but I couldn't keep him as well, I'd snapped.

What? Like I was going to let him walk away from me? No way was I going to let him leave me. Not when there was the chance that one day he might come take my daughter from me. Not when he was so willing to discard me like an old toy he had no more use for.

He had to die, and he brought it on himself.

Just like James brought his death on himself. I wasn't going to stay married to someone who refused to try for another baby. James said losing our daughter broke him, but what about me? He didn't care that it almost destroyed me. Being divorced wasn't something I ever wanted, but being a widow? People don't judge you for that. They support you. They take care of you. So I killed him. Nobody understands how much I wanted a baby. The lengths I was willing to go to have one. Just like they don't judge you for being a single mom when your husband dies. And, until now, nobody has thought twice about both of my husbands dying.

I don't want to believe that she's telling me the truth about Jordan, but if she was really married to Lawrence and accidentally got pregnant... I guess there's a chance Jordan is hers.

But that doesn't matter because I'm not giving her back.

Sophie leans against the counter, her question pulling me out of my thoughts. "Explain why Lawrence would give you a baby when you and I both know he didn't want to be a dad."

"You don't understand," I begin, but she cuts me off.

"Stop it! No more lies. No more spinning the truth so you look good. Jordan is mine." Her eyes are wide with rage, and she stabs her fingers through the air at me. "Tell me why Lawrence gave her to you. How did you talk him into that?"

I can see her mind at work. She's thinking through this faster than I would have thought possible. And then what will I do? How will I keep Jordan for myself?

"I didn't talk him into anything," I grit out. "Lawrence showed up with a baby and gave her to me. He's the villain in your story, not me. I had nothing to do with him taking Jordan."

She barks out a laugh. "And you honestly think nobody would ever question you suddenly having a child? That they wouldn't ask for—"

"For what? A birth certificate?" I grin at her. "I have one, in case you forgot."

"You can't photoshop a birth certificate and think it will hold up in court." She spits the words at me.

"Sophie, I'm sorry, but I have no idea what you're talking about. You saw a—"

"You know exactly what I'm talking about. You photo-shopped her a birth certificate." Her cheeks are red with anger.

"Where?" My eyes are wide, my voice innocent. I know full well where she found it, but I want her off-balance. She has the upper hand right now since she wasn't in a car accident, but that doesn't mean I can't come out on top, and part of my plan involves pushing her as close to her breaking point as possible.

"Your computer."

"Lawrence's computer," I correct. "Why would he have something like that on his computer?"

"Because you made it." She takes a step closer to me, her hand resting lightly on the back of Jordan's head. I have to drag my eyes away from her touching my child.

She's dangerous. I had a bad feeling about her spending so much time with Jordan, but I ignored it, and now I have to figure out a way to deal with her.

"Show me." I turn and gesture for her to lead the way.

"I will." She sweeps past me, out of the kitchen and down the hall, taking my daughter—still strapped in the Ergo carrier—with her.

A moment later, I join Sophie in Lawrence's office. If she were to turn around, she'd see the smile playing on my lips, but no, she's too focused on what she thinks she's found.

"I saw the file," she says, opening Photoshop and going to the most recent projects.

It's not there.

I see the moment Sophie realizes her plan isn't working out the way she wants it to. She closes Photoshop and opens it again.

"Everything okay?"

"Shut up and let me look." Again, she tries to open the most recent files, but again, the birth certificate isn't there. "It was here—I swear it was here."

She clicks around faster, opening and closing Photoshop three times before I reach out and lightly put my hand on hers.

Maybe I can turn this around. Get Jordan away from her long enough so we can escape.

"Sophie," I say, "when's the last time you slept?"

"Last night," she croaks.

"I know you haven't been sleeping in your bed. It's as perfectly made as the day you arrived, so where have you been sleeping?"

She turns to look at me but doesn't respond.

"I bet it's on Jordan's floor. No wonder you're tired. And I know coming here has been really stressful. I know Lawrence... didn't always treat you the way you deserved to be treated, but you have to understand that I'm not the enemy. And although you came here with the best intentions, I think it's time for you to go. Leave my baby. Leave me alone."

She stiffens. Slowly, she turns, her eyes locked on mine. "Jordan isn't your baby. I made that clear."

"Oh come on, Sophie." My mind races as I think about how to get out of this. I have to play on her mind, have to get her off-balance.

Otherwise I might lose everything.

She clears her throat. "Jordan. Isn't. Your. Baby. You deleted the file. You had to."

"I've been passed out on the sofa," I say, but she shakes her head.

She doesn't realize that the one time I went to the bathroom, I snuck in here and deleted the file. No way will she find proof of it ever existing.

"No. I don't know how you did it, but you did something. And you... took her from me."

She pauses.

"Get out of my house." I draw myself up to my full height,

even though my bones scream for me to sit down. "Out. Leave us alone, Sophie. You're evil, and I want you out of here."

She stands up. Her chest is almost pressing into mine. I can feel her breath on my cheek.

"She needs her mother!" I scream the words at her, but she ignores me.

Fine. I'll get Jordan from her and flee this house. I don't know how I'll get my baby out of her baby carrier, but I have to—I have to save her. I'm not staying here a second longer with her. I'm not—

She grabs my bad arm, and I scream as she wrenches it back and to the side. As she twists, I feel my bones shift, my skin burn. I scream louder and try to turn to hit her with my good hand, but she moves faster than me, grabbing me around the neck with her other hand.

And then she squeezes.

Hard.

SIXTY-TWO

Sophie

Charlotte screams, the sound feral and bubbling, that of a wild animal caught in a trap, one willing to chew off its own leg to get the hell out of there, and I let go of her neck.

But I don't let go of her arm.

"Stop it!" I yank her back, my hand locked around her upper arm. She screams louder—*I must really be hurting her*—then her arm slips from my grasp.

She's not strong enough to pull away from me without help, and I take a step back as she falls to the ground. She tries to catch herself with her good hand, but the sick thud she makes when she lands makes my heart beat faster.

I didn't kill her, did I?

"Charlotte?" I kneel next to her. Now that she's no longer screaming, the hall is deathly silent. "Charlotte, you okay?" My hand is on her arm again and I grip it hard, then give her a little shake.

Nothing.

I think I killed her.

The thought hits me like a bullet, and I gasp.

I've never killed anyone before, never really thought seriously about wanting to do it, although the thought of killing Lawrence had crossed my mind. I'm not a murderer, not like Charlotte. She hurt Lawrence. She hurt James. She's evil and might not stop until she gets my daughter.

What do I do?

Sitting back on my heels, I try to get Charlotte a little room to breathe. Her neck is exposed, angry red marks there from where I squeezed and squeezed and squeezed until...

Until she died?

No. No way. I'm not that strong. I really don't believe I am. I'm that angry, and that protective, but I wouldn't actually kill someone, right?

Orange really isn't my color.

I push that thought from my mind and reach down, my hand trembling, to press my fingers into her neck. The skin is warm, and supple, and—

There.

A pulse. It's soft and a little fluttery, like a caged bird, but it's there, and I exhale hard before standing and wiping my hands on my jeans.

The right thing to do would be to call an ambulance. Charlotte needs professional care—I have no doubt that she does. I might have... broken something in her neck? Cut off too much oxygen?

I don't know.

I'm not a doctor.

"Oh shit." I stand up and put my hands on the back of my head. "Shit, shit, shit." I turn and walk down the hall, then back. Back and forth, my feet eating up the space, until Jordan starts to cry, the sound yanking me from my thoughts.

I leave Charlotte where she fell. What I will have to do is get down next to her and look at her face. I'll have to check and

see if she's breathing. Surely she is. Surely this was just an accident and she's going to sit up at any moment.

Point her finger at me.

Take Jordan back.

Maybe it would be better if she didn't sit up.

That thought runs through my head on repeat over and
over, the words mashing together, becoming a run-on sentence
that I can't ignore. I do my best, though, as I make a bottle for
Jordan.

I have to leave it on the counter to unhook the Ergo and lift
her out, and that's when I notice that she's wet and needs a
change. So stupid of Charlotte not to have any diapers down
here to make it easier to change her.

When she's mine, I'll have diapers all over the house if
that's what it takes. It's silly to have to go upstairs to change her
when she's wet here and now, but that's what I do.

I don't have any other choice. She needs me, now more than
ever. There's a small part of my brain screaming at me to hurry,
to take her and run, but I can't help but move slowly. I can't
help but take care of her.

I need to hurry. But Charlotte is hurt and out of the way,
and now I know for sure that this is my daughter, and I want to
spend time with her.

In her nursery, I let her hand close around my finger after I
get her onesie snapped back up. It's only when I think about
how much she looks like Lawrence that I snap back to reality.

"Now, what were we doing?" I pull her to my chest and cup
her bottom to support her. She was calm while I changed her,
but she starts crying again, and it hits me.

The bottle.

Back down the stairs, taking each step carefully. She's no
longer in the baby carrier, and I can only hold her with one arm
so I can grab the banister with my other hand. By the time we

get to the first floor, she's screaming, and I hurry into the kitchen and pop her bottle into her mouth.

"There you go," I coo, kissing her on the forehead while she eats. "That's better, isn't it? You were so hungry, my brave girl."

My brave girl.

Because she's mine. Always has been mine. And now I'm going to take her, and nobody will be able to stop me.

What I should do is go look at Charlotte and make sure she's... what? Do I want her to be okay? The alternative is terrible, but if she were dead, she couldn't stop me from taking Jordan.

Nobody could stop me.

I read the obit. Charlotte's parents are dead. Nobody will mourn her, and, more importantly, nobody will try to take Jordan from me.

I could take her. There's no reason to call the police. I have money. I'll take her and run, and by the time someone finds Charlotte, the two of us will be long gone. Besides, my blood runs through her veins, and I can prove she's mine.

My heart beats faster at the thought. My palms grow sweaty. It's not right to think that way, but the thought has been there since the moment I entered the house and saw her for the first time.

I could. I don't have to hire a lawyer and fight Charlotte for her. She'll make my life miserable. I have money, but until they can determine who she really belongs to, she'll go to foster care, and she doesn't deserve that.

Or I could just... take her. Especially if Charlotte's gone. If she's dead, she's... mine.

Resolve flows through me, and I hold her closer to me, like a football I'm afraid someone will knock free from my arms. Little Jordan here won't ever have to worry about whether or not someone loves her.

My mind is made up.

She finishes her bottle, and I toss it carelessly into the sink. Really, I don't need to pack anything. I could, of course. I could make her a little suitcase and then sweep her out of this life, but I have all the money in the world. There's no reason for me to waste any more time when I could just... take her.

Save her.

My stride is long. Confident. I hurry through to the foyer, Jordan still tucked close to my body as I think about what it will be like to finally have her back.

I'll make sure our lives are perfect.

Nobody will ever hurt her or take her from me again. I pause to drop a kiss on the top of her head and two things happen at once.

One: the doorbell rings.

And two: my eyes fall on the floor where I left Charlotte.

She's not there.

SIXTY-THREE

Her

Lawrence is an idiot if he really thinks I'm going to leave well enough alone.

In taking my child from me, he took everything from me. I don't even know if I had a son or a daughter since he won't talk to me about it. If I want answers, I'm not going to get them sitting at home.

I'm only going to get them by going out and getting them.

It's dark out, and while I normally don't like driving in the dark, I'm willing to tonight since it means I'll be able to follow Lawrence to her house.

I don't know who the other woman is, not yet. All I know is that she's taking over my life. I can't help but be a paranoid wife, just like all the other ones before me who check their husbands' collars for lipstick.

Only I don't draw the line there. I sniff his clothes, snuggling into him as soon as he comes home under the guise of missing him and wanting to be closer to him. But really I'm trying to see if he's got anyone else's perfume on him.

In the morning when he's in the shower, I sneak downstairs and into the garage. I feel insane getting in his car and looking for any sign of another woman. A whiff of perfume would do it, sure, but also a stray bobby pin. A dropped mascara. A tampon.

Anything could be something. Any long hair stuck to his seat, a forgotten lip balm where I usually sit. I've scoured every inch of his life looking for signs of who the other woman is, but I haven't found any.

Until now.

The house he pulls up to is fine, but it's much smaller than the one we live in. What pisses me off? It's only about half an hour from ours. Anger rips through me when I think about how easily he could stop over here on his way home after work. He could even swing by on his lunch break for a quickie.

Forcing myself to take deep breaths, I keep my eyes locked on him. He doesn't park in the garage but in the driveway, and I slow to a stop a few houses down and across the street.

It's a nice neighborhood although the houses aren't nearly as nice as ours. There aren't any streetlamps, which means I don't have to worry about someone seeing me sit in my car. As long as I'm still and quiet, I don't think anyone will notice me.

The light on the front porch of the house he drove to turns on. The front door swings open. I take a deep breath as a petite woman steps out. She waves at my husband, but I can see a scowl on her face.

He moves slowly as he gets out of his car. There's still tension in his body, the same tension that had been there when he received a text at dinner. I know immediately she has to have been the one who texted him.

But who is she? Why would he hurry to her side?

I'm not close enough to hear what they're saying, but I can see her face. She's not happy and, for a second, my mind sees something that isn't there.

His arms wrapped around her, pulling her close.

His hand resting on her lower back. Possessive.

Her pulling back, laughing, happy.

They're happy together.

No. I blink hard, clearing the daydream and coming back to the present, to how they're facing off a few feet from each other, their muscles tense with anger. They don't like each other now, but I bet they *were* happy together.

It feels like someone stabbed me through the heart when I realize that. How long has it been since he came home and was happy to see me? I'm sure, if I asked, he'd tell me he'd be happier to see me if I cleaned up, if I changed out of my old pajamas, if I made an effort with my hair and makeup.

But I don't think I can.

Slowly, like my hand is on autopilot, I start my car. The engine barely hums to life, and neither one of them look towards me. I back up, fully intending to use someone's driveway to turn around, but then I stop.

Their body language is different. It was tense, but now it's angry. Lawrence's hands are on his hips, and he's hinged forward like he's really laying into the woman. She can give as good as she can get, judging by the fact that she's not moved away from him. She plants one hand on her hip and then raises something and shakes it in his face.

He looks like he's going to hit her. I'd do anything to make out the expression on his face, but it's too dark. Still, I see the way his right hand swings back some, the tension in his shoulders, how he pivots a little to the side.

She beats him to it. She smacks him across the cheek and then takes a step back, clapping her hands over her mouth in shock. Something falls from her hand, but I barely notice it, I'm too busy watching what's happening next.

Lawrence doesn't respond. I fully expect him to lash out at her, to hit her back, to get into a screaming match with her, but instead all he does is kick the thing she dropped.

It spins away from them, rolling a bit of the way down the driveway before coming to rest on the road. It's much closer to me now and I squint to see what it is.

Small. White? It's hard to tell unless—

The woman stalks down the driveway, her cell phone's flashlight bobbing ahead of her. Just before she bends to pick it up, I finally make out what he kicked.

A baby bottle.

SIXTY-FOUR

Sophie

Where the hell did she go?

Panic grips me, the feeling now familiar, a tight squeezing around my throat that makes it difficult for me not only to think straight but to breathe.

Something thunks behind me, and I whip around, adrenaline pumping through my body and making me want to flee. My eyes flick from corner to corner of the living room.

Nothing by the sofa.

Or the window.

The far door? I step into the room, my ears pricked, holding my breath as I search for what made that sound.

Charlotte—it was Charlotte moving around who made that sound. You know it was; you just don't want to admit it—

Nothing. She's on the move, but she's not in here, and I feel myself relax a bit.

But where is she?

"Charlotte?" I'm too quiet for her to hear me. I clear my

throat and try again. "Charlotte? Are you in here? Are you okay?"

The doorbell rings again, and I whip around. I'd forgotten someone was out there. Charlotte distracted me. She's not even here in the same room as me and she distracted me. In my arms, Jordan whimpers.

"I have to answer the door," I tell Jordan. "I have to see who's out there."

Jordan makes a little hiccupping noise but quiets back down when I start to bounce on the balls of my feet.

The doorbell rings again. This time, it's accompanied by someone pounding on the door.

"Coming!" Another quick glance over my shoulder, but no Charlotte.

I hurry to the door and take a deep breath before unlocking it and throwing it open. As quickly as possible, I plaster a smile on my face.

"Did you call the police?" The officer standing on the porch has a large, pockmarked nose. He's tall, towering over me, his eyebrows crashing together as he stares at me.

I don't immediately respond, and I see the way his hand shifts, just a little, coming to rest on the butt of his gun.

"No," I finally say, after I manage to unstick my tongue from the roof of my mouth. "Sure didn't. Sorry, you must have the wrong house."

His eyes flick to Jordan, then back to my face. "Anyone in the house with you?"

"Nope. Just me and my baby." I bounce on the balls of my feet to keep her from crying. It's coming—I just know it. It's in the way she's breathing, sucking in little bursts of air like she's prepping for the big show.

"Mind if I look around?" He smiles as he asks the question, but it's clear to me that he's not asking my permission.

"Um," I say, bouncing harder. "It's almost time for this little one to take a nap. You know how schedules can be." I glance at his left hand. No ring. He might still have kids though.

"Ma'am, what's your name?"

I swallow hard. "Does that matter? I don't know why you're here, why you're asking me these questions, and I don't think I should have to answer them. I—"

"Are you home alone?"

I look him right in the eyes when I lie to him. "Yes."

"Step outside." Again, his hand flicks to his gun. I see the movement out the corner of my eye but don't look down at it. The last thing I want to do is give him the satisfaction of knowing I'm scared.

"Okay." I do as he asks, my eyes trained on him as I step out onto the porch. Across the street, a neighbor watches, a cup of coffee in their hand. I do my best to keep from glaring at her, then reach behind me to close the door.

Wherever Charlotte is, I hope she stays there. Permanently. The cops came, and that's clearly her fault—she must've called using Lawrence's cell, given hers is still smashed on the living-room floor—but maybe she's hurt worse than she thought. Maybe she was able to make a phone call but is now curled up somewhere, licking her wounds.

I'll finish dealing with her after I've handled things with this cop. I'll—

Something closes on my wrist.

I screech and try to jerk my hand away from the door, but fingers tighten around my skin. Her grip is stronger than I would have thought possible, and I gasp, turning and jerking my hand from hers.

"Let go of her!" The officer bellows the words, and I'm not surprised when he's suddenly right next to me, his hand on Charlotte's arm.

But then his hand is on mine as well. We're separated and he stands between us, his cheeks red. "What the hell is going on here?" A quick glance between the two of us and I see it all start to click in his mind.

"You called, didn't you?" he asks, releasing Charlotte.

She nods, whimpering a little bit as she steps out onto the porch. Her bad arm is tucked up close to her chest, her good one by her side. Tears well in her eyes.

"I did." Her voice is quiet, and I glare at her.

When I thought she might not be alive, when I thought she couldn't stop me from taking Jordan... I'd been so happy. It had hit me, for a moment, that I could finally have the life I've wanted for so many years.

I could put the past behind me, the problems with Lawrence, no matter how perfect he seemed on the surface, how he treated me. I could even move past the fact that I wanted a child more than anything in the world and he was willing to do whatever it took to keep that from happening. I thought it was all over, that I was finally going to get what I deserved.

"She stole my baby." Charlotte's voice shakes a little, but her hand doesn't as she levels it and points at me. "She took my daughter and hurt me."

The officer had let go of my arm, but it's clear he wishes he hadn't. He shifts position, turning his body towards me and putting himself between the two of us. I can still see Charlotte, but it's clear he's going out of his way to make sure she's protected.

From me.

Like I'm the bad guy.

I'm not the bad guy. I came here to help, that's all, but everyone's acting like I'm the evil one in this situation.

"This isn't her baby," I tell him, pulling Jordan closer to my chest. My eyes never leave his face. I need him to look at me and see me for who I am. I need him to understand that Jordan is the only one here who matters, that I would do whatever it takes to keep her safe.

"Then whose baby is it?" His voice is low. While he waits for me to respond, his hand slides up to his radio and he calls for backup.

This can't be happening.

"Jordan is mine," I say, and Charlotte scoffs. I should keep talking to him, should keep her out of it, but I can't help the anger that rises in me when I see the expression on her face. It's hot and furious, an explosion of it. I glare at her. "You're not her mother! I am! You stole her from me!"

"She's insane," Charlotte says, but she's not speaking to me. She's turned to the officer, and I watch as she reaches out and carefully rests her hand on his arm. She seems to curl in on herself like a dying bug, something so in need of protection that he won't have a choice but to help her.

"She photoshopped the birth certificate," I say, stabbing my finger through the air at Charlotte. "She's lying to you!"

"I can get her birth certificate," she says, her voice level. Calm. "But please, get my baby away from her first."

The officer turns to me. His jaw is set; his entire upper body looks tense. If I thought for a second that I was going to be able to talk my way out of this, I can tell now that that window has closed.

"Ma'am. Give me the baby."

I don't move.

I *can't* move.

"This is my baby," I whisper. "She's not the mother. I am."

SIXTY-FIVE

Sophie

Charlotte places the fake birth certificate on the kitchen table with a flourish, then steps back. She throws me a grin, and I have to take a deep breath to keep from lunging at her.

The officer put Jordan in her swing. Her eyes are closed as she snoozes, and I have to fight to pull my attention from her and focus on what Charlotte has put on the table.

"It's fake." I say the two words with all the confidence I can muster so that hopefully the officer looking at it will give it more than a cursory glance.

He picks it up and runs his finger over the official seal, which is, *obviously*, flat because it's fake. She can try to gaslight me all she wants, but I know what I saw on the computer.

"It's a photocopy," Charlotte says, sounding apologetic. "The original is in my safe deposit box, but obviously I can't get to that on such short notice. This is the copy I keep here just in case." She pauses. "That's why that seal is flat."

"Right." The officer puts the paper back on the table, but he doesn't look at me. "I don't see—"

I take a deep breath to try to stay calm.

I'm losing this. And I'm going to lose Jordan.

I don't know how to get this officer on my side, not when Charlotte is so calm and seems in control. She's doing a great job spinning this all to make herself look like the perfect mom and me like I'm crazy.

"But you don't have any maternity photos!" I throw the words at her, pointing at her face. "And I do!"

The officer looks at Charlotte. I see the look of pity that passes between them, and I want to scream. *He's not getting it.*

Time to make sure he understands what I'm saying.

"Jordan isn't her daughter," I say, speaking slowly so each of my words has a chance to sink in. "She kidnapped her. From me."

Charlotte starts laughing. "What the hell are you going on about? Of course Jordan is my daughter." She glares at me. "Do you have any proof of her being yours? Did you file a police report when she went *missing*?" She makes air quotes around the word.

Rage bubbles up in me, and I look to the officer, but he's no help. He's looking at Charlotte like he believes her.

"Please," I say, drawing his attention from her. "You have to believe me. That baby is mine. We didn't mean to get pregnant. But I did, and then my husband was so upset. I didn't have a choice but to give my daughter up for adoption. My husband made me. I wouldn't have, but I didn't have a choice."

"Can you prove it?" His voice is kind, but there's an undercurrent there, that he's placating me or leading me on, or just interested in seeing how this all plays out.

I take a deep breath and slowly let it out. My mind races as I try to think things through, but no matter what I tell him, I don't know how to make him see my side of things. I try another tactic.

"She was sleeping with my husband—" I begin, but Charlotte cuts me off.

"And she knew about it. They had an open marriage, but she can't handle the fact that he had a family with me and not with her."

The officer frowns. I'm about to lose him.

"He died under mysterious circumstances," I begin, but again Charlotte cuts me off.

"Lawrence dying was terrible, but it wasn't mysterious." She wipes away a tear. "Bad heart. He fell asleep and never woke back up." She looks at the officer. "You can read the autopsy report, if you want."

Insulin. An insulin overdose would put you to sleep like that.

"Please." My blood whooshes in my ears. "Please, you have to believe me. Her first husband died too. She killed them—I know she did." I hate the desperation in my voice. He's going to hear it and think I've lost it—I'm sure he will.

Charlotte turns to him. When she speaks, her voice is lower. "Officer, she needs help. She showed up and told me she was Lawrence's sister."

He glances at me. "This true?"

"It is, but—"

She continues. "When she destroyed some of my property, I neglected to press charges and asked her to leave. As you can see... she won't. Can you get her out of my house?"

"No!" I shriek the word, and Charlotte takes a step back. She puts her hand up between the two of us like she has to protect herself.

She's doing a great job making me out to be the bad guy.

"I don't know what drugs she's on, but she's erratic, and I wouldn't be surprised if she's taking something," Charlotte tells him.

"Would you stop?" I have to stop yelling, but it feels impossible. She's lying through her teeth to get him to think I'm crazy.

"Ma'am, it's time for you to leave." The officer puts his hand on my shoulder, silencing any thoughts. "You and I are going to take a ride. Talk some things out."

"You can't arrest me." I take a step back from him, but he moves with me, keeping his hand on me. "No. I didn't do anything wrong. Let me go!"

"You're trespassing," he says, and while his voice is level and calm, any kindness I thought I heard there earlier is gone. He means business.

"She let me in," I say. "You can't be trespassing if someone invites you in."

The three of us are silent. Charlotte stares at a spot on the ceiling, too much of a coward to look at me. The officer stares at me, waiting for me to make a decision.

"She got into a wreck with the baby in the car," I blurt out. "You can't tell me she's a fit mother if she's doing stuff like that."

The officer doesn't blink.

"I did," Charlotte said, and her voice is thick. "But it was an accident. Never in my life would I put Jordan at risk like that."

My mind races. His hand tightens.

"Ma'am. Turn around and put your hands behind your back. We're going to the station. We'll get you some help."

I feel like I'm in a fog as I turn and do what he asked. Do I have a choice? Could I make a run for it, maybe grab Jordan and get out of here?

But before I can formulate a plan, the handcuffs are on. They're tight, and I grimace.

He starts Mirandizing me as he leads me out of the kitchen. I jerk from left to right, trying to lay eyes on Charlotte one more time.

"Let's keep going." The officer tugs my arm, already turned

back to the front door, but I can't drag my eyes away from Charlotte. She's staring at me, her chin lifted, the sorrow that was on her face a moment ago already gone. "We'll get you some help, okay?"

"She's lying," I say, but the officer shakes his head. I don't want to walk with him, but he's pulling me harder now and I don't have a choice. "She's lying! You have to believe me! Jordan isn't her daughter, she's mine!"

The handcuffs cut into my wrists. I twist my arms a little, trying to loosen them even though I know it's futile. I'm not getting out of this.

Not for a long time.

But I will. Somehow. And then I'm coming for Charlotte.

SIXTY-SIX

Charlotte

Jordan coos as I lay her down in her crib. It's a little too early to put her down for the night, but I need some time to myself. What just happened... well, it would be enough to shake anyone, and I honestly feel like I'm coming out of my skin.

Downstairs, I pour myself a glass of wine. Maybe not the best way to deal with the stress of the day, especially when I'm taking this many painkillers, but I'm looking at it as a celebration. A little food would help settle my stomach, but after Sophie spiked my meal, the thought of eating anything makes me feel sick.

Letting Sophie into my house was the stupidest thing I ever could have done—I know that now. But I honestly had no idea who she was.

Lawrence's wife.

His real wife. His legal wife. The woman he chose before me. His executor, I'm sure of it, even though she always acted dumb when that was brought up.

I shake my head. How could someone who I loved so much treat me the way he did?

Those words keep rattling around in my head, but I can't make them make sense. I loved him. *Love* him.

The day he showed up with Jordan in his arms... I've never been that happy. Well, until he told me it was him or the baby, that is. It was then that I saw what he was trying to do: break it off with me but keep me placated while cleaning up a mess he had made.

And as soon as I realized that, I knew what I had to do. Lawrence was selfish, and there wasn't any way I was going to let him walk out of my life, out of Jordan's life, and do whatever he wanted to do. Not that I knew he'd be running right back to Sophie.

I had no idea he was married. I thought he just wanted to be free of the commitment of marriage, that he thought a baby was a good trade for his freedom.

But then there was Sophie, and she was like a dog with a bone once she figured out who I was. She was on a mission, and I have no doubt that she would have taken steps to ruin my life no matter whether I'd invited her in or not.

I'd just been so damn tired. I'd needed help. I'd needed someone who missed Lawrence like I did, and even though there was a voice in the back of my head telling me that I was screwing up, I'd ignored it.

And I almost lost Jordan because of my actions.

That can never happen.

I already had to kill twice to be a mother.

Killing James still fills me with regret. I don't think I've ever loved anyone the way I loved him, and it's not just because he was my first love. He was strong, and passionate, and adored me.

But when I lost the baby and he said he didn't want to try again—that he *couldn't* try again—I knew I had to do something, had to take steps to make sure I would have the baby I wanted some day. If he'd been willing to try again, even if we'd had to adopt, I would have been happy being his wife for the rest of my life.

But he wasn't willing to try again. And I needed to be a mother.

And then there was Lawrence. He had to die not only because he was going to leave me, but also because he knew where Jordan really came from. He was the link to someone who might try to take her from me.

You'll be happy as a mother, he'd said, like a baby was a consolation prize for your marriage falling apart.

Your marriage that wasn't even real.

I close my eyes. The thought is unbidden and painful. My marriage wasn't real. If he hadn't left me with Jordan, he wouldn't have left me with anything.

Jordan's fake birth certificate is on the kitchen counter where I left it after showing it to the police officer, and I take it to file it away in the office. It really looks real. I may not have ever gone to college, but you can learn most skills you need on YouTube.

It was good enough to get me out of trouble today anyway. Maybe I should consider a change of career. I'm not saying I'm the best at Photoshop, but I could learn.

No doubt there are other people in similar positions to mine who need to prove a child is theirs. Or hide who they really are. I could help them. Make a career out of it.

It's not a bad idea actually.

I stop before filing the birth certificate, debating what to do next. My mind races as I look down at the paper.

Hiding damning evidence works for a while, but what if Sophie comes back? I bet she will. She was determined to take Jordan from me, and if she gets a judge to listen to her, to issue a court order for a DNA test, then I could really be in trouble.

I'll need to take out a restraining order on her. I'll have to be vigilant. At work, the store, driving around with Jordan, dropping her off and picking her up from daycare? There are a thousand places where Sophie could come for me.

She knows my secrets. I don't think she can prove that I killed James and Lawrence, but what if she causes a scene? Goes to the news? Keeps harping on about what happened until someone takes her seriously and they come to investigate me and take my daughter away?

Maybe I should move.

I look around the house, my heart hammering in my throat as I consider that. The house isn't in my name. I'm not on any of his accounts. It's crossed my mind before that I might need to pawn my jewelry for some cash.

Slowly, I turn my wedding ring around on my finger. How long will Sophie be locked up? I can't imagine that they'll keep her for very long once she stops her insane rambling. She's not crazy, she's...

She's right.

As much as I hate to admit it, she's right. And even though the law isn't always completely reliable, and sometimes the person who's in the right fails to come out on top, is that something I want to risk?

Is Jordan something I want to risk? No. Not after what it took to finally become a mother.

A bolt of excitement shoots through me. There's an obvious answer to my dilemma, but I won't make it happen standing here and thinking about it.

I didn't do anything wrong, but I have to run.

EPILOGUE
THREE MONTHS LATER

Charlotte

A cool breeze washes over me as I stand on the front porch of our little rental. From here I can't see the ocean, but I can smell it. Yes, I wish we lived closer to it, but this is all I could afford. After selling all the jewelry Lawrence gave me and gathering any cash I had, the move to Florida almost wiped me out completely.

Honestly, I was just lucky that my landlord felt bad for me as a widowed single mom. I was right all along—widows and single parents get more sympathy than someone who's divorced. Nobody has to know that Lawrence and I weren't legally married. I can only imagine how that would go over.

And if someone ever found out that Jordan isn't my biological child? They'd come for me with pitchforks and turn me in to the police before I could even think about how to stop them.

I take a sip of my coffee. The wood planks under my feet are gritty with sand from when Jordan and I visited the beach yesterday. I'd kept her covered up so she didn't get a sunburn, of course, so she didn't get to see much of the water, but I want her to love it the way I do.

We're right on the outskirts of a big city, which is exactly what I begged Lawrence for when he was still alive. I wanted more from life, and I finally have it. Sure, waiting tables all day is exhausting and my feet hurt, but at least I have freedom from living under his thumb, and Jordan and I are together.

Besides, I have a plan. I'm not staying in this tiny rental forever. There's someone at work who's interested in me—I know he is. I see the way his eyes follow me around the dining room, how he always asks to be seated in my section. He doesn't care that I'm a single mom, although he knows nothing beyond that fact.

And he won't. Not until I'm ready for him to.

He has money, I can tell. Enough to support me and whatever children I might have.

Every morning before Jordan gets up and I take her to daycare, I go online and search for Sophie. Her company's website has been taken down, and while that made me nervous the first time I noticed it a month ago, I'm pretty sure she's just licking her wounds.

For all I care, she's dead. I hope she's dropped off the face of the earth and I never have to hear from her again. It's been months since I saw her, but I still wake in the middle of the night with a terrible fear that she's right down the hall, that I'll creep into Jordan's nursery and see her sleeping on the floor, or —worse—awake and rocking my baby.

More than once, I've gotten up around 2 a.m. and crept into Jordan's nursery myself. I don't take her from her crib and don't wake her up, but just seeing her and knowing that she's okay is enough to let me get sleep.

Speaking of... I glance at my watch and confirm what I thought. Even though I took the day off work, I still have something I have to be on time for. So while I'd love to stand here and enjoy the slow way the sun lightens the sky, how the birds wake up and shake off their sleep to call out, how good my coffee is, I need to get a move on. Jordan has to be up and fed before I can leave.

I won't be long. I've been planning this out since we arrived in Florida, since I went to the park and saw how so many mothers ignore their babies so they can stand around and chat.

I sigh with contentment and take the final sip of my coffee before hurrying back inside. I leave the mug in the kitchen sink, then walk down the hall to Jordan's nursery. I'd be lying if I said that part of me didn't miss having Sophie around to help with her.

It's hard. It's what I wanted, what I killed for, but it's hard.

Would I give it up? Not in a million years.

Do I regret killing Lawrence?

I pause as I think about that. I don't regret it because it wasn't fair of him to try to make me choose between being with him and having a child. I wish he'd wanted a family with me, but he was too selfish to be a parent. This would be too hard for him.

It's the kind of hard that helps me fall asleep as soon as I get into bed each night. The kind of hard that makes me wish I had a second child because I know Jordan is going to grow up faster than I ever thought possible, and I want to really enjoy it. Soak it in.

I want her to stop growing up so quickly. And—just as much as that—I want her to have a sibling. If I had another child now, the two of them could grow up together. They'd be insepa-rable. I remember how hard it was to be an only child when my parents died, and I don't want that for Jordan.

I pause outside the nursery and take a deep breath before opening it. She's moved on from sleep sacks to footie zip-up pajamas, and I love choosing the different prints for her. Of course, I bought all the ones she has second-hand at the local thrift shop, but it doesn't matter. She doesn't know, and her sitter doesn't care.

Inside her nursery, I turn to the right and approach the crib. I put my hands on the rail and then look down into it.

It's empty.

My heart beats faster as I stare at the empty mattress, the sheet slightly wrinkled. There's a sleep sack in the corner, and I barely glance at it before turning and leaning against the crib.

What am I going to do?

Jordan. She's dominated every waking moment I've had since Lawrence laid her in my arms. And now...

Now what?

I turn back and stare down into the empty crib, tears burning my eyes.

I should move. The last thing I need is to stand here, to remain motionless when I have so much to do. Today is the day.

I have to make this happen.

There's a shuffling noise behind me, and I whip around.

Jordan coos as I approach her crib, leaving the empty one behind me. Right now, my daughter needs me, and I'll take care of her.

I'll hold her, rock her, feed her, change her.

And then I'll put her back down in her crib. I'll swaddle her up nice and tight, so she feels like she's being held. I'll make sure nothing is in the crib that could possibly be a danger.

And then I'll leave her here while I do what I have to do. Having a child seemed like a dream that would never come true. Having two? It seemed completely out of reach. Impossible. Unachievable.

But I have a plan.

The chance of someone offering me another child? Slim to none. That will never happen.

But that's fine. I'm willing to take one.

Sophie

I watch as Charlotte locks her door behind her and hurries to her car. Jordan's not in her arms, and I feel myself stiffen with excitement.

Today is the day. After so much money spent finding her, after moving to this crap Florida town to be close to her, after the waiting and waiting and waiting... the day is finally here.

I'll stop at nothing to get my daughter back. When Charlotte pulls away from the house in her crappy little car, I sink low in mine.

I ditched the luxury car for a beater so I would blend in. Just as I thought, Charlotte hasn't looked in my direction once, but I haven't been able to take my eyes off her.

I've watched her go to the store. I've watched her take my daughter to the beach. More than that, though, I've watched her at the park. Seen how she's stared at other babies, how she's offered to hold them when their mothers have to pee, how greedy her expression becomes when she looks at them.

I know what she wants.

She's dangerous. Even before I moved in with her, I knew she was a problem, but that's become more and more obvious. Taking my child when Lawrence gave her to her was one thing, but she has something else on her mind now.

She wants another child.

I have no doubt in my mind that's what she wants, especially after I broke into her home and found the matching cribs in her nursery. She's always been obsessed with babies and apparently that hasn't changed, not even after she took mine from me.

The right thing to do would be to go to the police. I could take Jordan back the official way. A DNA test would clear things up, but that's not how I'm going to handle it. How many hoops would I have to jump through when I could end this now? And what if she somehow managed to convince a judge that Jordan is really hers? Since he bribed a doctor to handle the birth and everything was done in secret, there's no official record of me giving birth or even being pregnant. Sure, by doing it this way, another child might be taken.

But it won't be mine.

Instead of driving away, like I have every other time for the past few weeks when I see Charlotte take Jordan with her, I roll my shoulders back and hurry up to the house. The last time I was here, I found the spare key under the fake rock in the scrubby grass of her front yard, and I grab it and let myself in.

From the back, I hear Jordan start to whimper.

I don't hesitate. I go and get my baby.

Dear reader,

I want to say a huge thank you for choosing to read *What Every Mother Needs*. If you did enjoy it, and want to keep up to date with all my latest releases, just sign up at the following link. Your email address will never be shared, and you can unsubscribe at any time.

www.bookouture.com/emily-shiner

At first glance, a book about two women fighting over a baby might not appear to have anything to do with a hurricane, and I completely understand the confusion regarding the dedication. Where I live, nestled in the North Carolina mountains, we're not ever supposed to deal with hurricanes, but that's what happened September 27, 2024.

My family was lucky. We had flooding and lost power for ten days, but we were able to get out and help the people who lost everything. When we weren't boiling water to drink and cook or helping pack food boxes or cutting fallen trees, I wrote.

And let me tell you, this book was in rough shape when I finished the first draft. My amazing editor offered an extension on it, but between you and me, I needed to see the tail end of it. I needed normalcy, which is something that a lot of people in the area still don't have at the time of me writing this.

Were we warned there was going to be rain? Sure, we were.

But nobody could have guessed that we'd end up with water filling houses to the roof, that grocery stores would have six feet of water in them, that the very mountains that make us feel so safe would funnel every drop straight down into homes and neighborhoods, washing away homes, roads, and bridges.

It can be easy to feel discouraged and like we can't do anything to help, especially when the need is so overwhelming. This book helped me when everything was falling apart. When I woke up at 4 a.m. in the pitch-black, I'd light a candle and write. In short: writing this book gave me the same thing reading gives so many of us—an escape from the reality of the world.

Ten percent of everything I am paid for this book during its lifetime will go straight back into relief efforts for victims of natural disasters. I'm keeping it close to home at first, helping out the people in our mountains who lost everything, and will donate to others when the needs here are met. That includes KU reads, eBook, paperback, and audiobook sales, as well as any movie or TV adaption that may occur. (We might as well think big!)

This book is important to me, and I hope you love it. I hope it offers you an escape when you need it the most, whether that's from work stress, family, or just because the world sometimes seems to be too much. I get it, believe me, and I'm so happy to create that escape for you.

I hope you loved *What Every Mother Needs*, and, if you did, I would be very grateful if you could write a review. I'd love to hear what you think, and it makes such a difference helping new readers to discover one of my books for the first time.

I love hearing from my readers—you can get in touch on my Facebook page, through Instagram, Goodreads or my website.

Thanks,

Emily

KEEP IN TOUCH WITH EMILY

authoremilyshiner.com

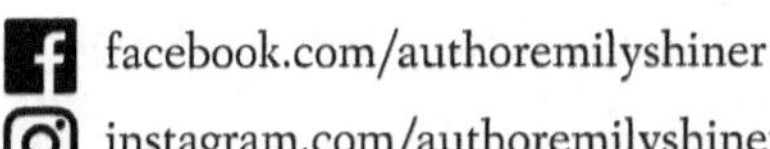

facebook.com/authoremilyshiner

instagram.com/authoremilyshiner

bsky.app/profile/authoremilyshiner.bsky.social

ACKNOWLEDGMENTS

Every time I get to sit down and write acknowledgements feels like a blessing because writing books really is a dream come true. Each book is special and different, but this one really feels that way.

Knowing that I wanted to donate proceeds from this book pushed me to make it as good as possible (yes, I do that with every book, but you know what I mean!), and that wouldn't be possible without my favorite team. Kelsie Marsden, Donna Hillyer, and Laura Kincaid—thank you. You three consistently help mold my books into the amazing stories we know they can be. I can't think of many other people who would willingly suffer through reading my first draft. (Or second, third, fourth…)

The rest of the Bookouture team is the most amazing group of people I've ever had the opportunity to work with. They're kind and focused and believe in great books and the people who write them. Where would I be without each of you?

A huge thanks to my family for unending support each and every time I sit down to write. I may not have a dedicated office, but y'all always honor my time in my carved-out spot in the living room.

To Blue Lotus Chai who has no idea I exist but makes the speediest tea ever. (Pretty sure I've thanked them before, but let's be honest. They're amazing.)

And, as always, my readers, who are delightful. I love y'all.

PUBLISHING TEAM

Turning a manuscript into a book requires the efforts of many people. The publishing team at Bookouture would like to acknowledge everyone who contributed to this publication.

Audio
Alba Proko
Melissa Tran
Sinead O'Connor

Commercial
Lauren Morrissette
Hannah Richmond
Imogen Allport

Cover design
Aaron Munday

Data and analysis
Mark Alder
Mohamed Bussuri

Editorial
Kelsie Marsden
Lizzie Brien

Copyeditor
Donna Hillyer

Proofreader
Laura Kincaid

Marketing
Alex Crow
Melanie Price
Occy Carr
Cíara Rosney
Martyna Młynarska

Operations and distribution
Marina Valles
Stephanie Straub
Joe Morris

Production
Hannah Snetsinger
Mandy Kullar
Ria Clare
Nadia Michael

Publicity
Kim Nash
Noelle Holten
Jess Readett
Sarah Hardy

Rights and contracts
Peta Nightingale
Richard King
Saidah Graham

www.ingramcontent.com/pod-product-compliance
Lightning Source LLC
Chambersburg PA
CBHW030534190726
48283CB00006B/1917